"It was another kin

The worst kind, he could
It was a nightmare that would haunt him for the rest of his life.

Chloe lay awake long after Ben had gone back to sleep. Not for the first time, she sensed that he had deeper, sadder memories than he wanted to reveal.

To be honest, she was glad he hadn't told her about them. Once he let her in on what was bothering him, she'd feel duty-bound to make things right. And at this point in her life, that wasn't supposed to be an option. She was trying her hardest to focus on herself, never mind that she'd taken on the responsibility for her niece. That was turning out to be easier than she'd expected.

Ben was another story. She was planning to stay uninvolved in his problems, whatever they were, and no matter how sympathetic she might be.

That didn't mean she didn't care—far from it. Ben was far more important to her now than she could have thought possible when she'd first arrived at the Frangipani Inn.

The key was to keep things in perspective. Wasn't it?

Dear Reader,

This is Chloe's book.

Chloe Timberlake appeared briefly as my heroine's best friend in my last book, *Breakfast with Santa*. I didn't intend for her to remain in my consciousness after I finished writing the book. After all, she was a minor character, named after one of my favorite cats.

But sometimes writers create characters who just won't let go. Chloe was at a juncture in her life; she was on the brink of leaving her hometown of Farish, Texas, to strike out on a new venture. I kept wondering what would happen to her. And besides, she was alone, and she seemed too nice not to have someone special in her life.

Fortunately, I found exactly the right guy for her. Ben Derrick is someone she knew long ago—a man who, as it turns out, appreciates Chloe's quirky qualities. He's suffered great tragedy in the past and has finally managed to start putting his life back together. Enter (ta-dah!) Chloe.

Their love story illustrates that sometimes you have to wait a long time to find true love, but that the greatest riches of all are the treasures of the heart. Enjoy!

Love,

Pamela Browning

P.S. Please visit my Web site at www.pamelabrowning.com.

THE TREASURE MAN

Pamela Browning

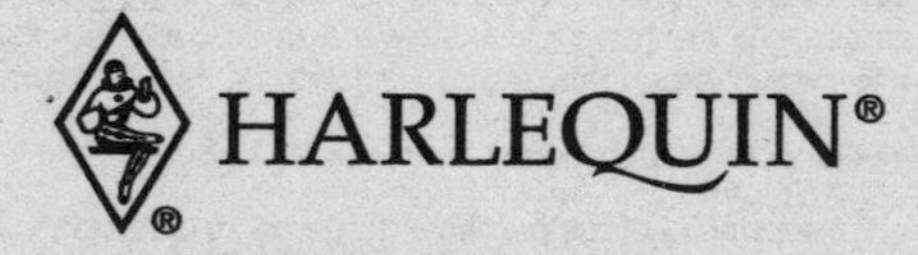

TORONTO • NEW YORK • LONDON
AMSTERDAM • PARIS • SYDNEY • HAMBURG
STOCKHOLM • ATHENS • TOKYO • MILAN • MADRID
PRAGUE • WARSAW • BUDAPEST • AUCKLAND

ISBN 0-373-75115-X

THE TREASURE MAN

This edition published by arrangement with Harlequin Books S.A.

www.eHarlequin.com

Printed in U.S.A.

For the Florida hurricane victims of 2004,
and for those who came to the rescue...thank you.

Books by Pamela Browning

HARLEQUIN AMERICAN ROMANCE

854—BABY CHRISTMAS
874—COWBOY WITH A SECRET
907—PREGNANT AND INCOGNITO
922—RANCHER'S DOUBLE DILEMMA
982—COWBOY ENCHANTMENT
994—BABY ENCHANTMENT
1039—HEARD IT THROUGH THE GRAPEVINE
1070—THE MOMMY WISH
1091—BREAKFAST WITH SANTA

Prologue

Afterward, Ben couldn't recall when he first smelled smoke. He had a vague memory of a whiff of it as he left Ashley in her seat at the front of the auditorium, but it was intermission at the Chico Chico concert, and a lot of people had gone out for a cigarette. If he'd noticed it then, he would have thought it was people smoking.

A long line of concertgoers wended their way through the lobby to the refreshment stand, and he hoped there would be some root beer left by the time he reached the counter. Root beer was his thirteen-year-old daughter's favorite drink, and since it was her birthday, he didn't want to substitute cola or 7-Up or whatever else might be left. Still, he hung back, figuring it was more important for the kids attending the show to buy their drinks and hurry back to their seats; he could always slip into place beside Ashley after the performance resumed.

And then he saw it—a huge black billow of smoke rushing toward him down the aisle. Simultaneously, someone in the theater yelled, "Fire!" A woman screamed over the cacophony of voices, and people started to pour into the lobby.

Ben knew this was bad trouble. With the acrid odor of smoke stinging his nostrils, the crackle of flames in his ears, he fought his way past the first wave of panic-stricken concertgoers.

"Daddy! Daddy! Help!"

It was his daughter's voice. He'd recognize it anywhere. People pushed past him, running, screaming, crying. He tried to forge a path through the crowd, but there was no space. He noted with alarm that flames were now licking at the stage curtains, and the ceiling was ablaze.

Someone struck Ben a glancing blow on his forehead, but he kept pushing. It was like swimming against a fierce current, something he'd done many times in his work as a diver. Despite his anguish, he was driven away from Ashley, not toward her.

Desperately, he shouted her name, choking on the smoke. "Ashley! Daddy's coming!"

He fell to his knees, struggled and stood, was bowled over again.

"Out of the way, man! The place is burning!" A man tried to help him to his feet but was swept into the melee.

Ben accidentally tripped a woman, but together they managed to regain their footing. Her progress toward the door left a small hole in the sea of people, and he pressed toward Ashley. He had to make sure she was safe, had to reach his daughter.

The heat of the blaze scorched his face, seared his lungs. Glowing sparks swirled in the air above his head—a surreal dance performed amid chaos and destruction. An usher's shirt was on fire, and he screamed as he tore at the blackened fabric. Through a gap in the crowd, Ben saw that the seats where he had left Ashley only minutes ago were engulfed in flames.

Eyes streaming with tears, he crawled over several fallen bodies and managed to grab on to a theater seat so that he wouldn't be carried backward. Now the smoke was so thick that he could see nothing through the tunnel of fire ahead, and it hurt too much to breathe. He went down again but clung to the seat to pull himself to his feet. His gut wrenched with the certain knowledge that he was losing strength.

A father's main job was to protect his child, and he hadn't been able to do that. As the blackness all around began to blot out his consciousness, Ben prayed that Ashley had found a way out of the building. They had been sitting near an emergency exit, so perhaps she had kept her head and escaped. He held that hope in his heart as he slid slowly to the floor, the roar of the flames echoing inside his head until he heard…nothing.

Chapter One

Chloe Timberlake knew that she had truly reached the end of her long journey to Sanluca, Florida, when the earthy scent of the Everglades muck gave way to the fragrance of the Atlantic Ocean wafting on the breeze. She leaned her head out the car window and let go an exuberant whoop that was heard by no one except perhaps a few tree frogs chirring in the scrub oaks overarching the road. And her cat, of course.

"Come on out, Butch," she said. "We're a long way from Farish, Texas. The Frangipani Inn is straight ahead." She nudged open the tattered carpetbag where the big orange tomcat liked to sleep when traveling.

Butch poked his head out and twitched his whiskers. No litter box for him; Butch was toilet trained and hadn't forgiven her for that last grungy rest stop on the Glades Highway. He looked down his nose at her before indulging in an indolent stretch, then sniffed appreciatively at the brine and seaweed.

When the car emerged from the shelter of the trees, Chloe turned off at 1200 Beach Road, the shell-rock driveway crunching under the old blue Volvo's tires. Ahead of them, her father's family home was surrounded by an encroaching tangle of vegetation, growing thick and lush now, in late May. Nearby, a boardwalk led down to the beach.

"I wonder whose Jeep that is," Chloe mused as the headlights swung past a decrepit vehicle, its pockmarked sides spattered with mud. As she braked to a stop under a gumbo-limbo tree at the rear of the inn, a lithe shape detached itself from the side of the building and moved toward her. Chloe was wary; the inn, her cousin Gwynne had assured her, was unoccupied.

The shape morphed into a man and, still suspicious, Chloe rammed the car into Reverse for a quick getaway. His presence rattled her, even though Sanluca's crime rate ranked so low it wasn't even on the charts. Yet why was this fellow, who was now sauntering toward her car, lurking in the shadows of the Frangipani Inn?

He stepped within the circle of headlights, and with a jolt, she recognized him. She hadn't seen Ben Derrick in years, not since that summer when she was sixteen; but she would have known him anywhere. He'd been unrepentantly handsome and sexy as sin, though he'd never seemed to realize it. Now he was barefoot—ill-advised considering the incidence of sandspurs in the native scrub. Baggy shorts rode low on his hips, and his hair—dark, generously sun-streaked and needing cutting—was tousled by the breeze from the ocean. He looked scruffy and nondescript, and he was sixteen years older than when she'd last seen him, but he was still Ben Derrick. And still a heartbreaker, no doubt.

He squinted into the glare. "Gwynne?" he said.

Of course. He'd always preferred her cousin, teasing her, joking with her and ignoring Chloe. When Ben had disappeared late in that summer of her sixteenth year, Chloe had been devastated. She'd been shy in those days, had never done anything to draw attention to herself, had been content to hang out in Gwynne's shadow. She'd never told anyone that she'd fallen hopelessly in love with Ben Derrick.

Chloe rested a restraining hand on Butch's head so that he wouldn't take it into his fool head to make a grand leap from the car. "I'm Chloe Timberlake," she said over the stutter of the Volvo's engine. "Gwynne's my cousin." She didn't add, *You remember—I was the redheaded, flat-chested girl who hung on your every word, who followed you around like a lovesick fool for two whole months. And you couldn't have cared less.*

Ben leaned down and peered in the window, studying her. "You're Chloe?" His voice was a rumble in his chest.

"Right," Chloe said. "I was here one summer a long time ago. Actually, I visited a lot of summers, but we only ran into each other that year." He'd worked as a diver for Sea Search, Inc., the local marine salvage company whose search for sunken treasure had been the subject of many *National Geographic* television programs.

"I boarded here sometimes when Gwynne and her mom ran the place as a bed-and-breakfast."

"I remember." Oh, yes. He'd been a charismatic character in those days, tall and tanned and utterly charming.

If Ben recognized her, he gave no sign. "I've just rolled into town and was counting on Gwynne and Tayloe's having a room for me."

"You didn't call first?"

"I got a recorded message about the number not being in service at this time."

"That's because the Frangipani Inn is no longer a bed-and-breakfast."

"I'm sorry to hear that." For someone who needed a place to sleep for the night, he delivered the line with a bit too much nonchalance. He slapped absently at a whining mosquito. "Where have Gwynne and Tayloe gone?"

"Gwynne's off finishing her master's degree in speech pathology, and my aunt Tayloe remarried last year and lives in Mexico with her husband. I'm here to work for the summer. I design jewelry."

This was the season for thunderstorms riding in on warm

moist air from the Gulf of Mexico, and over the sound of her voice, Chloe detected a rumble of thunder in the distance. Tonight's predicted stormy weather was fast closing in.

"I don't suppose you'd rent me a room anyway," he said.

The crash of the breakers on the other side of the dunes filled the silence. She gazed up at the clouds scudding past the turret of the inn for a long moment before answering. "I'm not planning to run the house as a B and B."

Chloe felt the first spatter of rain. As she raised the window and cut the Volvo's engine, the scene went dark, and all she could see was the white stripes of Ben's shirt a few feet away.

"C'mon, Butch," Chloe said. She grabbed the cat and her backpack. Fortunately, the clouds from the oncoming storm had not yet obscured the moon, and as she slid out of the car she was able to get a good look at Ben Derrick. His eyes were murky in the darkness, and she couldn't recall their color. Strange, since she'd thought she'd never forget anything about him. Were they blue? Gray? She had no idea.

"Can I help you with that?" He reached for her pack, but she sidestepped quickly and whipped it out of his reach.

"No, I'll handle it. Thanks."

"I'd better check out the house with you this first time," Ben said gruffly.

"I don't think so," Chloe retorted. She turned, wondering what it would take to make this guy get in his Jeep and go. Couldn't he take a hint?

"The reason I suggested going in with you," Ben said with great patience, "is that if the house has been vacant, no telling what's inside."

Chloe was mindful of Gwynne's stated reasons for offering to let her live in the sea-worn old mansion. She'd mentioned concerns about vagrants, beach bums, kids partying inside and no one detecting their presence until much harm had been done. Maybe it *would* be a good idea to let Ben check out the place.

"Let's hurry. It's beginning to rain," Chloe said tersely. She started along the winding sandy path to the house as huge raindrops began to fall. The wind kicked up, and the air took on a sudden chill as rain sluiced down in great torrents, drenching them both.

They ran past thrashing clumps of sea oats and salt grass. When she reached the haven of the porch, Chloe set Butch down. The cat, spooked by the change in weather, shook himself and immediately bounded into the bushes below.

"Butch! Get back here!" She could barely make herself heard over the wind and rain.

Of course the cat didn't. Chloe wasn't concerned that Butch would try a disappearing act, since he knew who his food came from, but she wished he hadn't left her alone with Ben.

Who conveniently produced a flashlight from his pocket and beamed it on the rusty old lock. Chloe, clumsy in her haste, fumbled with the key, inserted it and swung the door open on a cavernous front hall.

A flock of dust bunnies scattered in the fresh gusts admitted through the open door as something dark scurried toward the nether regions of the house. Chloe groped for the light switch and flipped it. The lone bulb remaining in the overhead fixture flared and died.

"I'll turn on a lamp," Chloe said, wiping her face with her forearm before dropping her backpack on the hall settee. As she spoke, Ben trained the flashlight on the parlor to her right.

The house had been in her father's family since the early part of the century, and she and her older sister, Naomi, had spent many glorious summer vacations in the big Victorian mansion when she was growing up. A year ago when she'd last visited, the Frangipani Inn hadn't been in this state of disrepair. The furniture, layered with white covers, loomed eerily as she felt her way into the parlor's depths, where she knocked into a table, caught herself before keeling over and managed to turn on the light over the piano. It cast the shrouded shapes into gloomy shadows.

Dust was everywhere, and cobwebs trailed spookily from the high ceiling. The windows were coated with a thick coat of salt spray, and the air smelled musty. As she stood taking in all the decrepitude of a place that she remembered as bright, light and uplifting, Ben said, "Things deteriorate rapidly near the ocean. The place has been unoccupied for how long?"

"Almost a year," Chloe told him, her voice echoing because of the high ceiling. In order to see what was what, she shoved aside white muslin to reveal a wicker chair that belonged on the porch. One of its wooden rockers was split, and she tugged the cover back over it. As she did so, something scrambled frantically across her toes, something warm and furry with quick little feet.

At the same time, a flash of lightning and an earsplitting clap of thunder rent the silence. Chloe screamed and would have bolted if Ben hadn't caught her and held her steady.

"Easy," he said. "That was only a field mouse." His arms were hard-muscled and strong, she noticed through her panic. His heart beat steadily beneath his damp shirt, and his wet skin was slick beneath her fingers.

"I h-hate mice," she stammered.

He released her, and she saw that his eyes were a deep, velvety brown. He smelled of sun and salt, of the sea and sand, bringing back memories of that summer so long ago.

"There are bound to be one or two mice in here," he said, the voice of reason.

She recovered enough to scoff at that. "One or two? Ha! They breed," she said. She stalked toward the door. "I can't live with mice. I'm leaving."

Ben cocked a head toward one of the windows, which was rattling in its frame due to the energetic pummeling of the elements. "It's raining hard now, and there's lightning. Besides, there's nowhere else to go."

"Where is that cat when I need him?" she muttered. She threw the door open. "Butch? Butch!" Rain blew in her face; it tasted of salt. There was no sign of a big orange cat, no glimmer of his white bib under the shelter of the rubbery round leaves of the sea grapes.

Ben walked up behind her. "I saw him run under the house. He'll have a grand old time there chasing the mice and palmetto bugs."

"Palmetto bugs?"

"The state insect of Florida. See, there's one on the curtain." He pointed at a huge cockroachlike bug in the library on the other side of the foyer. It was an ugly dark brown, almost two inches long and waving curious feelers in their direction.

Chloe shuddered. She'd rather eat roadkill than bunk near that creature. "I'll sleep in the car. I'll—"

"No need to do any such thing. I'll run over to the other part of the house and get the bug spray." He started toward the kitchen.

Since she had no intention of being left alone with the palmetto bug, Chloe wasn't far behind. "Okay, but what about the mice?" She was seriously questioning her recent and possibly foolhardy choice to start a new life in this place.

"I'll take care of them, don't worry."

"Humanely, I hope."

He glanced at her over his shoulder, the corners of his mouth twitching. "Oh, of course. I'll invite them to leave in a pleasant voice, and I'll reassure them it's not them, it's me. I'll say that I hope we can still be friends, and even throw them a farewell party if you'd like."

"Please," she warned, "don't make light of this." She wasn't in the mood for humor.

"I thought maybe kindness to rodents ran in your family. Tayloe used to trap live mice and release them in the thickets, which I warned her was silly, since they—and their loved ones—would only come back for a return engagement, but that was the way she wanted it."

"You know where to find the mousetraps?"

"They're in the hall leading to the caretakers' annex."

They went along turning on lights until they came to the kitchen, Chloe doing her best to unstick her wet blouse from her skin along the way. Someone had broken a window in the back door and had evidently camped out there, abandoning dirty dishes and silverware in the sink, which was dripping a steady stream of rusty water.

"Here we are," Ben said, throwing back the bolt to the door of the annex, where a small apartment was built down close to the dunes. "Bug spray. And traps."

"Could you deal with the palmetto bug first? He creeps me out big-time."

While Ben was rummaging in the hallway, Chloe gave up on her wet blouse and resigned herself to its present see-through state until she could find a dry towel. She ventured a cautious peek into the pantry, which turned up nothing more than an unopened jar of pickles and several warm cans of cola. "I have food in the car, a bag of canned goods and a cooler," she called to Ben. "I could offer you something to eat in exchange for your trouble."

"It's okay," he said on his way back through the kitchen. "I'll be satisfied with a glass of water." He avoided looking at her—which, considering the transparency of her wet clothes, she appreciated.

She followed him. "The water softener isn't hooked up, so

we won't want to drink the water yet. I brought a bottle of wine in my backpack. It's a really good Estancia pinot grigio."

"No, thanks. And if you don't want to witness instant death, I suggest you leave the palmetto bug to me."

Since bug killing held no interest as a spectator sport, Chloe decided to locate a dry towel. The staircase was dusty, the white paint on the banister chipped, and upstairs the bedrooms, like the parlor below, were swathed in white muslin.

The linen closet was located on the landing, and although the towels smelled musty, they suited her purpose. As she towel-dried her hair, she wandered around, reacquainting herself with the second floor.

Her aunt had assigned each bedroom a name. The master suite was Sea Oats and decorated in golden tones. The room that had always been Chloe's was the turret room, Moonglow, and after she'd removed the dust covers and piled them in the hall, it appeared exactly as it had every year. She opened the windows an inch or so, enough to admit fresh air but not much rain.

Nostalgia swept over her as she took in the curved walls, the pretty blue-painted bureau, ornate wicker headboard and dotted-swiss curtains. She and Naomi had enjoyed many good times here with Gwynne—reading under the covers at night after Tayloe had told them to go to sleep, racing down the wide staircase in a flurry of anticipation when Zephyr the Turtle Lady tossed seashells against their windows early in the morning and invited them down the beach to inspect the newest turtle nest. Being in this room made her feel like a little girl again. Considering that she was over thirty and more worldly wise than she would have liked, that was a good thing.

"Chloe?"

Leaving the towel draped across her shoulders, she poked her head out the door, and saw Ben standing at the bottom of the stairs.

"The palmetto bug is history," Ben reported.

"Good. Now maybe I should squirt some of that stuff around my room."

"I'll be glad to spray the rest of the house. Then I'll set out the mousetraps."

"We don't have anything to bait them with," she said, coming out to the landing. "Unless mice are into dill pickles."

"I'm prepared to donate the cheese crackers in my pocket. That should work." He pulled out a package and opened it.

Chloe descended the staircase. "Not so fast. We might have to eat those ourselves."

"Are you hungry?"

"A little." Self-consciously, she ran her fingers through her hair, hoping it wasn't standing up in spikes.

Ben handed her a cracker. "That's to tide you over until I can run out to your car and bring in the food."

"You don't have to—"

"Hey," he said. "I can't stand to watch a woman starve. No big deal." He brushed past her up the stairs, carrying the can of insecticide, and she heard him humming tunelessly to himself as he went from room to room, anointing each one in turn.

Since there were eight bedrooms, each with its own bath, this took quite a while, during which Chloe inspected the dining room and removed the covers from the big mahogany dining-room table and chairs. The breakfront was devoid of its usual heirloom silver trays and goblets, which made the room seem bare, and Chloe recalled Gwynne's telling her that she'd put them in storage. The elegant bone china was still there, and so was the antique crystal, all under the surveillance of numerous saturnine Timberlake ancestors glaring down from ornate gilt frames.

When she'd finishing in the dining room, Chloe retreated to the kitchen and munched gloomily on Ben's cracker. The inn was a disappointment. True, her memories were based on idealized moments from past vacations. She hadn't been prepared for the general disrepair of the place, but she definitely couldn't go back to Texas. Her grandmother, with whom she'd lived for the past five years, had sold her house and moved to an assisted-living facility.

During the years with Grandma Nell, Chloe had saved her money in order to give herself a chance to do what she did best—design jewelry. Her cousin's offer to let her live here had been a godsend. But Chloe's work would suffer if she was forced to spend all her time cleaning and repairing the Frangipani Inn, not to mention that she didn't have a clue how to go about it.

When Ben returned, she wordlessly handed a can of warm cola up to him. He popped the top, sat down on a chair beside hers and drank, his throat working as he swallowed. "You don't remember me, do you?" she asked him suddenly.

He lifted a brow. "Cute. Red hair. Gwynne's cousin."

"Well, thanks for the cute, anyway," she said wryly.

"It was a long time ago. You were how old? Fourteen? Fifteen?"

"Sixteen," she told him, remembering the pain of longing for a guy who hadn't recognized her existence. He'd called her Carrots because of her red hair, and she'd hated that nickname.

"I was twenty-one and in my first season of diving for Sea Search, Inc."

"You seemed much older to me."

He snorted. "Honey, that summer I was getting older by the minute." His curt laughter didn't convey humor.

She got up to plug in the refrigerator. "I've been thinking," she said.

"Oh?" His eyebrows shot up.

"About your request to stay here. I wasn't anticipating sharing the place with anyone else because I have work to do, but if you'd help with repairs in exchange for rent, you could live in the annex. You'd have your own entrance and everything, and—"

"Hold it," he said. "You don't have to talk me into it. I have nowhere else to go, and I'm a decent handyman."

"That's good, because I don't know one screw from another."

He blinked at her, and she realized what he must be thinking. She felt her neck coloring. "We could give it a trial," she said quickly to cover her embarrassment. "Maybe a week or two?"

"That suits me, since I'm waiting for a job to come through and money is tight."

"You don't work with Sea Search anymore?"

"I haven't been employed there for over a year." Ben drained the can in one easy motion and stood up, crumpling it in his hand. "The rain has let up enough so that I can retrieve the food from your car," he said before tossing the can into the trash bin beside the door.

Chloe, her cheeks still flushed from her gaffe, handed over her car keys and watched from the window as Ben loped through the curtain of rain. He soon returned carrying bags of groceries that she'd bought before leaving Texas, sprinkling wet droplets around the kitchen as he shook water from his eyes.

"I spotted your cat. He's sitting under the porch steps."

"Butch will be okay on his own. He loves it here." She set a box of cat crunchies out on the counter for later and started to stash the rest of the food in the pantry.

"Would you like a sandwich?" she asked.

"No, I'd rather inspect my new digs."

"You'll have to plug in the refrigerator in there, and I'm not sure the hot-water heater works. Gwynne mentioned something about it."

"I'll check everything." He rose, and she found herself staring point-blank at his bare damp torso, exposed when his shirt had come unbuttoned. His physique, even though he was older than when she saw him last, was close to spectacular. Wide shoulders tapered to a narrow waist, and his legs were muscular and nicely formed.

"I'd better call Butch one more time," she said, mostly for something to do besides stare at the line of hair pointing toward his navel.

She stood and went to the door as Ben disappeared into the annex. Butch didn't appear when she called. Since she wasn't interested in flailing around beneath the porch in the hope of chasing him out, she went back inside and opened the can of tuna.

After her solitary meal, she climbed the stairs to her room and stripped off her wet clothes, noticing that the stream of water from her bathroom sink ran nonstop, a knob was missing from the vanity and the hook from the closet door lay on the floor. Thank goodness Ben Derrick had shown up. With him to help her, she might be able to make her ambitious plans for the summer work after all.

She was brushing her teeth when she heard a door open downstairs. "Chloe?"

"Uh-huh," she said through a mouthful of toothpaste. She grabbed a glass of water, rinsed her mouth and spit; the water here had a foul sulfur taste, but the water softener would take care of that.

"You're right. The hot-water heater isn't working."

She wrapped her robe tightly around her and went to the top of the stairs. Ben was standing in the foyer below.

"I'll look at it tomorrow," he said.

"Okay," Chloe said, her heart sinking. She didn't have extra money to pay for major repairs, and anyway, she wasn't sure whose responsibility they would be, hers or Gwynne's.

"I figured I'd better report it."

"Thanks. I think. Hey, you'll be needing a hot shower, won't you?"

"That would be nice, but I don't want to inconvenience you."

"The bathrooms up here are all supplied by the water heater under the attic stairs," she said, inclining her head in that direction. "It's working fine. I have personal knowledge of this."

"If you wouldn't mind—" Ben began, but she shushed him by holding up a hand.

"Use the bathroom off the master suite to my right. You won't be in my way."

"Cool," Ben said, and for a moment she could have sworn that he was ogling her bare legs below her short terry-cloth robe.

"No, hot," she said, referring to the water, but as he raised his eyebrows, she realized that he thought she was making a flirtatious comment about him.

"Good night," she mumbled in embarrassment, turning on her heel and fleeing to her own room, knowing that she hadn't mistaken the humorous glint in his eyes.

"Good night, Chloe," he replied, a hint of laughter in his voice.

Her room was filled with the sound of the rain on the roof and Ben taking his shower on the other side of the wall, which divided her room from the master bath. She couldn't stop visualizing Ben standing under the shower spray, soaping himself all over. The more she tried to banish him from her mind, the more vividly her imagination embellished his image.

"Ridiculous," she muttered as she fluffed her pillow for the fourth time. "I'm not here to get involved with a guy."

Except that it was a strange thing about not wanting to meet men. Sometimes all you had to do was decide that you didn't want any part of them, and suddenly, they were everywhere.

Popping up in your headlights. Crawling out of the woodwork like palmetto bugs. Showering in the room next door. Reminding you of when you were sixteen years old and eager to find out what love was all about.

Too bad that you couldn't just squirt men with something in a spray can and make them go away. Although even if that were possible, she wouldn't get rid of Ben Derrick.

Not that anyone could ever recapture the thrill of a first crush. No, better that Ben never realize that she'd cared for him. Better to hunker down at the Frangipani Inn, get to work and forget all about that special summer.

Chapter Two

Chloe's goal in taking up residence at the inn was twofold. The solitude would allow her to get her fledgling jewelry business off the ground, and she could stop solving other people's problems. It was difficult, after years of accepting the roles that other people expected her to play in their lives, to disengage. Grandma Nell had understood.

"You can't create space for new experiences and new people in your life if you're giving all your energy to people who drag you down," her grandmother had said. "It's time for you to leave behind unproductive and outmoded situations, Chloe. Go to Sanluca. Stay awhile."

The resounding message was that she needed to concentrate on herself for a change. After several rescue operations involving unsuitable men, Chloe couldn't have agreed more.

Of course, there would always be room in her life for Butch, who woke her the morning after she arrived by jumping on her feet and nibbling at her toes. Hoping to get back to sleep, she yanked one foot away, then the other. This only caused the cat to settle on her chest, purring loudly as he kneaded sharp claws in and out of her shoulder.

"All right, I'm awake," she told him grudgingly, treating him to a vigorous rub behind the ears before sliding out of bed and padding into the bathroom.

"How did you get in, anyway?" she asked, knowing that Ben must have opened the door for the cat. A glance at her watch told her that it was almost nine o'clock, late by her standards. Usually, when she was here, she was awake at dawn, since the rising sun's rays easily penetrated the thin curtains of her room.

Butch meowed and pawed at her leg. "Okay, okay," she said, lifting the toilet lid. Butch was toilet trained because she'd been relentless in her expectations. She took a dim view of scooping cat litter, and so did her grandmother, who had been skeptical about adopting a pet in the first place. Chloe had insisted that they keep Butch after he'd ventured out of the woods behind their house, skinny and scared. Now he weighed in at a hefty twenty pounds and was afraid of nothing.

Since Butch preferred privacy when he performed, Chloe wandered into the bedroom. She opened the windows to let in the breeze, marveling at the sight of the waves lapping on the shore. Though born and bred in the heart of Texas, she'd always felt a kinship with the sea.

Ben was sitting at the edge of the ocean, staring toward the horizon. She almost called to him, but something about the set of his shoulders gave her pause. She read discouragement in the way they slumped, and something else. Sadness? Sorrow? She wasn't sure, but she sensed that he was weighed down by some indefinable burden. He seemed different from when she'd first met him. In those days, he'd been full of personality, convivial and gregarious. People had been naturally drawn to him, and he'd basked in his own popularity. The change in him tugged at her heart even as she cautioned herself that whatever Ben's problems were, she wanted no part of them.

She returned to the bathroom, where Butch was now waiting

at the edge of the sink for his morning drink of water. After turning on the tap for him, she flushed the toilet, a skill that the cat had unfortunately not mastered. After one lick at the dripping faucet, Butch gave a disdainful little *brrrup!*—his equivalent of "yuck"—and jumped down.

Chloe started a shopping list. *Bottled water,* she wrote at the top as her cell phone rang. The caller ID revealed that it was Naomi, who, until she'd married her husband, Ray, the summer of high-school graduation, had accompanied her to Sanluca during their childhood summer vacations.

Naomi wasted no time getting to the point. "Chloe, guess what Tara's done now."

"I couldn't say right off," Chloe said cautiously as possibilities sequenced through her mind. Her teenage niece had recently decided that she didn't want to go back to high school in the fall. "Taken up skydiving? Joined a convent?" Chloe figured the only way to calm Naomi down was to make light of the situation.

"She's run away from home, that's what! Ray and I are frantic with worry. Tara finished her final exams and split. No one has a clue where she is."

"Did she leave a note?"

"She propped a sweet little card on her pillow, telling us not to worry."

"As if you wouldn't."

"As if," Naomi agreed with a sigh.

"At least Tara took her exams," Chloe pointed out.

"Why do you find this funny?" Naomi asked with remarkable forbearance. "We're beside ourselves with worry."

"Tara confided before I left Farish that she'd reformed. My guess is that she's hiding at a friend's house and they're pigging out on hot-fudge sundaes. You used to do that when finals were over, remember?"

"We're checking with all her friends, and in the old bunkhouses on some of their parents' ranches, and every other possible place. The police don't consider her disappearance a criminal matter because Tara left a note, went of her own accord and kids run away all the time. They believe she'll be back. I'm not so sure, Chloe. Tara and I had a big argument a couple of days ago."

Chloe's heart sank. "I'm sorry to hear that. Care to tell me about it?" She'd hoped that Tara was sufficiently chastened after her latest transgression of hosting an unchaperoned party when her parents weren't home. But then, Chloe knew about rebellion for rebellion's sake. She'd been a difficult teenager herself.

"On Sunday, Tara wanted to wear this really horrible outfit to church. I mean, it was so short that it would have raised the eyebrows of every little old lady in the congregation, including Grandma. Especially Grandma. And no bra, and—"

"I don't wear a bra sometimes." Like maybe never, Chloe was thinking, if the weather didn't cool off.

"You're a grown woman, free to make your own decisions about how you dress. Tara's still a kid. I told her that over my dead body would she leave the house in that getup, and she said that she hoped I wasn't planning to assume room temperature any time soon, but she was going, like it or not. And I said she wasn't, and she said I was a bitch, and—"

"She called you a bitch?"

"As well as other names I would rather not repeat. Then she stormed out of the house, wearing a dress no bigger than a sticky note. Ray and the twins and I waited for her to come home and were late for church because she never showed up. Or at least, she didn't come home until we were gone. I didn't figure out until late that night that she'd taken a duffel. She packed clothes, Chloe, and her teddy bear. She never goes anywhere without that bear."

Chloe sighed. This sounded like an updated version of her own difficult adolescence, though she hadn't had the comfort of a stuffed animal when, during Christmas vacation in her senior year of high school, she hitchhiked to visit a boyfriend who had recently moved to California.

"That's awful, Naomi. You have my heartfelt sympathies," Chloe told her.

"We've set off alarms in every direction. I've alerted Marilyn and her group in case she shows up in Dallas." Marilyn, their cousin, and her husband, Donald, had five kids. Tara had been close to that branch of the family most of her life.

"You'll call when you find her, won't you?"

"Sure. Let's hope it's soon."

"I'm sure it will be. She's a good kid, Naomi."

"I keep expecting her to walk through the front door—" Naomi broke off her sentence, a sob catching in her throat.

"I'm so sorry, Mimi." Chloe was the only one allowed to call Naomi by her old childhood nickname.

"I'll keep you posted. I wish I were in Florida with you. I worry about you being all alone there."

"Well, don't. Ben Derrick showed up."

"Who?"

"You wouldn't remember. You were already married to Ray the summer that Ben boarded at the inn and I was here."

"He's nice?"

"Also helpful."

"Age?"

It took a moment for Chloe to figure this out. "Thirty-seven."

She could picture her sister narrowing her eyes on the other end of the phone. "You haven't taken up with him already, have you?"

Chloe let out an exasperated sigh. "I've been here less than twenty-four hours, Naomi. Surely you jest."

"I am not in the mood for joking, Chloe. I'm falling apart. I can't even pull myself together long enough to throw a load of laundry into the washing machine."

"Do you want me to come home, Naomi? Help you out?" She waited with dread for her sister's answer, knowing that she'd go if Naomi needed her.

"No, Chloe," Naomi said. "We'll get through this. But thanks."

Chloe, all but heaving a giant sigh of relief, decided to broach a new topic. "How are Jennifer and Jodie?" she asked. Naomi and Ray's twin daughters were ten years old and never gave them any trouble. So far, anyway.

"J and J are upset that Tara's disappeared, like all of us."

"Give them my love."

"I will."

"And Grandma Nell—is she adjusting to the assisted-living home? Or is she still trying to decide if she likes it?"

"Chloe," Naomi said patiently. "Stop assuming responsibility for other people's well-being. Our grandmother is doing fine. She's made a new friend, and they watch their favorite TV program together every day. The friend's family treats them to dinner at the country club. Grandma's happy. Repeat after me. Grandma's *happy.*"

"'Grandma's *happy*,'" Chloe recited as if by rote.

"You've got it. You've got it! Listen, Chloe, I'd better hang up in case Tara tries to call home on this line instead of our cell phones."

"Okay. I'll talk to you soon."

"Love you," said Naomi.

"Love you, too."

She heard the sliding glass door to the annex grinding along its track. It was located under her bedroom window, and a glance outside told her that Ben was no longer sitting and staring morosely out to sea. While she dressed, she heard the Jeep's engine roar to life as Ben left. Briefly, she wondered where he was going, but she didn't have time to mull it over. She had work to do.

Downstairs, she threw all the windows open and hauled the wicker rockers outside to the front porch, where last night's rain had washed everything fresh and clean. A row of red hibiscus bushes bordered the porch, their flowers as big as saucers, and overhead, in a nearby palmetto tree, a mockingbird's white feathers flashed as it flitted to and fro. Beyond the rolling dunes, the sea was glassy and calm. This day, like every day in summer, would be scorchingly hot. The sun was already blazing down on the sand.

Unfortunately, the Frangipani Inn wasn't air-conditioned. Tayloe had been adamant that the winds off the ocean cooled it enough; she'd insisted that if the natural breezes had been good enough for her grandparents, they were good enough for her. Chloe wasn't so sure. Sea breeze or not, air-conditioning seemed like a really good idea in this hot and steamy climate.

Once she'd opened the house, she tackled the dirty dishes in the sink, then measured the small study off the library, where she intended to set up her workshop. The space was cluttered with an old treadle sewing machine, a box of dusty jelly jars and various other debris. She'd place a workbench at one end of the long, narrow room A telephone outlet behind Tayloe's old desk would make it convenient to connect to the Internet. Between the workshop and the kitchen, a large closet, formerly a butler's pantry, would house her jewelry-making supplies. The closet contained a safe, where she'd keep the precious and semiprecious gems she used in her one-of-a-kind designs.

All that decided, she was finishing off a slice of peanut butter toast when someone began hammering on the front door.

Through the sidelight, Chloe spotted a tattered white sailor hat with the brim pulled low. She threw the door open to Zephyr

Wills, one of the most senior of Sanluca's senior citizens. Known as the Turtle Lady, she felt that it was her obligation to safeguard the big loggerhead turtles that nested up and down the coast.

"Chloe!" Zephyr cried, her round wizened face crinkling into a broad smile. She was under five feet tall and as frail as a bird. "Gwynne told me you were driving all the way from Texas, gal. What's the matter—you tired of cowboys?"

"And how," Chloe said with feeling.

"Well, no wonder. All those sweaty horses, all that nasty dust. I knew a cowboy once, but never mind about that right now. Thought you'd never open the door. With Tayloe and Gwynne, I always walked right in. Didn't think you'd care for that, though."

"I, um, wouldn't have expected it," Chloe admitted.

The Turtle Lady wore her customary white long-sleeved shirt, which she donned every day for protection from the hot sun. Chloe could have sworn that Zephyr's plaid shorts were twenty years old, which was almost as long as Chloe had been vacationing at the Frangipani Inn. Zephyr carried a ruffled parasol; it was her trademark.

"Come for a walk with me, Chloe. We'll check out the latest nests."

Zephyr had always liked company on her morning nest-hunting expeditions. Tayloe was usually willing to oblige; Gwynne, too.

"I'd love to," Chloe told her, nudging Butch back inside with her foot.

"Get a hat. You don't want to have a sunstroke. Is your cat coming with us?

"No, he doesn't much like the beach."

"That's just as well. No telling what trouble he could get into out there."

Chloe found a hat on the rack inside the door and skipped down the steps with a kind of heady anticipation. In her girlhood, she had listened with fascination to Zephyr's explanation of the habits of loggerhead turtles. During their summer breeding season, female turtles lumbered onto land to lay eggs in a shallow nest in the sand. Then they returned to the ocean, never to see their own offspring, which hatched in a matter of weeks and clambered down the beach to the ocean, subject to predators and often so confused by the lights on land that they headed the wrong way. Zephyr considered it her mission in life to make sure the babies found the sea, and she sent them off with a little blessing and prayer for their safety.

Due to the nearby coral reefs being constantly ground to bits by wave action, the sand on this beach was famously pink. The ocean at this hour was still a deep cerulean blue, but as the day progressed and the sun climbed higher, its color would change to a cool, inviting turquoise. An onshore breeze, picking up now, fluttered the brim of Chloe's hat and ruffled her hair. As they walked, Zephyr cast inquisitive glances at her from under the parasol.

"You used to be a redhead," Zephyr stated. "What happened?"

"Uh, well, magenta and bronze and green and a color called Desert Dream, which I've settled on, finally. I want to look like a normal person for a change." She wore her hair in a straight bob slightly longer than chin length, having dispensed with the spiky style she'd tried last year.

"You always were kind of different," Zephyr ventured. "Gwynne was predictable, Naomi was sedate, but you were always turning cartwheels down the beach or ripping off all your clothes and jumping in the water."

Chloe laughed. "I doubt if I'll be doing any nude swimming around here now. There are lots more people on the beach these days."

"We have the new wilderness preserve to thank for that," Zephyr told her. "Lost Galleons Park, they call it, after the 1715 Spanish fleet that wrecked on the reefs while transporting gold and silver from the New World to Spain. Strange juxtaposition if you ask me—galleons in the New World and space launches right up the coast trying to find other new worlds. We're going to have a space-shuttle launch later this summer. You going to be around?"

"I'm sure I will. I like the name Lost Galleons Park."

"Ha! It's a descriptive name, but I wish they'd named the park after the turtles. Someone at the state capitol must have decided treasure is more important than loggerheads, though I don't see how."

"So much of the economy around here derives from the search for treasure," Chloe said. "Sanluca owes a lot to those sunken ships."

"Oh, it's 'treasure this and treasure that,'" Zephyr agreed. "Since I was knee-high to a sandpiper, those old ships have been the sole local industry."

"Gwynne told me the Frangipani Inn will become part of the park complex eventually."

"The house and its land will be absorbed into the system once Gwynne and her mother die. That's the way Tayloe wanted it. Can't say if it's a good idea of not. Bunch of tourists browsing through that grand old house! The park people intend to use it for a museum or some such."

"That's better than tearing it down and building a condominium," Chloe said with conviction. She regretted that concrete-and-glass condo buildings had sprung up along much of the Florida coastline. The tall towers blocked the very thing that people had moved here to enjoy—abundant sunshine.

"Ben, now, he'd agree with us about condos," Zephyr said.

Chloe kept planting one foot in front of the other. "You've seen him lately, I take it."

"I ran into him on the beach last night before the storm. First met him years ago when he first came to Sanluca from a little town in the Glades. I already knew his mama and daddy from a time when I lived out there. I hadn't seen him in a long while. Hardly had a chance to talk with him before the wind and rain came up. Bad storm, that. Knocked a bunch of mangoes off the tree at my house. Look over there now and you'll see the latest turtle clutch."

Chloe shaded her eyes from the sun when she spied the orange flag signaling a turtle nest. Zephyr gestured at the mesh net, about two feet high, that she'd placed around the nest to keep raccoons, possums and other land predators from disturbing the eggs. "Last night, I was watching the mama turtle and waiting for her to finish when Ben came along with his metal detector," Zephyr said. "The man startled me, I'll grant him that. I was paying attention to the eggs dropping into the sand when up walks someone I didn't recognize at first. Never saw Ben Derrick with a beard before."

"It's not quite a beard, only the beginning of one."

"You ask me, he's going for the whole megillah. You should talk him out of it."

"Like he'd pay any attention," Chloe retorted as they headed back toward the inn. "I hardly know him." She wished her friend would talk more about Ben, but she was disappointed when instead, Zephyr changed the subject.

"Say, about that cat of yours. You'll need to put a bell on him if he's to run loose. Prevent him from sneaking up on the shore birds," she said.

"He'll have enough to do with keeping the mice at bay in the inn."

"Never saw a cat that didn't stalk birds."

"Butch is different." She decided against telling Zephyr that Butch was toilet trained. Zephyr probably wouldn't believe it anyway.

They started up the boardwalk, which meant that if Chloe was going to learn anything more about Ben, she'd better get Zephyr talking. "Ben's been away from Sanluca a long time, I guess," she prodded.

"Couple of years. Had to leave after he got fired from Sea Search. Not that I pay much attention to what people say, when all's said and done. People say too much. That's why I like animals a lot more."

Keeping Zephyr on the topic was hard. "Ben was fired?" Chloe asked. This was electrifying information; she'd had no idea.

"That's all I'll mention, though he's lucky to be alive after that accident."

"What accident?"

"Not on that motorcycle of his, if that's what you're thinking."

"He drives a Jeep now."

"It was a diving accident. He surfaced from one of the shipwreck sites too fast. They get the bends, divers do, if they don't take time to decompress on the way up."

"They can die," Chloe said, remembering how Gwynne had explained it to her one summer, complete with facial grimaces and elaborate descriptions of how a diver's blood could boil and their hearts could burst. Now that she was grown-up, Chloe suspected that Gwynne had embellished her story for effect, but the bends—or DCS, which stood for decompression sickness—was still nothing to fool with.

"Dumb thing, that," Zephyr said. "Ben not taking care of himself, I mean. Losing his job. By the way, I've got some of those windfall mangoes in my car. Thought you might like a few to eat. I'll get them for you."

"Great," Chloe said with little enthusiasm as Zephyr left her to go to the parking lot. She wondered why Ben had surfaced too fast from a dive. As an experienced diver, he would have known better.

Zephyr returned with the mangoes, and Chloe invited her inside for a while.

"Nope, I've got to get back home. Maybe some other time. I'm glad you're here, Chloe. The inn has been vacant too long."

"The whole place needs tidying up," Chloe confessed, "but I'm too busy right now setting up my workshop. Maybe I'll get around to cleaning in a few days." Privately, she doubted she'd have time.

"You want that big place clean you should hire locals to do it. Too many people are without jobs these days. Citrus harvest is in the winter, and in the summer the packing houses are closed. Teenagers especially need work," Zephyr said. She gestured down the boardwalk, where a group of girls and boys were horsing around, slapping one another with damp towels and shrieking. "They get up to no good if they don't have enough to do for three months. Ben may know someone. Maybe even those kids."

"Perhaps I'll ask him," Chloe said, and left it at that.

THE FIRST THING Ben did when he left the inn the morning after his arrival was to stop by Keefe's Dive Shop, where local divers congregated and bought equipment as well as supplies. Dave Keefe, the genial owner who had outfitted Ben with scuba gear years ago when he'd first come to town, greeted him effusively.

"Ben, I'm glad to see you," he said, after clapping Ben on the back and shaking his hand. "You've been gone too long. What are you doing with yourself these days?"

"Trying to earn a living. I don't work for Sea Search anymore."

A shadow passed over Dave's face. "I heard."

"The thing is, Dave, I'm still a certified scuba instructor. I'd like to pick up a class or two. It would help me make ends meet."

Seeming thoughtful, Dave circled back behind the counter. “I can help you out,” he said slowly. “I’m teaching a group of beginners, but I’d like some time off. Would you consider taking over? The class is on Thursday evenings, seven to ten, in the pool out back. I teach the basic stuff.”

“You’ve got a deal,” Ben said, his hopes rising. Maybe reestablishing himself around here wouldn’t be so difficult to after all.

“See you next Thursday? I’ll introduce you to the students and bug out right away.”

“Sure.”

Dave rummaged on a shelf under the counter. “Here’s the scuba manual. I can’t teach you much about diving, but you should be familiar with questions the students will ask.”

“No problem,” Ben assured him.

His spirits were high as he drove down Loquat Street, which passed for the main drag in Sanluca. The town’s appellation was a corruption of San Luca, which was the name of the spring-fed river that drained into the Intracoastal Waterway, known in these parts as Spaniard’s Lagoon. Back in the days when Florida belonged to Spain, the lagoon, protected by several barrier islands and accessible from the ocean through a natural inlet, had been a popular safe anchorage for ships that plied the shore.

A sign at the edge of town welcomed visitors: Sanluca, it proclaimed. Home Of Sea Search, Inc., And Not Much Else. Underneath, in smaller letters, it said, Proudly Undeveloped. True, because on Florida’s east coast, to find any place that hadn’t been overbuilt, straining schools, social services and infrastructure, was rare. Sanluca had avoided that fate because the town was small in area and most of it had been set aside as a nature preserve.

Besides Dave’s dive shop, Sanluca’s business district encompassed a post office, a gas station, a combined art gallery and gift shop, a small treasure museum and the Sand Bar, which was a local hangout at the city marina. For nostalgia's sake and in celebration of landing the teaching job, Ben acted on impulse and stopped in at the Sand Bar to order a burger, medium rare, with cheese and onions.

"Want a beer?" asked Joe Devane, the beefy bushy-haired bartender. He and Ben went back a long way, to the first year Ben worked at Sea Search.

"No, a glass of water will do," Ben told him, reacquainting himself with the Sand Bar's decor, which consisted of fishnet draped around dried starfish hung on the wall. An old ship's wheel was mounted above the pool table, and outside was a thatched hut where you could belly up to the bar and listen to pickup jazz sessions at night.

Joe slid a glass across to Ben, leaving a slick, wet trail on the polished wood. Ben drained the drink in almost one gulp. It was easy to get dehydrated in this tropical climate. The sun baked the moisture right out of a person's skin.

"You working for Andy McGehee again?" Joe asked.

Ben shrugged. "I've talked to him about it. He's full up. Got enough divers, he says." He wasn't surprised at Joe's question. At the Sand Bar, local treasure hunters talked casually and often about the business.

"There're always one or two divers who quit in the course of a summer. He'll hire you."

"Maybe. In the meantime, I'm going to be teaching a scuba class for Dave Keefe."

"That's great, but don't give up on Andy. He was in here the other day with some of the guys on his crew. They were talking about last year's hurricane and how it uncovered new sections of the wrecks offshore."

"Couldn't help but do that," Ben agreed. A good storm was a treasure hunter's dream.

"He'll need all the divers he can get."

"Yeah, well," Ben said. He understood Andy's unwillingness to hire him after he'd let him go during what Ben privately thought of as the bad time. Andy was probably unconvinced that Ben had since shaped up, and that was understandable.

"Are you staying around here somewhere?" Joe asked. There weren't many options, even in the off-season. The Sanluca Motel was a dilapidated scratcher with ten dimly lit rooms where people rarely wanted to spend more than one night. The nearest real hotel was twelve miles away and charged for one night's lodging twice what most locals earned in a day. The other alternative was an RV park where the owner, old Ducky Hester of the gnarled teeth and bodacious BO, might let someone stay for a night or two in the trailer of an owner who only occupied it in the winter; Ducky pocketed the money with the owner none the wiser. Ben considered himself lucky to have run into Chloe Timberlake last night, and even luckier that she was allowing him to stay in the apartment at the Frangipani Inn.

"I'm living at Tayloe and Gwynne's place," he said.

"I heard they closed up the inn and moved away."

Ben shrugged. "Tayloe's niece is looking after things," he said.

"That's good. For you, I mean."

Ben nodded and took a long drink of water as Joe moved away to greet another customer.

His hamburger was done perfectly, and Ben soon became aware that the waitress, who wore a halter top and sported a silver ring in her navel, was sending soulful looks in his direction. When she slapped the check on the table, she sidled a little closer than necessary. "Joe says you're hoping to sign on with Sea Search," she said. He made himself focus on a large white pelican, one of a flock that roosted on the pilings around the place.

"Yeah," he said. "That's the plan."

"My brother works for Andy McGehee. I could put in a good word for you."

The pelican flew away, flapping its wings as it soared awkwardly above the lagoon. "Sure," he said easily. "If you want." He waited for her to reel in whatever strings were attached.

"Okay, I'll mention it. You're Ben, right?"

"Ben Derrick," he said.

"I'm Liss," she said. "Liss Alderman."

He vaguely remembered a young guy named Alderman. The kid had hung around the city docks a lot, and in fact, Tommy Alderman had still been in high school back when Ben had worked for Andy McGehee.

"Nice to meet you," Ben said. He didn't mention that he'd met Tommy. That would only encourage her.

"Same here." Liss favored him with a blindingly white smile and flounced away, twitching her derriere. Damn, but she was young. Only twenty-two or so, and that was too much of an age difference. He didn't dare bring women around to the inn anyway, since his landlady might object.

Not that Chloe was interested in him, though she'd warmed up considerably after he played Bwana of the Jungle and wiped out a couple of palmetto bugs. He smiled, recollecting how she'd flown into his arms when the mouse ran over her foot. She'd reacted like a scared schoolgirl, like his thirteen-year-old daughter, for Pete's sake.

That thought sobered him quickly, and a mantle of sadness settled over him. After two years, he should have stopped obsessing about what had happened. About how it was all his fault.

He tossed money on the table, gave Joe a salute of sorts, and, head down, hurried to his Jeep. Better to stay busy doing something, anything, than to start thinking. Booze used to work, but he'd given it up after drinking had almost scuttled what was left of his life deeper than any of those old shipwrecks out on the reef. But, finally, he was sober again. The trick would be to stay that way. Some trick.

"'Bye, Ben," Liss called through one of the open windows.

He waved halfheartedly in her direction, wondering what days she didn't work. No need to come back if she was going to put the moves on him.

He'd managed to avoid Chloe this morning. If his luck held, she'd be out when he got back to the Frangipani Inn. That way, he wouldn't have to talk to her. Not that she was hard to talk to, really. He even liked her, sort of. He almost remembered her from the year when his life had changed, the year when he'd married Emily.

Marrying Emily had taught him not to get close to anyone. He'd abandoned that precept when Ashley was alive, but those circumstances had been different. Ashley had been his adored daughter, and it had been easy to give her his heart.

Never again. He didn't want to love anyone that much. Saying goodbye was always so painful. And sometimes goodbyes happened whether you expected them or not.

"BEN!" CHLOE CALLED.

Ben stuck his head out of the closet where he was installing a new heating element in the annex water heater. He'd hoped he'd be through in here and could make himself scarce before Chloe stopped pushing and dragging things around Tayloe's old study. He'd heard her at it when he returned home after lunch, and he'd called out an offer to help, which she'd turned down. Well, he had enough to do, and he wished Chloe hadn't chosen this moment to pay a visit.

"Back here," he replied. "In the annex."

Chloe appeared in the hall from the kitchen, her hair piled on top of her head and damp tendrils trailing down her neck. She was wearing a sleeveless tie-dyed T-shirt cut off above her waist, and a pair of the shortest shorts he'd ever seen. Last night he hadn't paid much attention to her, except for that remark about his being hot. Well, she hadn't meant him—he was pretty sure of that by the way she'd slunk off to her room afterward—but now, well, she was the hot one. He made himself pull his gaze away from the swell of her breasts under that tight-fitting shirt.

"What's wrong with the water heater?" she asked.

"The thermostat. Not too difficult to repair, but it gets hot in the closet." There was that word again. Hot. It had popped out without his thinking about it. Embarrassed, he wedged himself back into the stifling space.

"We could open these windows wider," she said, walking past him and heading for his bedroom. He didn't like her trespassing on what he now considered his territory; it was only a bedroom, a living area and a small kitchen, but he'd spread his meager possessions throughout, and it would be his home for a while. He hoped.

"Euwww, there's a lizard in here." Chloe made tracks back toward the kitchen.

"He won't hurt you," Ben said curtly. "In fact, he'll help keep the insect population down."

"Well, I guess a lizard's not so bad. I was used to them in Texas. Didn't you spray insecticide in this apartment?"

"Nah, I don't like the smell of it. Me and my lizard buddy will make out fine. Say, could you see if there's a rubber gasket lying around anywhere? I'm missing one."

"Here it is." She handed it to him, which meant that she had to step inside the closet, which meant he got a close-up view of most of her.

She had a freckle in the white of her eye, an adjunct to the liberal dusting of freckles on her upturned nose. This fascinating combination caused him to stare at her a tad longer than made her comfortable, if fidgeting was any indication.

"The fridge in the apartment works okay?" she asked. She lifted a straggle of pale hair off her face.

"Sure. I put bottles of water in there earlier. Help yourself."

"Got any beer?"

"Nope. Sorry."

"That's okay." She wore multiple earrings, which jingled as she went to the kitchen, and he heard the sound of her opening and closing the refrigerator door. "Can I bring you anything?"

"I'll be through in here in a minute." He cast a glance out of the closet and saw her sauntering to the glass door. He liked the way she looked silhouetted against the sand dunes outside, all legs and pout. Not a perturbed pout, just one that occurred naturally when she was thinking. What would she be thinking at the moment? He had no idea.

He edged his way out of the closet and mopped his brow with a rag. She turned toward him. "I've arranged for the phone to be hooked up, and the water-softener folks are sending a man out as soon as possible."

"Good, since I've never owned a cell phone and hope I never will," he replied. "Plus bottled water can get pricey after a while."

"Also, Ben, keep track of your expenses for the water heater and everything else that you do. I'll see that you're reimbursed, but whether it'll be me who does the reimbursing, I don't know. I'll have to ask Gwynne."

"You talk to her much?" He brushed past Chloe into the kitchen. Her hair was the prettiest shade of blond, shimmery like sunbeams. It wasn't her natural color—he remembered her as a redhead. Not that it mattered. She was one of those women who was born to be blond. In the sun streaming through the window, her skin, damp with perspiration, gleamed.

She kept her head turned away. "Gwynne doesn't answer her phone."

While he washed his hands at the kitchen sink, Chloe wandered over to a shelf built into the wall. "What's all this?" she asked with interest.

"A collection of artifacts that I've recovered over the course of my career." He didn't add that they were small and could be transported easily when moving around a lot. They were his connection with his chosen line of work, the only remembrance he'd kept of his past life before the bad time.

"I've never seen anything like that statuette," she said.

"It's a clay dog, probably a toy made by descendants of the Mayans in Mexico. That's a silver bosun's whistle beside it, and a pewter shoe buckle in the front. All those objects date from the 1700s."

"This must be a wine bottle," she said, studying it.

"Not too many bottles survived in perfect condition like that one," he told her.

"And this?" She gestured at a slim gold ring intricately carved and set with three emeralds.

"Recovered from a wreck of a merchant ship in the keys. It was so beautiful I've never wanted to sell it. See, the emeralds aren't cut with the precision we've grown to expect in modern times. They're rough, without many facets. That only adds to the charm as far as I'm concerned." He'd planned to give the ring to Ashley when she was older, and now it made him sad.

He went abruptly to the refrigerator, twisted off the top of a bottle of water and drank deeply.

"It's beautiful," Chloe said, still appraising the ring. "Artistically crafted."

He surmised that since she designed jewelry, the ring was of particular interest to her, but he didn't want to discuss it anymore.

"I could use a swim about now," he said. It was a remark meant to distract, not necessarily to produce results.

"Race you to the beach."

In a matter of seconds, Chloe had wriggled out of her shirt. Her breasts were covered—if you could call it that—by a wisp of a bikini bra in a delicate shell-pink. It was almost the exact shade of her skin, and he did a double take before he figured out that it wasn't her underwear but a swimsuit.

Next, she stepped out of her shorts, revealing an even briefer excuse for a bikini bottom.

"Let's go!" she said.

"I—well, I have to put on swim trunks."

"Okay, meet you down there." She set the empty water bottle on the table beside a chair and headed out the sliding glass door, leaving him agog in her wake.

Nothing shy about Chloe Timberlake, that was certain. He wondered if she was as easygoing about the rest of her life, like making love, for instance.

Why this occurred to him he couldn't imagine, though he supposed that her near-naked body might have something to do with it. His memories of her when she was a kid were spotty at best, but he was sure that she hadn't been this well-endowed, her breasts high and firm, her derriere rounded in the right places.

He pulled on his trunks in record time, grabbed a towel and followed her. The sky above was laced with slow-moving clouds, and the sun-baked sand burned his bare feet. As he jogged out of the dunes, he spotted Chloe lolling in the shallows close to shore where last night's wave action had scooped out a tidal pool right below the high-tide line.

"Hi," Chloe said, interrupting his reverie. "Come on in. I'd forgotten how this is like having our own little swimming pool right down here on the beach."

He waded in. The water was too warm, more like the temperature of a bathtub than the ocean, and it was translucent, so that every shell and rock on the bottom was clear.

"I know what I want," Chloe said, leaping to her feet and scrambling out of the water. That swimsuit of hers was almost transparent; the outlines of her nipples were visible. He glanced away, his mouth suddenly dry.

"I'll be right back," she said. She ran up the beach and disappeared into the dunes.

I know what I want, she'd said. He tried to stop thinking about what *he* wanted, which was, let's be honest here, a tumble with her.

Once, he wouldn't have put it in those terms. Each woman he'd met before the bad time was new territory to be explored, and he didn't only consider their bodies. No, he'd always been vitally interested in what went on in their heads. He'd been fascinated with the dimensions of women's minds, how they brought different perspectives to life than men, how they never failed to surprise and delight him. There had been many women after Ashley's mother, from whom he'd been divorced shortly after their daughter was born.

All the women after Emily had enriched his life immeasurably, but he'd never remarried. He'd flitted here and there like a butterfly, alighting in one place for a while and then moving on to something that promised to be sweeter but often wasn't. He wouldn't ever do that again. It was a way of life requiring optimism, a quality that was missing in his makeup these days.

So why was he feeling positively hopeful as Chloe Timberlake reappeared on the path?

Chapter Three

Chloe, he saw as she moved closer, was carrying a couple of deflated beach rafts over her arm.

"I discovered these in the hall closet," she said as she sat on the sand at the edge of the pool. "Here, one's for you." She tossed it to him.

Chloe made a comical sight with her cheeks puffed out as she prepared to blow up the raft. This was a woman who was as unselfconscious as they came.

"I'm looking forward to floating around in the water and getting a suntan," she said between breaths. She acted as if anything she suggested should be all right with him.

"Okay," he said. Her plan didn't sound half-bad, though he didn't need a tan. He could understand why she wanted one. Her skin was as pale as a tourist's.

"You'd better put on sunscreen," he cautioned.

"Already did," she said in that jaunty way of hers, the faint aroma of coconut-scented suntan lotion wafting in his direction.

Ben concentrated on inflating the raft, wondering if it wouldn't have made more sense to use the air compressor in the annex closet to do the job. But then he wouldn't have had the pleasure of watching Chloe puckering up, a sight that put him in mind of other reasons she might do so. He'd bet her lips were soft and pliant, capable of eliciting the most delectable sensations.

Damn, he'd better stop thinking in such terms or this raft wouldn't be the only thing that inflated.

"There," Chloe said with satisfaction. She launched the raft with a little push. A couple of fish skittered away, but Ben scarcely noticed now that Chloe was splashing into the water and preparing to board.

Ben knew for certain that there was no graceful way to get on a raft that was floating in the water. You could belly flop, or you could straddle it, or you could shove it under your body and hope it didn't go all cattywampus. But somehow Chloe managed to arrive stomach-up on the raft with remarkable grace, holding him spellbound in the process.

When she was settled, one hand trailed in the water, the other rested on her abdomen. Her eyes, he discerned in the bright sunlight, were not blue but a delicate shade of lavender, with long dark lashes. Ben usually wasn't a fan of women with pointy chins, and he couldn't exactly say that Chloe's was pointy, but it wasn't rounded, either. In the middle of it was a dimple that fascinated him because it went away when she smiled, which was exactly the opposite of what dimples usually did. And her eyebrows had a coquettish slant to them, which he didn't think came from plucking or waxing.

"Is something wrong?" Chloe asked suddenly.

"No, no," he said too hastily. "I was just watching that guy with the parasail over there." Down near the inlet, someone was floating effortlessly above the ocean, dangling from a multicolored nylon parachute.

"Right," Chloe said, after gazing in that direction for a moment, but she sounded unconvinced.

"When the tide comes in, this pool will disappear," he said, mostly for conversation's sake. He launched himself onto his raft stomach down, then paddled toward the far end of the pool, which was perhaps twenty-five feet away.

"That's why it's important to take advantage of it," Chloe said as she drifted along beside him. "I intended to go for a quick swim, cool off a bit before getting to work, but it's going to be difficult to concentrate. I keep worrying about my niece. She's AWOL, and my sister is beside herself."

"They live in Texas?"

"Back home in Farish." Chloe outlined how Tara had disappeared.

"Like you say, she's probably fine," Ben said.

Chloe sighed. "Things had seemed to settle down with her, but I should have known better. I had a difficult adolescence myself."

"I was into trouble most of my teenage years," he told her. "Riding with a group of kids on motorcycles, finding all kinds of mischief. I lived in Yahola, a small town inland from here. Lake Okeechobee was to the south, a bunch of cattle ranches situated to the north, and I was bored out of my gourd." He slanted a look at her to assess how she was taking this. She seemed interested rather than critical.

"Me, too," she said. "To me, Farish, Texas, was the most nowhere place in the world. Our Main Street started at the courthouse square and ended in a cow pasture." She laughed. "I can't believe I've voluntarily moved to Sanluca, population two thousand. That's approximately six thousand fewer people than Farish."

"If this is where you can pursue your dream, it's worth it, Chloe. That's how I ended up here when I was nineteen."

"What got you from Yahola to Sanluca?" Curious, she glanced at him.

"I got a book at the library, and it showed pictures of people diving for treasure off the Florida Keys. After I read it, I hopped on my motorcycle and rode over to see a friend who had moved here, keen to find out if he knew anything about Sea Search. He introduced me to Andy McGehee. Andy said, 'Kid, you've gotta learn to dive before I'll talk to you,' so after that, I spent every penny I earned on scuba lessons and all my spare time diving."

"You had a passion," she said softly, shading her eyes with a hand for a moment to stare at him.

"I'll always be grateful to the librarian who recommended that book."

"That's probably the key to reaching Tara. Helping her find her niche, I mean. She's assured me she's over her past problems. Maybe she'll find her own passion."

"What kind of problems has she had?" he asked.

"Tara shoplifted on a dare and got caught. She lifted a pair of panty hose from a store in a mall in Austin. She was only thirteen at the time."

"I did worse than that myself. I set the local postmaster's rural mailbox on fire."

She lifted her head to stare at him. "You didn't!"

"'Fraid so. It's a federal crime. He was friendly with my folks, though, and didn't prosecute."

"Whatever possessed you?"

"I probably just wanted attention."

"Maybe that's Tara's problem. Her twin sisters are six years younger, and they tend to steal the show. When Tara got in trouble for shoplifting, Naomi and Ray were forced to notice her."

"Don't they usually?"

"They adore her, and the twins, too. Unfortunately, twins tend to take up a lot of time. It's even worse when they're adorably cute like Jennifer and Jodie."

"I hope Tara shows up soon, Chloe."

"Thanks. I shouldn't let myself obsess about her to the point where I can't work, especially since I'm sure she's hiding out someplace safe—maybe an older friend's apartment or the house of a family who's on vacation."

He turned his head toward her. "What kind of work do you plan to do here?" he asked. If she really was a jewelry designer, he couldn't imagine why she'd come to Sanluca.

"I'm into a new venture. Sea-glass jewelry." A glimmer of perspiration had appeared on her top lip. Ben quashed a desire to lick it away.

"Sea glass, huh?"

"Well, it's better than a couple of things I've tried in the past. Like gourmet dog biscuits and feng shui, neither of which went over too well in Farish."

"What's sea glass, anyway?" At least Ben knew what gourmet dog biscuits were; he wasn't sure about feng shui.

"It's glass that has been tumbled and scoured by the sand and the sea. It comes in all different colors—cobalt-blue, turquoise, the deepest purple or amethyst, celadon, jade. I got the idea when I was visiting Gwynne last summer and we picked up the most lovely specimens down here on the beach. I fiddled around with it, learned to encase it in cages of sterling silver or fourteen-carat gold. I've designed earrings around sea glass, and rings, and bracelets, and necklaces, and slides, and all sorts of things."

He'd noticed the small pendant she wore. "Is that one of your pieces?" he asked. The jewellike shard of translucent celadon couched in silver was cradled in the hollow of her throat.

"I found this bit on a day that I was beachcombing with Tayloe and Gwynne. It's the first necklace I made. Now I craft more intricate designs, compositions of sea glass intermingled with precious and semiprecious stones."

"Very clever. Can you actually make a living doing that?" he asked.

"It depends. My grand plan involves placing my more elaborate pieces in high-end stores."

"I bet that's not easy to do."

"I have a couple of ideas in mind. Gwynne's godmother, Patrice DesJardin, owns a shop in Palm Beach. I've called and left her a message about my jewelry. Gwynne thinks Patrice will be interested." Her raft rose and fell with the gentle motion of the water. They didn't speak for a few minutes.

"When will you find out if your job's going to materialize?" she asked after a while.

"In a few weeks, I hope. I've been talking to Andy McGehee about working with him at Sea Search again. In the meantime, I'll be teaching a scuba class."

"Andy's something of a local legend. Do you know him well?" She seemed to be choosing her words carefully.

"I worked for him for a long time," he said, unwilling to give anything away.

"Tayloe mentioned that he's made a lot of money with Sea Search," Chloe said. "I've passed by the treasure museum in town where he displays some of the loot, and Gwynne told me he's built a huge compound for his family on Manatee Island." The island, reachable by Beach Road over a bridge from Stuart's Point, which was about four miles north of the inn, was where many celebrities kept large and exquisitely appointed winter homes.

"Andy is a millionaire several times over. He started treasure salvage in the early days, when not many people believed it could be done. 'What's lost is lost,' they used to say around here, but Andy proved them wrong."

"How do the divers in one of these treasure-hunting outfits divvy up the find? I've always wondered."

His raft was drifting closer to hers, and if it continued on its course, they'd collide. Ben kicked lazily with one foot until he'd turned around where he could see her. "A lot of people ask that. After we bring the treasure up, it's all kept in one big pile, so to speak. At the end of the season, the state of Florida takes its percentage due under the law. The rest is parceled out equally among the group."

"Have you ever found anything really valuable?"

"One year I found a chunk of coral that broke away to reveal a beautiful gold crucifix. I sold it to a collector for sixty thousand dollars."

"No kidding!" Chloe raised her head. Her earrings, all three pairs, glinted in the sun.

"There's a lot more out there," he said. "That's why I've got gold fever."

"And sea water in your veins," Chloe added.

"Right," he said, amused.

They floated silently for a while, listening to the soothing sound of waves breaking nearby. Every so often, a flock of gulls circled, soon soaring away in search of something more interesting. After a couple with two children and a dog ambled past, Chloe flipped over onto her stomach, the motion sending a wake across the pool.

"I'm going to the store later," she announced suddenly. "We could cook steaks for dinner if you'd like to join me."

"Steak sounds good," he heard himself saying, though he'd figured he could grab something at the Sand Bar.

"Great. Seven o'clock, and I'll provide a salad, too."

"I'll bring a couple of baking potatoes," he offered.

Chloe levered herself off her raft into the water and submerged for a moment. When she came up, her hair was plastered to her head and her skin glistened with water. Tiny drops beaded her eyelashes, shimmering in the sun. The effect was enchanting.

Ben found it impossible to pull his eyes away as Chloe towed her raft toward the edge of the pool. Her wet bikini clung to her form, delineating every curve. When she half turned toward him, he swallowed, wishing that he didn't have such a ready response to this woman. For her part, she seemed totally unaware of her electrifying effect on him as she bent to pluck something from the water.

"This is a wonderful example of sea glass," she said, holding it toward him. The breeze blew a few drops of dripping water onto his warm forearm. In the palm of her hand was a slim half-moon shape, slightly curved, its color as delicate as a lilac petal.

"It's almost the same shade as your eyes," he blurted, and the look she gave him indicated an awareness that hadn't been there before. An awareness of—what?

Her fingers closed over the shard, and he stared at her from behind his sunglasses, overcome with regret that they had become so sexually aware of each other in such a short time. He needed someone he could talk with, hang out with, maybe who would like to take in a movie occasionally. He most certainly didn't need the complication of a woman and all the accompanying hassles.

"Dinner," she said, aiming a coquettish grin at him. He was convinced that she didn't mean to flirt. Those glances, the sparkle in her eyes, that sinuous walk meant nothing.

"Right," he replied.

She waded out of the water, and Ben was relieved when she disappeared beyond the dunes. She might not realize her effect on him, but he certainly did, and he was wary of starting anything with her.

On the other hand, why not go for it?

Because you can't care about her in any meaningful way, he told himself. That should have been sufficient reason, but as he watched her progress toward the inn, it wasn't at all.

CHLOE WAS GLAD Ben had accepted her dinner invitation, which she had half expected him to refuse. He had a way of keeping a his distance, like a lot of loners, and the loner species of male wasn't one that she wanted to cultivate. Certainly he was polite enough, and today they'd established a personal connection when he'd revealed something about his troubled youth.

"I wouldn't be alone, even without him," she said to Butch, who bounded out of the nearby stand of Australian pines and met her at the spigot near the bottom of the porch stairs, where she'd stopped to wash the sand off her feet. "I'd have you, wouldn't I?" She shook the water off and dried her feet on a towel.

Butch, after allowing himself to be petted, led her into the house, tail high. He jockeyed into position near his food dish for a handout, so she relented and gave him the leftover tuna that she'd saved from last night.

"I can't figure out how you manage in that fur coat of yours," she said to Butch. "This weather is so hot, even for me." She headed for the shower, her second of the day.

Afterward, she slipped into a clean sleeveless blouse and comfortable khaki shorts, and went to put the barbecue together. She'd noticed the pieces strewn around the back porch earlier. With a good deal of effort, she managed to insert the legs into their slots on the bottom of the grill pan but couldn't figure out how to get the rack to fit evenly on top.

Butch sat on the back porch railing, all but rolling his eyes at her clumsiness. "I've already broken a fingernail, not that it matters, and this stupid thing doesn't fit," she fumed as she fussed this way and that with the rack.

"Can I help?"

Ben strolled with unhurried ease out of the long shadows bordering the house. He wore pale blue jeans with a white shirt open at the throat, Top-Siders with no socks, and his hair was freshly washed and blown dry. He'd shaved off the beard stubble, which revealed his strong jaw and made him look five years younger. This put her in mind of the night she'd first met him all those years ago. She'd found him incredibly handsome, and he'd been completely uninterested in a gangly teenager with a Texas accent.

"I'd appreciate it if you'd check it out," Chloe said matter-of-factly, gesturing toward the barbecue. "I need to wash my hands."

"Here, you can take these into the kitchen when you go," he said, thrusting a dish in her direction. It held two Idaho potatoes, already baked.

"They're cooked," Chloe said in surprise.

"They'll be even more so before we eat them. What's the matter with the grill?"

"The thing that holds the meat doesn't fit on top," she said. She was on her way through the door to the kitchen when her cell phone rang. She balanced the dish with the potatoes in one hand as she yanked it out of her pocket, hoping the call would be good news about Tara.

"This is Patrice DesJardin calling," said a pleasant voice. "Is this Chloe?"

"Yes, it is," Chloe said, setting the potatoes on the wicker porch table before sinking onto the swing. It gave a disconcerting wobble, and she stood up quickly. The grommet, or whatever it was that held the chain on the back of the swing, was loose, threatening to dump anyone who sat on it.

Ben turned at the sound of the swing smacking against the railing and frowned.

Patrice said, "I remember meeting you at the Frangipani Inn a couple of years ago. We had a delightful time."

Chloe recalled that day well. Tayloe had made orangeade and egg salad sandwiches for lunch, and they'd listened long into the night as Patrice and Tayloe reminisced about their college days when they'd been roommates.

"It was fun," Chloe said, unsure how to segue into a sales spiel about her jewelry. Patrice could be a great help to her, since her boutique on Palm Beach's famed Worth Avenue was patronized by the rich and famous whose interest or lack of interest in Chloe's designs could either make or break her budding venture.

"Tell me about this exciting new direction of yours," Patrice said warmly, and that made it easy.

With the phone to her ear, Chloe wandered into the house, followed by Ben, who disappeared down the hall to the annex. "It all started right here on this beach," Chloe told Patrice, going on to relate how the lovely colors of sea glass had always fascinated her. "After I made my first pendant, so many people complimented me that I designed more and more, realizing in the process that I didn't want to do anything else."

"I'd love to see what you do," Patrice said. "The jewelry sounds like something that my customers might really like." Before they hung up, they agreed on a day and a time when Chloe would drive to Palm Beach.

Ben emerged from the annex as Chloe clicked off her phone.

"You seem much more cheerful than you did a few minutes ago," he observed as Chloe followed him outside.

She leaned back against the railing, watching as, with a variety of tools, he attacked the swing and the chain that held it. "That was Gwynne's godmother. She invited me to show her my designs. Patrice is key to my plan, so I'm very happy about it." *And relieved,* though she didn't add that.

"Good for you." Ben finished his work with the swing and gave it an experimental push before chucking the tools into a corner. "I brought a different rack that should fit. That one—" he nodded toward the rack responsible for Chloe's broken fingernail "—belongs to another barbecue that got thrown away. I recall something about it."

Chloe lowered herself to the top step as Ben dumped charcoal into the barbecue and doused it with charcoal lighter. "You must have lived at Frangipani Inn for quite a while," she observed.

"In spells, every now and then," he said.

She digested this, wondering if he was being intentionally vague. She well remembered how suddenly, that year she'd fallen in love with him, he'd disappeared from the inn. She'd heard rumors that Ben was still working at Sea Search. Someone ran into him on the beach but learned nothing about where he was living. In the fall, when Chloe was back in Farish, Gwynne had written that Ben was married. The news had devastated Chloe.

"You haven't been here much as an adult yourself, have you?" Ben, unaware of her thoughts, accompanied his question with a curious glance.

"Only once in the past five years, since I didn't like to leave Grandma Nell alone. Last summer, Gwynne was still at the inn, but Tayloe had gone to live with her new husband in Mexico." Chloe brushed away a grasshopper who wouldn't survive long if Butch caught a glimpse of him.

"Tayloe's gone from the inn for good, I take it."

"I think so. Gwynne, too. Once she gets her master's degree, she'll have the credentials to work with kids who have serious speech problems. I wouldn't be surprised if she wanted to live in a larger city."

"Good for her." Ben touched a match to the charcoal and

stood back while it caught fire. "Now that we've got this going, I'll finish cooking the potatoes," he said.

Ben started up the steps, and she trailed him into the kitchen, where he asked for milk, butter and salt. From his pocket he produced a packet of cheese. Before scooping the potatoes out of their shells, he dumped all these ingredients into a bowl.

Chloe watched, fascinated by his kitchen skills. She wondered if he'd cooked for his wife when he'd been married. She wondered how long the marriage had lasted.

"We're making twice-baked potatoes," Ben said. "You can help me put the filling back in the shells." He handed her a spoon.

She wasn't much of a cook herself, though Tara had often said that she made the best fajitas in the world. Ben's delegation of duties took her by surprise.

"I'm not sure I—"

"Of course you can," he said, demonstrating how to spoon the filling out of the bowl and smooth it into the potato skin.

"I've always been such a klutz at things like this," Chloe said apologetically.

"You must be manually dexterous, or you wouldn't be good at making jewelry," Ben pointed out, looking over her shoulder. "You're doing fine."

Chloe decided that she liked the job after all, and when she set her stuffed potatoes beside Ben's, no one could have told the difference.

"High five," he said, holding up his hand, and she slapped him one in exuberance. She was beginning to feel really comfortable around him, as if they'd known each other for a long time. Which they had, of course, but now they related as adult to adult.

"I'd say we're due for a celebratory glass of wine," she said. She dug around in one of the cluttered kitchen drawers for a corkscrew.

"None for me, thanks," he said.

She swiveled her head in surprise. "Are you sure?"

"Positive. I'll drink water."

"I'm planning to lay in a stock of beer soon," she said.

"Not on my account, I hope."

"I'm sorry. I don't have anything stronger." As far as she was concerned, she was merely making polite conversation, but a pained expression flashed across Ben's features.

"It's okay, Chloe. You see, I don't drink anymore. I can't."

"I'm sorry," she said, confused by this admission.

Ben met her gaze squarely. "The reason I don't drink anymore, Chloe, is that I'm a recovering alcoholic."

She stared at him for a long moment. "Is that why you got fired?" she asked in a rush, and then, realizing that she shouldn't have asked, she caught herself up short. "Whoa, I'm sorry. None of my business."

"Who told you about that?" he asked in an even tone. "Zephyr?"

"I shouldn't have listened."

"Why?" he said, his eyes dark with an emotion somewhere between pain and sorrow. "It happened. I almost caused the death of another diver. Andy was right to boot me off his team."

"Like I said, it's none of my business."

"Let's go outside," he said. "We can watch the fireflies come out. I'll tell you about it. I'd like to."

She followed and sat down beside him on the back porch steps. The stairs' narrowness made it necessary for the two of them to sit so close that their shoulders touched. Chloe didn't mind that Ben took her hand, didn't consider that his status as a recovering alcoholic should make her think twice about how much she wanted to hear. For a moment, she was transported back to her sixteenth summer, when she had fled around to the back of the house and into the nearby stand of Australian pines to escape the group of guests laughing and talking on the front porch. It was the night that she had learned that Ben had left Frangipani Inn and she wouldn't see him again. Her heart had been breaking.

Well, now she was thirty-two years old, and her heart wasn't breakable anymore. But it was full, just the same, as Ben began his story.

Chapter Four

"Andy hired me after I developed the diving skills I needed for Sea Search," Ben said. "That summer when I met you, I'd been working for him for over a year. We'd salvaged a merchantman galleon in the Keys, came back to Sanluca and continued to dive the 1715 fleet offshore. Andy's enthusiasm spilled over to everyone on his crew. Those were exciting days."

"Isn't it still kind of a thrill? To find items of beauty and value?"

"Of course. I was dedicated, determined. Andy liked that about me. But, Chloe, things happen to people. Over time, it's possible to be discouraged, disheartened, lose that initial drive and—well, the reason these things happened to me isn't important. I drank too much. I was wrong when I thought it wouldn't affect me."

Chloe held her breath, figuring that Ben would make excuses for himself. In her experience, people either did that or threw the blame onto someone else. But Ben surprised her. He didn't offer any justification at all.

"I kept diving. For a while, I was able to hide my alcoholic bingeing. A few people might have realized how bad the problem was, but they didn't say anything about it. Then I did the unforgivable. I stayed drunk for a couple of days before my friend Rick and I went on a deep dive on the *Santa Ynez*.

"Rick was my best friend, the one I could count on to be there whenever I needed someone. I'd hid my drinking problem from him, never let on that I was falling apart. Rick had a family, a beautiful wife and two cute little boys. To make a long story short, that day on the *Ynez*, I was a mess. Alcohol affects reaction time. It made my thinking foggy and slow.

"Rick had a problem with his air supply. It was my fault. I was so hungover that I'd failed to check the equipment properly. The current was strong, and I was ill-prepared to fight it because I was in such bad shape."

"You mean, from drinking?" she asked.

Ben nodded, the lines in his face tense. "That, and fatigue from a dive a few days before, plus the exertion of kicking against the strong current to get to the wreck. All are contributing factors to DCS. When Rick needed help, I lost my head. I was responsible for the two of us surfacing too fast, and as a result we both had the bends. Rick almost died."

"What kind of treatment did you have?" Chloe asked.

"We both ended up in a hyperbaric chamber, which recompresses the body, gets the nitrogen out of the tissues. I recovered pretty fast, but Rick didn't. I was horrified at what I'd done. I'd been careless, and it might cost him his life, leaving his wife a widow and his children fatherless." He swallowed, and for a moment it appeared he wasn't going to say any more.

"Well, that's what happened. Andy fired me. Said he couldn't keep someone on his crew who put other people's lives at risk. The hell of it was that I understood. I would have done the same if I'd been in Andy's place."

Chloe absorbed all this. "You moved away after that?"

"I couldn't bear to walk down the street in Sanluca with

everyone knowing I'd almost killed one of our friends and neighbors. I lived on savings for a while, had to move because I couldn't afford the rent at the house where I lived. Stayed at the inn with Tayloe and Gwynne for a couple of months. Went to visit my brother until he got shipped to Iraq—he's in the air force. Rattled around the Caribbean, trying to pull myself together. Did odd jobs. Never wanted to dive because I wasn't up to it. Finally, I woke up in a motel in Mexico, clueless about how I got there. That's when I borrowed enough money to get back to Florida and start a treatment program."

"And came here," Chloe said softly.

"I've still got a way to go before my life is totally on track. You've helped, Chloe. You gave me a place to stay and work to do while I wait for Andy to hire me again."

"Will he?" she asked with trepidation.

For the first time since he'd started relating the story, he smiled, easing the tension around his eyes. "Of course he will. I can't let myself believe otherwise."

"Good for you," Chloe said, admiring how he'd met his problem squarely and embarked on a plan of action.

Ben became quiet, and she sensed that he felt as though he'd said enough. Again, Chloe sensed an immutable sadness, a deep sorrow.

She waited in case he wanted to continue, but he only heaved a sigh. "Well," he said, "I'd better get those steaks on the grill." He stood up, dropping her hand as if he'd just realized that he was holding it. When he went into the kitchen, she didn't follow.

Perhaps the darkness in Ben, the melancholy that she'd glimpsed in him, was his guilt rising to the surface. Or maybe it was his natural reaction to being fired; losing a job meant loss of status, embarrassment, fear of the future.

Ben Derrick was toting a lot of baggage. But he wasn't asking her to help carry it. Most of the guys in her life had been all too happy to hand the job over to a willing woman, but this time was different.

Chloe wasn't willing, and Ben wasn't burdening her. The thing was, she had no idea how to handle this. In the past when she sensed compatibility in a man, the way she signified interest was to become available. She listened, she empathized, she threw herself in the path of whatever train wreck was heading down the track. Usually, she got run over.

Now she'd listened and empathized, but no one was tying her to the tracks. Ben didn't expect her to solve his problems for him.

And because of this, she felt a great deal of uncertainty about how to relate to him.

THE NEXT MORNING when Chloe woke up, Ben was gone.

His Jeep wasn't parked in its usual spot under the gumbo-limbo tree. She checked the view from her turret windows, half expecting to see him sitting at the edge of the ocean as he had the day before, but the only people in evidence were two teenagers, one of whom was trying to learn to surf. Chloe watched them until she tired of it, then went downstairs to feed Butch and to cook herself a soft-boiled egg and toast.

When her cell phone rang, she clicked it on immediately. It was her sister.

"We found Tara," Naomi said without preamble. "She's with Marilyn in Dallas."

Chloe carried the phone into the parlor and settled herself comfortably on the wide sofa. "See? I told you she'd be fine."

"We were so worried, but I'm at my wits' end. Ray and I adore Tara. She's our firstborn, the daughter I always wanted, the apple of her daddy's eye. I don't understand why we can't get along anymore."

Naomi sounded so woebegone that Chloe's sympathies were

immediately engaged. "Tara's going through a stage. What did Marilyn say?"

"She's happy to have her, and Tara can stay as long as she likes. Marilyn's going to take Tara and her kids to a Memorial Day celebration at the park, and Scott, her eleven-year-old, is having a birthday party this week, so Tara will help with that. The kicker is that Marilyn says Tara will have to follow the house rules about curfews, chores and conduct."

"You and Ray must be so relieved."

"We all are, and before I forget, Marilyn said to wish you luck on your new jewelry venture. By the way, how's it going with the guy?"

"With Ben?"

"Are there any other guys you want to tell me about?"

"Of course not. He's a recovering alcoholic, Naomi. He's got Issues, with a capital *I*. And for once, I'm not providing *Solutions.*"

"Glad to hear it, but how do you stop yourself? With every wounded warrior you've dated, you jumped right in and started slapping on emotional bandages."

Chloe scoffed. "That only results in my getting hurt. I'm out of the rescue business, believe me. For once in my life, I'm looking out for Number One, and that person is me."

"If you start to get involved with him, will you ask him to leave?"

"Should I?"

"Why not?"

"He has the most arresting brown eyes I've ever seen. And very broad shoulders. And a few other attributes that I find appealing."

"Chloe, he sounds dangerous."

"Not at all, since he's in the process of rescuing himself and isn't looking for pity."

"This sounds refreshingly responsible," Naomi said.

Chloe recalled Ben's matter-of-fact recounting of his drinking problem. "He's a fine person with a lot to offer some lucky woman—but it isn't me. But enough about Ben. Do you mind if I call Tara? Tell her I'm thinking about her?"

"Of course not. She loves you and respects you and considers you the best. You should have kids of your own, since you seem to have a special rapport with them."

Chloe sighed. So far, she'd preferred leaving the raising of the next generation to her sister. "Let's talk again soon, okay?" she suggested, figuring it was past time to end this discussion.

"Right now I'm going to rush out and buy some hair coloring that will get rid of the new gray hairs brought about by Tara's latest caper. Any recommendations on color?"

"Try magenta. It worked for me."

Naomi groaned. "One thing for sure, something fab and flirty would convince Tara that I'm not hopelessly unfashionable."

"I'm not so sure. Magenta is so passé these days."

As they hung up, they both were chuckling.

Chloe poured herself a second cup of coffee and carried it out onto the back porch, where Butch showed up after a few minutes and curled up at her feet in a patch of sunshine. She bent over to pet the cat as Ben wheeled into the driveway and parked the Jeep in the shade. After he got out, he reached in back and pulled out a metal detector.

"Did you find anything this morning?" she called to him.

"No, but it's good exercise. I rode down to the jetty at the inlet and tried my luck." He walked to the steps and rested the metal detector there, regarding her with a half smile.

"I've seen a lot of folks looking for treasure on the beach in front of the inn," she said. "What's out there, anyway?"

"The *Ynez* wreck is slightly to the south. The afternoon thunderstorms in summer keep the ocean stirred up, and the ballast stones around the wrecks tend to shift to expose the goodies underneath."

Ben unzipped a pocket in his shorts and dug in it to produce a gold coin. "I found this the day I arrived. My metal detector beeped just before I ran into Zephyr."

Chloe turned the coin over in her hand. It was about an inch and a half in diameter and gleamed in the bright sunlight.

"It's what we call a cob," Ben explained, moving closer. "You'll see that it has no date on it. This was created from the end of a gold bar, stamped with the design by slave labor. It's an eight *real* coin minted in Mexico. The design is a full cross and shield."

Chloe inspected the other side. "It's beautifully intricate. What will you do with it?"

"Sell it, most likely, especially if Andy doesn't hire me soon."

Chloe handed the coin back to him. "I'm impressed."

"There's more where that came from. Say, do you have any of that coffee left?"

She nodded toward the kitchen. "Help yourself."

"I don't mind if I do." He smiled at her and went inside.

When Ben returned, he was carrying coffee in a mug. He sat on a chair and propped his feet on the porch railing. A fly buzzed around his head, and he waved it away. Unexpectedly, Chloe recalled how she had regarded him when she was just a girl; he had been a remote god, worthy of worship but totally unattainable. The possibility of ever sitting here and enjoying a cup of coffee with him would have sent her into paroxysms of joy, *paroxysm* having been her favorite new word that summer.

"I think I'll repair the window in the kitchen door today and take a look at the front-door lock with an eye to replacing it," he said.

"Your choice," Chloe said. She immediately regretted her tone. Too blasé. Too unappreciative.

Ben, sipping reflectively at his coffee, didn't seem to notice; Chloe kept rocking. Ben appeared perfectly happy to sit nearby, saying nothing himself. As she slid a sideways glance at him, she felt herself flushing at the sight of his bare chest, the prominent pectorals, those wide shoulders.

She stood abruptly, setting the rocking chair into a flurry and Butch scuttling off the porch. "I should get to work," she said.

He stood, too. "I'd better go to the hardware store," he said.

"See you later," she said.

"Right."

Chloe heard Ben drive away and return some time later, when she was in her workshop. He began to chisel the broken glass out of the window in the back door; she could hear that, too. Finally, she got up and closed the workshop door.

She'd expected that the ensuing quietness would help her to concentrate, but all it did was increase her isolation. After a while, she opened the door again, but by that time Ben had gone, and she couldn't hear him at all. All she heard was the rhythmic rush of sea to shore, and the querulous cries of seagulls overhead.

CHLOE WAS UP EARLY the next morning and wandered into the library to find something to read. She'd hooked up an old hammock between two posts on the front porch and intended to avail herself of its comfort when she took breaks from her work.

The library was big and airy, all four walls lined with books. She studied Tayloe's collection of Harvard Classics, deciding that they were heavier reading than she required, before moving on to Gwynne's collection of paperbacks.

A romance was what she needed. She and Gwynne had devoured them by the boxload during the summers when they were teenagers. She chose one with a familiar cover and realized she'd read it before. But that didn't matter. Sometimes reading a familiar book was like reconnecting with a dear friend. And then a slim paper notebook fell from between the covers, and Chloe stared at it in her hand.

Property of Fire Timberlake, she read, which made her smile. She and Naomi and Gwynne had given themselves aliases when they were kids. Naomi had been Earth because she was so settled and serious, Chloe had been Fire because of her red hair, and Gwynne was Ocean because she liked that name better than any other. Sometimes they'd driven Tayloe crazy by refusing to answer to their real names, but when she complained, they'd retaliated by naming her Wind, which Tayloe had considered extremely unflattering.

Chloe opened the notebook and recognized a diary she'd kept during her sixteenth summer.

Diary of My Sixteenth Summer, she had titled it. Pensive at the sight of her girlish handwriting, she carried the diary to the hammock and settled down to reacquaint herself with the person she had been all those summers ago.

Dear Diary (oh, what shall I name you? You're going to be important to me, and you need a name. I promise I will think about it.)

You won't believe it, but I am in love. Yes, I'm finally over that stupid Todd Volmer, who doesn't have any interests but the stupid calf he's raising for 4-H. I have met a true man among men. A swashbuckler of a guy. An adventurer above all adventurers.

His name, dear diary, is (here a big smudge where she had erased) Gold. I'm calling him that because he has value. (!) And besides, his job is finding it. Gold, I mean. He's a diver for Sea Search.

He's very handsome. He's fun. He is so different from the boys I know in Farish that he might be another species altogether! Did I forget to tell you how old he is? Well, he's 21. My parents would kill me if they knew.

I haven't told Ocean, either. And certainly not Earth, who is eighteen and married and can't be expected to understand how anyone older than she is could be attracted to me!! But I think (hope) he is!! Gold smiled at me especially today before he left for work. He lives at the Frangipani Inn because it's the best place in Sanluca and my aunt is a good cook. She fixes a special breakfast every morning for him because she says he works hard and requires a lot of carbohydrates. I made the toast for him this morning, but he didn't know it.

More later… Ocean and I are going to wait where Gold parks his motorcycle and ask him if he wants to play Parcheesi after dinner. Ocean says he's played checkers with her before and she beat him.

'Bye! from Fire (Chloe D. Timberlake)

Chloe smiled wistfully to herself, wondering that she had ever been so young and silly. She had no recollection of meeting Ben when he parked his motorcycle at the inn after work that day, though she didn't doubt that she and Gwynne had done it. They'd always been up to something, and chasing after a guy that one of them liked was standard operating procedure.

Chloe quickly shoved the diary into her pocket when Ben passed by and hoped he wouldn't notice that she was flustered to see him. She jumped up from the hammock and spared him a casual wave, expecting him to keep walking.

He surprised her by halting at the bottom of the steps. "Hey," he said, "I thought you might like to walk on the beach with me."

"I have work to do," she began, but seeing how his face fell, she kept talking. "But I could take a short break."

"Great," he said. He grinned at her. "We'll take my metal detector and head toward the *Santa Ynez*."

While he went to get the metal detector, Chloe ran inside and smoothed her hair. Reading about her teenage self had stirred up all her old emotions for Ben, and it wasn't easy to put them out of her mind. If he'd ever discovered how she felt about him back then, she wouldn't have been able to face him now, she was certain of that.

Schooling herself to look disinterested, she met him at the beginning of the dune path, noting how different and yet how much the same Ben was now. He was still tall and tanned, still someone she'd turn to stare at on the street. But the sun had taken a toll on his face; deep grooves ran from his nose to his mouth and tiny lines feathered out from his eyes. This weathering only made him look more rough-hewn and rugged, both appealing attributes. Still, a new gravity these days overlay his attractiveness.

"How many wrecks are out there?" she asked as they started through the dunes.

"Eleven," he said. "Sea Search has the rights to salvage all of them, too."

"All in good shape?"

"They've been down there for almost three hundred years," he told her.

"I'm surprised there's anything left."

"The hulls have rotted, sand has shifted around, ballast is strewn over the ocean floor. The plate fleet of 1715 was the first fleet to head for Spain from the New World in four years, so it was loaded with gold and silver."

"All there for the taking?"

"The Spanish sent divers to bring up the treasure soon after the ships sank, but with their primitive methods, they couldn't get it all. Some of the divers secreted caches on the beach, planning to return to collect them in the future. Most of them never made it, and the changing shoreline spits up items of value from time to time."

A flock of brown pelicans skimmed in loose formation over the rippling blue water. One dived into a wave, came up with a fish. Farther along, Stuart's Point and Manatee Island stretched into the misty distance. North of there, but so far away that none of it was visible from here, was the Kennedy Space Center at Cape Canaveral.

They stopped beside a pile of seaweed while Ben explained how to use the metal detector. "This model is made for locating underwater finds as well as those in the sand, but because this is a state park, we can only operate lawfully between the high-water line and the dunes. Put on the headphones." He handed them to her. "The technique is to swing the detector back and forth over the sand and wait to hear a beep. Then you dig."

Intrigued, she followed Ben's instructions. The headphones fit tightly over her ears, and although the metal detector was heavier than she'd expected, she got the hang of swinging it back and forth in an easy rhythm. Once, the headphones transmitted a beep, but the find turned out to be an old corroded bolt, modern in nature. Another time, the metal detector beeped so crazily that she was sure she'd discovered something major, but it was only a quarter and fairly new.

When Ben took over, he had better luck, unearthing a chain marked fourteen-carat and missing a link. Chloe had to admit that being in on the discovery of this bit of jewelry was exhilarating, and she told Ben on the walk back to the inn that she now understood how people got hooked on this hobby.

He treated her observation seriously. "Some folks expect to

find important treasure from those wrecks out there right away. They're almost always disappointed. Sometimes, their metal detectors aren't state-of-the-art. Often, they get disgusted when they only find beer bottle tops or kids' sand shovels."

"From the way some people talk, there's treasure lying around waiting to be plucked out of the sand."

Ben laughed. "Amateurs should be satisfied with turning up the kind of thing that is readily available. The chain we found today, for instance."

"That *you* found, you mean."

"We," he said firmly. "It's a pretty piece."

"Agreed." Chloe glanced at her watch, surprised that so much time had passed. "Yikes! I've spent all morning out here." Usually, nothing was allowed to interfere with her work.

"We'll head back," Ben said.

They were more than halfway to the inn when Chloe felt a sharp pain in her big toe. Looking down, she realized that she'd stepped on a jagged piece of aluminum and cut her foot.

"Oh, no," Ben said, drawing even with her, his brow furrowing in concern.

"It's only superficial," she said hastily. Her foot was bleeding, sand clumping around the wound.

He bent for a closer inspection. "You're probably right, but we'd better take care of it. I have a first-aid kit in my apartment."

As Ben stepped into the lead, she limped after him, trying to hold her toe up so the cut wouldn't attract even more sand. This made walking awkward, and she wished she'd paid more attention earlier to where she was putting her feet. The wound was beginning to hurt.

When they reached the annex patio, Ben opened the sliding screen door and waited until she had passed through before closing the door behind her and setting the metal detector in a corner. The apartment was now very neat, with few personal items strewn around. Only the collection of artifacts on the built-in shelves, which she'd admired on her previous visit.

"You'd better wash that off," Ben said, gesturing at her foot. "The tub has a detachable shower spray." He nodded toward the bathroom.

"Really, it's not that big a deal," she protested, but he came up behind her and rested his hands on her shoulders to steer her in the right direction. The bathroom was small and cramped, and he turned on the shower.

"Wash it off," he ordered, disappearing into the bedroom and returning in a few moments with a plastic first-aid case. He produced a tube of antibiotic and some bandages while she removed the hand-held nozzle from its bracket and hosed off her foot.

"You can sit there," he said, indicating the edge of the tub.

"You don't have to—" she began, but he eyed her sternly.

"Please, Chloe, stop arguing," he said, handing her a towel. "You'll need to dry that cut off, and then either you put on the antibiotic or I do."

Chloe did as she was told, tending to the wound herself, though Ben stood by and watched. When she'd finished with the antibiotic, he had an adhesive-and-gauze patch ready and bent to apply it to the cut. Chloe had the ironic revelation that her discomfort in this situation was possibly due to the fact that people usually didn't take care of her; she took care of them. What was it Naomi had said? Something about her always being ready to slap bandages on other people's hurts?

She had a half smile on her face when she stood up, and Ben smiled back. "All better?"

"Yes. Thanks," she said. As an afterthought she added meekly, "Could I please have a drink of water?"

He laughed then, the sound booming as it echoed off the tiles of the tub and shower surround. "Sure. It's not as if that's a major request."

He led the way to the kitchen, where she hitched herself onto a bar stool and regarded her bandaged toe. Then he opened the refrigerator door and handed her a bottle of water, which she uncapped and drank almost all in one great gulp. As she lowered the bottle from her lips, she saw the clothes she'd shucked when she'd invited him for an impromptu swim neatly folded on the stool beside her. The idea of Ben's handling them, folding them, seemed too intimate by far.

Ben went on talking. "I noticed a wasp's nest up under the edge of the roof on the side of the house near the driveway," he said casually. "They're nasty little things, and we'd be wise to get rid of them."

"Things with lots of legs and venom are exempt from mercy," she agreed.

"I'll spray them right away."

She tossed the empty water bottle in the wastebasket. "Thanks for the treasure-hunting expedition. It was fun."

"You'd better take the antibiotic with you. You'll need it." Instead of handing the tube across the counter, he walked around so that he stood directly in front of her. His eyes were warm, and he was so close that she was reluctant to make a move for fear that she'd brush against him.

She went very still as she stared up at him. Without realizing it, she had been leaning in his direction, and now her arm touched his. The contact seemed to bring him to his senses, and he shook his head as if to clear it before wheeling abruptly and retreating behind the counter.

"I'll see you later," she said, accepting this reprieve with considerable relief and all but stumbling toward the exit in her haste to escape. She grabbed her clothes off the stool on her way past.

"Dinner?" he said, only the one word. They hadn't discussed it earlier.

She shook her head. "Not tonight." She kept walking out the door, up the path, clutching her clothes to her chest.

You idiot, she chided herself. *You're making something out of nothing.*

Maybe she was, but it would be a long time before she forgot the raw hunger in Ben Derrick's eyes. And it wasn't that he only wanted dinner. She was sure that he had much more in mind.

The odd thing was that she was in a mood to give it to him, which could be disastrous. She was finally in a position to make a life of her own, and there wasn't supposed to be room in it for anyone else.

Chapter Five

During the next week, Ben kept his distance, consulting Chloe in a businesslike way from time to time about repairs. He claimed to have caught four mice and released them to the wild, but Chloe never saw them and didn't care to. He got rid of the wasps' nest, substituted fresh two-by-fours for several rotten pieces of wood in the front porch railing and took it upon himself to crawl all over the roof and replace loose shingles.

Gwynne, who had finally phoned to ask how things were going, set Chloe's mind at ease by telling her that she and Tayloe would finance any necessary repairs, but Chloe was still concerned about money. Gwynne suggested that Chloe consider opening the Frangipani Inn as a bed-and-breakfast again. Chloe insisted that she had enough to do without cooking for guests, not to mention that she couldn't expect anyone to stay in the house when all the rooms were so dirty.

"Let them do their own cooking. Hire cleaning help," Gwynne told her. But Chloe put off making a decision. All she wanted right now was a chance to work quietly.

And it *was* quiet, except for Ben's hammering and sawing and tramping around the house. Still, she discovered that she didn't mind the kind of noise he made, because she didn't feel so alone with him nearby.

Loneliness was something Chloe had not expected to feel after her long-anticipated escape from Farish. In retrospect, however, it wasn't so odd that she missed being around other people. Living alone was a skill that she'd never had a chance to develop. She missed her grandmother, who could always be counted on to say something that would brighten Chloe's day. She missed Naomi and her husband and kids, and she missed her friend Beth, who was newly married and expecting a baby. Most of all, and this surprised her, she missed her niece Tara.

She phoned Tara one sultry afternoon when Ben had disappeared down the beach and she couldn't concentrate on her work. First, Chloe chatted with Marilyn, who had to tend to an emergency with one of her numerous brood and quickly turned the phone over to her teenage houseguest.

"Hi, Chloe," Tara said brightly when she came on the line. "How are things in sunny Florida?"

"Hot," Chloe said, easing a finger around the collar on her shirt. "Blamed hot. How are you getting along, Tara?"

"Oh," Tara said. "Okay, I guess."

Something in her niece's tone set Chloe on alert. "Want to talk about it?" she asked.

"Mmm," Tara said, and Chloe heard a shuffling followed by the sound of a door closing. Tara lowered her voice. "I'm in a closet where Marilyn and the kids can't hear me. Honestly, Chloe, I'm beginning to wonder if this is such a good idea."

"What do you mean?" Chloe asked, playing for time. Maybe Tara wanted to go home to Farish. That would be a good move, in Chloe's opinion, and she was prepared to encourage it.

"It's Marilyn. I never realized that she was such a tyrant."

"You've got to be kidding."

"She makes everyone follow all these rules and gets mad if I don't. Like, we all have our chores to do and she yelled at me for not cleaning the shower yesterday. I'm like, well, I did it the day before, but she didn't want to listen."

"I'm sorry to hear that," Chloe said, trying to muster more sympathy. Tara would need to learn at some time in her life that she didn't live in a perfect world.

"Yeah, but what am I going to do?" Tara said in a bewildered tone. "My life was supposed to be way better here, but Marilyn and Donald have their own rules and they're as bad as my mom and dad's."

Live and learn, Chloe thought, but she didn't suggest the obvious: that Tara go home. "There are rules everywhere," she said as consolingly as she could.

"*You* live exactly as you please," Tara pointed out.

"It may seem that way, Tara, but remember when I lived with Grandma Nell? She wanted me to go grocery shopping only on Fridays because she was convinced that was when I'd get the best bargains. She insisted that I use that ugly old furniture in my bedroom because it belonged to her mother, and I wanted something bright and modern. I put up with Grandma's requirements because I had to be there to take care of her, and I love her. I can assure you that I would have rather had more freedom in choosing what I did from day to day."

"I didn't mean *then,*" Tara said. "I was thinking of *now.* I bet it's wonderful in Sanluca, isn't it? With the beach and all?"

The last time Chloe had been to the beach was the morning she'd gone metal detecting with Ben, and as for things being wonderful, the house was a mess and her social life was practically nil.

"It's very nice," she said, infusing her tone with an enthusiasm she didn't feel. No point in dumping on Tara, who apparently had enough to deal with at present.

"I'm glad you called, Chloe. I always feel better after I talk with you."

"Think of me as just a little ray of sunshine, going around and brightening things up. Phone me anytime, Tara. It's good to hear your voice."

"I'd better get out of this closet before someone figures out it's my hiding place. Besides, it's time to clean up the kitchen with Marilyn and Ella. I don't like Ella much. She's so prissy and never wants to get dirty. She said she was going to rat me out when I wore her favorite shorts and spilled strawberry pop all over them, but after I washed them she wasn't so mad."

"Ella is how old now?"

"Fourteen, but babyish. She's never had a date or anything." Clearly, Tara felt vastly superior to her cousin.

"There will be time for that."

"Do you see many hotties on the beach?" Tara wanted to know.

"Not one," Chloe said. By now, she was familiar with the group of local young people who frequented the beach, but she wasn't sure what Tara would consider a hottie.

"I bet they're out there. I could find a few."

"Probably," Chloe agreed, and she was chuckling.

"Uh-oh, I'd better hang up. Marilyn's calling me. 'Bye, Chloe. Talk to you soon."

"'Bye, Tara. Behave yourself, okay?"

A big sigh. "Okay," and Tara was gone.

It was time to get to work, Chloe decided. Her work centered her. She found depth and meaning in creating what some people said were magical compositions of sea glass, metal and precious gems. If she could earn a living by making things that brought pleasure and joy to others, so much the better.

She hadn't been at her workbench long when the sound of someone chopping wood outside her workshop suddenly made it impossible to think straight. Chloe got up and went to the window. A stand of tall Australian pine trees bordered the inn property on the west, and in the shade of them, Ben, newly returned from wherever he'd gone, was wielding an ax, his sweat-glazed skin dappled with sunlight that penetrated the thick fringe of needles. The muscles in his back were heavily braided and rippled enticingly.

He must have spotted her standing there because he turned toward her, leaning on the ax handle. "Just splitting some of the old logs left when the park service cut down the trees that fell during last year's hurricane. I talked to the park ranger and she gave me the go-ahead. The wood will make good fireplace burning in the winter."

"I suppose so, but does it get cold enough for a fire then? It sure doesn't seem like it could."

"It will get down to the low thirties in Sanluca. Are you planning to stay over the winter?"

"I'm not sure," Chloe hedged. "A lot depends on my meeting with Patrice DesJardin."

"When is it?"

"Monday. Five days from now." She had been working feverishly on sketches and had several finished pieces to show Patrice.

"I can finish chopping the wood later, if it's annoying you."

"If you wouldn't mind," she began, but he held up his hand.

"No problem. I'll make a special trip to the home-improvement store in Melbourne and pick up some supplies."

"That's a good plan," Chloe said. She moved away from the window, and shortly thereafter, she could hear Ben walking around in his apartment downstairs. She wondered briefly how he filled his spare time. He sometimes left the house at night, and she had no idea where he went. Not that it was any of her business, but she was still curious.

After a while, Ben drove away in his Jeep. Chloe, when she'd been working so long that she couldn't stay hunched over at her workbench for one more minute, ate a quick sandwich for supper, then went to her room and lay down to rest her back. When she had revived somewhat, she retrieved her old diary from underneath the pile of T-shirts where she'd hidden it. She'd avoided reading it since that first day she'd found it, believing that she was better off not reliving her fascination with Ben Derrick. But she was curious, not only about him but about the girl she had been.

Dear Trees,

I've named you Trees, dear diary, because I love the Australian pines out in back of the inn so much. And paper is made from wood, and you're paper.

Gold likes Ocean much more than me. I am devastated. How can he not see that I love him? That I dream of him all the time? I am feeling paroxysms (new word!) of grief, and it's so hard to keep Ocean from finding out how jealous I am of her. He brought her a candy bar. A Kit Kat. He got it on the dive boat. Says his boss keeps a lot of them on board. I want to go on the boat and see what it's like. Then I would know Gold much better than I do now. I would understand what kind of world he lives in. I bet it's wonderful.

I love Gold so much! I want to cry when he doesn't notice me. I had to rush into the pine grove so I could be alone today when he pulled my hair and called me Carrots. I hate my red hair! And my freckles.

I may be Carrots to him, but he's still Gold to me. Priceless beyond measure. When he looked over at me in the kitchen this morning (I was pouring his coffee), I wanted to melt. I spilled coffee on the floor, but he didn't notice. He just said, Thanks.

His voice is deep and sometimes I hear a smile in it. If he could know me, the real me, he'd love me. I'm sure he would. Sigh. Double sigh.

I'm going to buy that perfume we saw at the mall last week even though it will take all my allowance to do it. Love, Fire (Chloe D. Timberlake)

On the next page she'd drawn a picture of the pine grove, small but rich in detail, with a raccoon sitting in the cleft of two branches.

She got up restlessly when she heard Ben's Jeep in the driveway, shoving the diary back under the stack of clothes in her drawer. She'd been right not to read it; it was disturbing to recall how desperate she'd been for Ben's approval in those days. Desperate and in love; not a good combination.

She waited to hear the sliding door of Ben's apartment grating along its track, indicating that he'd gone inside. Did he like to walk on the beach after dark, or maybe sit on the porch swing and gaze up at the plentiful stars for a while before bed? The ocean would be beautiful, the big breakers rushing over each other to shore. And the stars were splendid. She could glimpse enough of the sky from her window to know that.

It was hot tonight even with the windows wide open to catch the breeze, especially in the upstairs part of the inn. After she was ready for bed, she turned off her light and tugged the curtains aside to admit more air. It was too hot to wear clothes, too hot to sleep, and she slipped off her nightgown and tossed it on the dresser. For a moment, as she stood in the window with the soft breeze playing across her breasts, she couldn't stop thinking that it would have been nice to walk with Ben for a while tonight. Just long enough to make her forget about the lack of friends in her life, but not enough to start wishing, as she had done when she was a girl, that he was one of them.

CHLOE WAS FERVENTLY thankful for a different kind of scenery in Sanluca than she knew in Texas. Though unremarkable in many ways, Sanluca leaned toward the picturesque: the white walls of the squat, square post office boasted a mural of the 1715 Spanish fleet; the old wooden store-building-turned-gift-shop sported melodious wind chimes hanging from the eaves; and even though the gas station had gone modern, you could still buy a packet of roasted peanuts to pour into a bottle of cola.

Sea Search, Inc. operated out of the city marina and maintained a long, low building housing the treasure museum nearby. The bridge to the barrier island, site of Frangipani Inn and Lost Galleons Park, was reached by a long narrow road that meandered along the shore of Spaniard's Lagoon and eventually intersected with the highway from the Glades.

After the day she'd walked on the beach with Ben and cut her toe, Chloe was even more aware of her growing loneliness, so she determined that she'd try to find people with whom she had something in common. When she stopped in the gift shop, she learned that Gwynne's friend Sierra, who had offered to sell some of her simpler, less expensive pieces in the shop, had a new baby in addition to the two toddlers Chloe had seen the last time she'd visited Sanluca. Sierra said, regretfully, that she didn't get out much.

One other possibility was Peggy, the cheerful postmistress, so after leaving the gift shop, Chloe walked to the post office across a parking lot whose hot asphalt oozed beneath her rubber flip-flop sandals. Though Chloe asked her if she wanted to have lunch sometime, Peggy was doubtful that she'd be available soon, since her husband was recuperating from major surgery and needed her at home when she wasn't working.

"Give me a call when you're free," Chloe told her. "You can come over to the inn and join Zephyr and me on our turtle walks."

Though Peggy agreed that this would be fun, Chloe still felt at loose ends, Wishing that she knew more people in town, Chloe drove home through the meltingly hot afternoon haze. When she reached the inn and saw Ben's Jeep parked in its usual spot, she acted on impulse. She walked around the annex to the glass door leading into Ben's apartment. Only a screen was between her and Ben, who was clearly visible sitting in one of the chairs, reading the newspaper.

Before she could chicken out, Chloe spoke in a rush. "I was thinking I'd go to the Sand Bar tonight for dinner," she said through the screen. "Then I thought—" She looked up at the sky, down at her feet. This would be easier if they didn't have the history of her ridiculous teenage crush, of which he was blessedly unaware. She took heart from that notion. "I thought you might like to go along," she blurted.

Slowly, Ben lowered the paper, regarding her with mild surprise. "That sounds good," he said. "What time?"

Up at the sky again, down at her feet. A small red ant was charging up her instep, and aware from experience that its bite could cause a painful welt, she shook it off. "Seven o'clock?"

"Sure."

"Okay." She afforded him a curt nod and started to walk away.

"Chloe," he said, and she whirled around. He had come to the screen and cracked it open a bit. "Is something wrong?"

"Nope," she said as casually as she could. He was looking at her as if he could see right through her clothes to her skin. Maybe she should have worn a bra, but she usually didn't when the weather was this muggy. Maybe she should have put on shoes instead of dilapidated rubber sandals, though they were the most comfortable shoes she owned.

"Okay," Ben said, still sounding surprised. "I'll be ready at seven."

She managed a smile before she turned and fled to the back porch, where she bent to pet Butch before they both continued into the house. Why had she been so tongue-tied around Ben? What made her care how she looked when she was around him?

Her previous crush on him, of course. That alone was enough to render her more self-conscious than usual.

Back home in Farish, Chloe was known for her offbeat style, and she felt less self-confident without her usual flamboyant wardrobe. She shuffled through her closet, wishing she hadn't packed so sparsely. Luckily, she'd brought a print scarf, which she threaded through the belt loops of her jeans. She selected a rhinestoned T-shirt, black. After she removed silver studs and looped a pair of sea-glass earrings through her earlobes, where they glimmered along with small gold hoops and another pair of green cat's eyes, she was pleased with the result of her labors. She was trendy but casual. Comfortable but chic.

She was slipping on her sandals when she saw her diary; it had fallen from the folds of the T-shirt, no doubt, when she'd taken it out of the drawer.

Dear Trees, Paroxysms of joy! Happiness! Thrills!

Ocean and I saw Gold at the gas station and he bought both of us a moon pie! I could swear that he winked when he handed me mine. Ocean says he only had a gnat in his eye.

Gold was there getting gas for his motorcycle. I asked him if he'd take me for a ride on it sometime and he said sure. Wind came along and heard this conversation and said over her dead body would I ride on the back of any motorcycle, but she was laughing when she said it. Then she made Ocean and me get in the car and go with her to buy fertilizer for the plants. We had to ride home with it in the back seat and it smelled bad. I didn't care because I opened my new perfume bottle and sprayed some on both Ocean and me and we giggled all the way home.

I love Gold so much! I wonder what it would be like to kiss him. He has the most sensual mouth! Thinking about kissing him is all I do lately.

Love, Fire (Chloe D. Timberlake)

Chloe had to laugh at herself as a teenager. Surely there had never been any shallower teenage girls than she and Gwynne, plus she'd had no more idea about how to attract a man's attention than she had of how to fly to the moon. Fortunately, she'd eventually figured it out.

Nervous with the kind of anticipation she hadn't felt in years, Chloe was ready half an hour before it was time for him to show up on the back porch. She'd spent extra time primping in front of the mirror, trying to recall what perfume it was she'd used to lure him that summer. To the best of her recollection, it had been something heavy with the scent of sandalwood and spice and not exactly suited to a sixteen-year-old would-be temptress. In fact, Ben needed only a whiff of it to wrinkle his nose in distaste. "Whew!" he'd said, clearly unimpressed. "What's that awful smell, Carrots? Do you have a dead buzzard in your pocket?" Chloe had been crushed.

Now Ben came loping around the corner of the house, and Chloe found it in her heart to forgive him for his previous lack of sensitivity. She reminded herself that she'd been in the throes of first love when she'd written those words in her diary, and these days, she wasn't in love with Ben. Seeing him tonight was mere social contact, something to keep her from going bonkers as she adjusted to being away from her friends in Farish. Dinner at the Sand Bar with Ben wasn't really a date. But it sure felt like one.

"TAYLOE USED TO BRING Gwynne and Naomi and me here a lot in the summertime," Chloe told Ben as they waited for their food in the booth where they were sitting. Both tables and booths were fully occupied on this sultry night, mostly by couples. Overhead fans languidly stirred the humid air, and the clack of pool balls resounded from an alcove where a game was in progress.

"I don't remember Naomi," he said.

"She got married right out of high school. She wasn't here the summer I met you."

"Is that what people in Farish do? Marry young?"

Outside, a flash of heat lightning lit up the sky. Chloe took a long time answering. "Not everyone," she said offhandedly. "I didn't."

"So you've never married?"

She shook her head, hoping he wouldn't ask why. She didn't want to say that all the men she'd dated were losers in case that led him to the conclusion that she was one herself.

"You went to college, majored in art and then what?"

"I worked for a jewelry designer in Austin and eventually quit my job to take care of Grandma. I learned a lot about antiques while I managed the shop she owned for many years, and I also developed a healthy supply of patience. Grandma's a dear, and I adore her, but I won't pretend it was easy to sign on as a caregiver at the age of twenty-seven."

"Sounds like you had a difficult time."

"Not really, but I was itching to become my own person by the time she decided to go to an assisted-living facility."

"I can understand that."

The waitress, a snippy blonde, sashayed over to the table, bearing their plates. "Holler if you need anything else, Ben," she said.

Chloe noted a certain tenseness in Ben as the waitress batted her eyelashes at him. At least the lashes appeared to be real; Chloe wasn't so sure about the boobs.

Ben seemed slightly embarrassed, and Chloe wondered if the waitress, whose name tag read Liss Alderman, was how he spent his spare time away from the house. She didn't detect any intimacy between the two of them, just an unusual level of interest on the part of Liss.

"Sooo," Chloe said, drawing the word out after Liss had disappeared into the kitchen, "here I am in Sanluca, alone at last."

Ben salted his burger, and she spooned a dollop of chili sauce on her fried oyster sandwich.

"It's good to be alone sometimes," he said.

"Gwynne said you got married," she replied carefully. "That summer when we met."

"It didn't last long." When she was silent, he elaborated. "Emily wasn't easy to get along with, but she was a fine person and I hoped we could work it out. Well, we couldn't, but we parted friends and still are."

She wondered why he'd married. He'd never brought Emily around to the inn that summer. His marriage had been sudden and unexplained. At least he and his ex-wife were on amicable terms. Chloe couldn't say that about any of her past loves. They'd all disappeared from her life when the romance was over.

"Emily lives in Colorado. I haven't seen her for a while."

"She used to live here? In Sanluca?"

He nodded. "Yeah. She worked at one of the citrus-packing plants. Head of telephone sales. How's your sandwich?"

"Great. It tastes like fried ocean."

He laughed at this.

"Say," she said. "Is there anyplace to get good Mexican food around here? I grew up on Tex-Mex and I think I might be going through withdrawal."

"There's a little place called Paquita Juanita's a few miles west of town. I don't think you'll be disappointed. The fajitas are pretty good."

"Not as good as mine. My nieces tell me that my fajitas are the best in the world," she said, daring to brag.

"Any chance I could talk you into cooking them sometime?"

"Maybe."

"Good, I'll hope for it." He grinned at her across the table.

"Everything okay here? You ready for more iced tea?" The waitress had shown up again, her shirt now tied under her breasts to expose a bit of midsection and a ring in her navel.

"None for me, thanks," Ben said. "Chloe?"

She shook her head. "I'm fine."

Chloe could swear that Liss had winked at Ben, but he didn't respond. Instead, after Liss swished away, he said to Chloe, "How's that toe of yours? All healed?"

"Just like new."

"Let's dance. Want to?"

A band had started playing outside in the thatched hut, and the music floated through the open windows. The song was slow, suggestive, with a blues beat, but Chloe, after a moment's hesitation, said, "Sure."

Ben followed her past the bar, where a couple of local yokels swiveled their heads when she passed by. She forgot all about them, however, when Ben turned to her and, with a smile, took her in his arms.

With him so close, she caught a whiff of aftershave, a scent with overtones of sandalwood and spice. She was accustomed to his smelling of sun and sea, but this was pleasant. Sexy.

"You're not relaxing," he pointed out when she stepped on his toe.

"Sorry," she said as she fielded an assessing glance from Liss, who was carrying a tray of drinks past the small dance floor.

"Just let the music take us away," he murmured in her ear, and even though she tried, she couldn't get past the dirty look that Liss gave her as she hurried back to the bar.

"I—I'm not accustomed to this kind of dancing," she said, holding herself away so that she could gaze up at him. She had never suspected that he was a good dancer.

"You're doing fine," he said. "Look, this is a blues beat. Step to your right, sway left—that's right—now we take that step to the right that we started but didn't finish."

"Cool," she said, because he made it easy to follow.

"Now we twirl around and go the other way. You're getting it, Chloe. You're good."

"Not really. My dancing skills mostly center around the Texas two-step."

"You're doing fine," he said, drawing her so close that her hair brushed his cheek.

"Some guys don't like to dance. They can't lead. You're different," she told him.

"That's because I have a teachable partner. Isn't this fun?"

"Yes," she said, though she would rather not have been in the line of vision of Liss, who was now glaring with no pretense of doing otherwise. So maybe he'd come on to Liss at some time, and she resented seeing him with Chloe. Or perhaps Liss had staked him out and didn't appreciate the interference of some other woman before she could make her own move.

The song ended, and the band struck up another number. Ben kept his arms around her. "Let's try that again," he said.

"I'll only step on your feet a few more times," Chloe said. She was ready to call it quits.

"Relax," he said.

If Chloe wasn't mistaken, Ben was dancing so that his back remained toward the aisle between tables where Liss had to traverse between the bar, kitchen and tables. That made it easier for the waitress to scan the crowd and locate them, which, of course, Ben didn't realize.

As they danced, Chloe tried to make up her mind; should she tell Ben about Liss, or was it better to ignore the whole thing? By this time, if Liss had been able to fire daggers from her eyes, Chloe would have been dead meat.

"You'll have to show me the Texas two-step," Ben said.

"And the cotton-eyed Joe, and a good old-fashioned schottische. We Texans are versatile."

"I gathered that. What else do people do in Farish?"

"Go to church. Eat Sunday dinner with the family. Follow the high-school football team."

"It sounds wonderful," Ben said, looking intrigued. "Tell me more."

"They gossip about one another, but usually it's nothing harmful. They stop in the aisles at the grocery store and say things like, 'If that Lucille isn't the darnedest thing! Did you hear she bought Jakey a new Corvette? I wonder how long it'll take him to wreck it! Why, just last week, he sideswiped Odell Higham's new mailbox out on the bypass in that old Ford of his.'"

Ben threw his head back and laughed. "That doesn't tell me much about Farish, except that I'd rather be Jakey than Odell Higham."

"You're right. Jakey is the favorite son in that family. And by the way, it took him only two months to wreck the Corvette. He's okay, though, and now his mom has bought him a motorcycle. I bet they're talking about it all the way to Kettersburg."

"Where's that?"

"A town about ten miles away. It's where my grandmother moved when she went into an assisted-living facility."

"How old is your grandmother, Chloe? I've heard Tayloe and Gwynne mention her when they discussed your family, but I don't recall much about her."

"Grandma Nell is eighty, and she broke her hip a while back. She had surgery, went through therapy and decided she wanted to move to the assisted-living place where her friends are. So she closed her antique store, and I no longer had a job."

"You sound as if you're happy about it."

"I was chomping at the bit to get back to designing jewelry."

"And you have."

As the song ended, he pulled her close. With her temple resting gently against his cheek, she felt excitement ripple down her spine, quick as the heat lightning in the distance. She would have passed it off lightly if she hadn't felt him tense, also. She glanced up at him. Deep in his eyes she read a longing, a bleakness, even as his arms tightened around her.

Before she could make sense of it, he released her. She tried to recall what they'd been discussing, couldn't remember, settled on a quick, glib, "Thanks for the dancing lesson." Then she turned abruptly and preceded him back to the table, where their empty plates had been cleared.

"Ready for dessert?" asked Liss, popping up from nowhere.

Ben raised inquiring eyebrows, and Chloe shook her head. "No, thanks," he said. "I'll take the check."

"I'm paying my share," Chloe said quickly as Liss retreated.

"No, you're not. My treat."

"I asked you out tonight."

"The man should pay."

"According to what you've told me, you're not in any better financial shape than I am," she retorted.

"Ah, but I just got paid for teaching scuba classes."

Liss brought the check and slapped it on the table.

He tossed down a bill. "Keep the change," he said.

"Yes, sir. And do come back soon." This Liss delivered in an unmistakably come-hither tone.

When Liss had gone, Ben regarded Chloe with a glint of humor in his eyes. "I can't help it if I'm irresistible to women," he said.

Chloe laughed. "I guess not. I get the idea that Liss wishes I'd disappear."

"Well, maybe so, but I don't."

"Is—um, is she a good friend of yours?" Chloe ventured.

"No, I've never had any conversation with her that didn't involve ordering food."

"Sorry. I shouldn't have tried to dig into your personal life."

"There aren't any women in it at present. Except you," he added after a few seconds.

She stood. "Who needs to get her beauty sleep. I'll be up early tomorrow morning, working on my designs to show Patrice."

On the way out, they had to pass Liss at the waitress station, and she shot Chloe a scowl that was pure venom before she flounced off to the kitchen. Chloe was tickled to see that Liss was trailing a long streamer of toilet paper from one shoe.

The night air was cool as they headed toward Ben's Jeep. The beat of the music followed them, and her arm brushed his. She wondered if he was thinking what she was thinking—that it would be so easy to escalate their relationship into something more. All it would take was not moving in the opposite direction when their arms made contact, so that their hands would meet and clasp. In the span of a heartbeat, they'd turn their heads exactly the right way and touch lips. Or maybe he would reach for her in the shadows of the poinciana tree and draw her to him. His hands would rest warm on her bare shoulders, and her skin would tingle from his touch, and suddenly, his lips would close over hers. Or she would seize the initiative and stop beside the Jeep, pin him back against the hood as she had her way with him. This made her smile, and though she meant to keep it to herself, Ben noticed.

"What's so funny?"

"Nothing. I was only having an amused moment."

"Something about me? About Liss?"

"Not about Liss," though her answer would have been different a minute or so ago.

"You're smiling at me, then," he guessed, but she shook her head.

They had reached the Jeep, deep under the shadows of the poinciana tree, where he made no move to kiss her. She climbed in while Ben walked around to the driver's side.

The drive home was short, past the dock, across the bridge and a half mile down Beach Road. When he pulled up at the Frangipani Inn, they heard a clatter and a scrambling from somewhere near the back porch.

"A possum," Ben said. "Look." An animal with silver-gray fur scuttled under the cover of the sea grapes.

The uninvited visitor had overturned the garbage can. Fortunately, they had frightened the possum soon enough that it hadn't torn open the bags inside and strewn their contents all over the place.

Chloe jumped out and went to inspect the damage. Ben followed and helped her restore the bags to the container, then clamped the lid on.

He turned to her. "Thanks for a pleasant evening. I enjoyed being with you, Chloe."

"It was fun for me, too," she said as Butch bounded out of the bushes. Chloe bent to pet him. "I'm glad he didn't tangle with the possum. They can be vicious."

"Butch comes down to see me in the annex sometimes," Ben said. "I hope you don't mind if I let him in."

"Of course not, but he could eat you out of house and home." The cat twined around her ankles and went to stand at the door, waiting to be let in.

Ben rested one foot on the bottom porch step. She was poised slightly above him on the next one, torn between wanting the evening to be over and wanting to prolong it.

"I opened a can of sardines for Butch last night," Ben said. "He ate all of them and wanted more."

"You have my permission to indulge him, but don't get him used to lobster or clams. They're a little pricey."

He stared at her, his eyes dark in the light of the rising moon. "Am I also allowed to indulge myself? Would that be okay?"

"I—I'm not sure what you mean," she said, though she had an idea.

"This," he said, one hand coming up to cup the back of her neck.

Caught unawares, she protested. "I—"

"Don't talk," he murmured before drawing her head down toward his. "Just do it."

His lips closed over hers, as firm as she'd expected them to be and even more tantalizing. His mouth was hot and hungry, but there was more, too. A certain jangling of the nerves, a breathlessness, a fierce yearning to feel more. As if this trembling, heart-pounding passion wasn't enough. As if she needed to savor it, pull it into her, breathe him in and out like the very air.

His hand on her neck—she wanted it elsewhere, exploring, exciting her beyond all caution and control. His lips—she needed them to trail down her neck, linger at her breasts, find the tender spot in the hollow of her throat.

They didn't, though. He wound up the kiss neatly and with an air of finality.

"Good night, Chloe," he said.

"Good night," she whispered. She could still taste him on her lips.

Stop it, she told herself. *Don't be silly. You don't want a romance, and this could be complicated.*

Could be complicated? She almost laughed out loud. It already was.

Chapter Six

Ben was sure that Chloe Timberlake, with her provocative glances, voluptuous body and tinkling earrings, was going to drive him to distraction. Not that it was all sex. He admired her. She was a gifted artist, original and clever. He'd appreciated her penchant for fun, the unexpected, the different.

Ben liked all women. He'd freely admit it. He didn't want to give his heart to one, that was all. At times when he was tempted, he usually took a hot shower; cold showers were vastly overrated as a deterrent to sex, he'd found. But with the weather so warm, taking hot showers only made him more miserable. So what was a fellow to do?

After that steamy kiss on the back porch when they came back from the Sand Bar, Ben had some very definite ideas. He'd wanted Chloe right then and there—on the porch swing, the kitchen table, the floor, anywhere at all. She'd responded to his kiss with enthusiasm and verve. So why hadn't he tried for more?

He didn't want to put her off him for good, and although Chloe was sassy and spirited, one of his favorite combinations, he didn't like to mix business with sex. Or romance, whichever this was.

In order to stop thinking about Chloe all the time, he took to hanging out at the Sand Bar, playing pool at night. He went to

AA meetings, which helped him in his determination to stay sober. In the daytime, he went for long rides in his Jeep, chasing sandpipers out of the way, sand crabs into their holes and dogs back to their masters. Some days he wandered the streets of Sanluca hoping he'd run into Andy McGehee, who would offer him a job on sight.

Yeah. Sure thing.

One night at the Sand Bar, Liss turned up, off duty and showing more skin than usual. For the first time he noticed that she sported a silver tongue stud. She was wearing a slinky top that gave away the secret that she had breast implants; a line of definition under her skin was a dead giveaway. She undulated over to his table and sat down, leaning forward so that her breasts were in danger of surging out of her top.

A deep bass rumbled from the speakers mounted on the wall over the bar, some funky driving beat intended to bludgeon all the good sense out of a thinking man's brain. Liss started to rub his knee, but he kept his hands strictly to himself.

"I just moved out of my parents' house this week. I've got my own place now," she said.

"Congratulations. That's a big step."

"I've planned to do it for just aeons." She lowered her lashes. "I could use some help," she said.

"What kind?" he asked, knowing he should nip this in the bud but still curious to see where it went. When you got to be his age, the attentions of a pretty young girl went a long way to enhance a guy's ego.

"Maybe you could help me move a big old couch from the living room to the second bedroom," she said. "I intend to make a den out of it."

"Where do you live?" he asked, figuring that he could still get out of this if necessary.

"I rented a trailer at Ducky Hester's RV park." Her voice had taken on a husky tone.

"I've got to get up early in the morning," he lied. "I can't stay out late."

Liss pouted and moved her hand a few inches closer to her goal. "You're the first person I've ever invited to my place. I sure would like to show it off."

Throwing reason to the wind, Ben followed her home in his Jeep. Liss drove a small sedan, and when she slid out of the car at her place, her short skirt hiked up to reveal almost everything.

"I'll get us something to drink," she said as soon as they were inside the mobile home. He had barely taken in the dark paneling and the fake fur rug on the floor when she slid her arms up and around his neck and kissed him full on the mouth. After they broke apart, he retreated to the other side of the room and said, "Is this the couch you want to move?"

"Sure, but no hurry," she said. "How about a screwdriver?"

For a second or two, the question confused him. He didn't need a screwdriver to move the couch. Then he caught on that Liss was talking about a drink made with orange juice and vodka.

To avail himself of such means to uninhibiting himself was tempting, but he realized that there was no such thing as drinking one. He'd soon want another and another and be back where he started. Andy would hear about it and would never rehire him.

"No, thanks," he said.

Liss poured vodka in a glass and drank it straight. "Forgot to mention I'm out of orange juice," she explained with a wink when she saw him looking at her.

He wasn't liking this scene one bit. "This couch can't be so heavy," he said. "If you'll take that end, we can manage it easily."

Liss walked around the dining-room table and rubbed her shoulder suggestively against his chest. "I didn't really want to move a couch tonight," she said, her voice low and suggestive. "I had something else in mind. It could involve a couch if you like." She laughed a long throaty laugh.

Suddenly, as his gaze angled down her neckline at those breasts that were spectacular but not real, Ben didn't want to do this.

He tried to soften the blow. "You're a beautiful girl, Liss. You deserve someone better than me."

"Say again?" she said in a disbelieving tone.

"Someone closer to your age who will care about you. Who has a good future, a decent job and is available."

"What are you talking about?" She was staring at him as if he'd grown an extra eyeball in the middle of his forehead.

"I need to go. I'm sorry if I let you think—" He shrugged, sure that she'd be angry and not blaming her a bit.

She wasn't, though. She quickly and cleverly changed her tack. "Would you like to talk about it? Is something wrong?"

"The two of us are wrong, Liss." Patiently, he removed her hand from his collar and kissed her chastely on the cheek. "'Bye," he said.

He walked out the door and toward his Jeep.

"Ben?" She called from the door. "Are you okay?"

"Uh-huh," he said, wishing she'd keep her voice down. The last thing he needed was for someone, maybe Ducky, to learn he'd been alone in her trailer with her, even though nothing had happened.

"Okay. See you around."

"Right," he said.

Liss was still standing at the door, gazing out into the night as he drove away.

Ben told himself that he shouldn't have left the Sand Bar with her in the first place, but at least he'd weaseled out of the situation before he did any real harm. He was sure that Liss's feelings were hurt, and she might badmouth him for a while, but his decision not to avail himself of her body was the right one.

He was in a melancholy frame of mind when he drove up outside the Frangipani Inn. It was late, and the house was dark. As he often did when he arrived home from his classes or twelve-step meetings late at night, he walked around to the front porch. The wicker chair creaked when he lowered his weight onto it, but he took care not to rock. Chloe's open bedroom window was right above where he sat.

He dozed for a while and woke up with a start when he heard the front door open.

Chloe stepped out into the moonlight. She was wearing a short robe, translucent, and it was open down the front. Certainly, she had no idea that he was sitting only a few feet away. She must have come down for a breath of air; the temperature of the upstairs bedrooms could be stifling on nights like this.

Chloe went to the edge of the porch and leaned against one of the pillars. Behind her the palms swayed in the light wind blowing from the east, and her robe fell away to reveal even more of her. All of her, in fact, because she wore nothing underneath.

His sharp intake of breath almost gave him away. Her breasts were full and shaded blue in the moonlight; her waist was narrow, her hips slim. Her tan was bisected by pale swimsuit lines. At the apex of her thighs, a tantalizing shadow hid what lay between.

Ben had never seen anyone more beautiful than Chloe in those moments. The chair creaked when he stood, and she whirled around, startled.

"It's only me, Chloe," he said quietly. Before she could wrap her robe around her, he strode across the porch. Her eyes were wide and luminous, her lips parted.

"Ben," she said, and that was all. She went into his arms willingly as he crushed her to him, and her skin was softer than he imagined, her lips more pliant. They parted beneath his, warm and wet, and he groaned. She wasn't timid but demanding, giving more than taking, and as hungry as he was. Could a woman know the same ache, the same yearning, the same lust? In his experience, no. But other women weren't Chloe.

His hands slid up past her waist, inside the robe, where her skin was so smooth. Her breasts rested lightly in his palms, the nipples sharp little points beneath his thumbs. Her hands feathered down the sides of his face, covered his, showed him how to pleasure her. She was provocative as hell, and if this went on much longer, he wouldn't be able to stop.

Not that he wanted to end this. No. Never. He forced himself to release her lips, but she kept kissing him, trailing kisses down the side of his jaw, pushing aside his shirt so that she could kiss his bare chest.

"Chloe," he said urgently, his voice a rasp. "Are you protected?"

She rested her cheek against his chest. "No," she whispered. "I didn't anticipate—didn't plan this."

"Neither did I," he told her as he struggled for his breathing to return to normal, for his heart to stop racing. They were twelve miles from a drugstore; that in itself would put a damper on things.

She stepped away, wrapped her robe around her and tied it. She slid her fingers through her hair, an unconsciously sexy movement, and he heard her sigh. "Then I guess this isn't going to happen," she said, a catch in her voice.

"Chloe, I—"

"It's better like this," she said on a note of resignation. "I want you to respect me in the morning."

From the way she said it, he understood that she was trying to inject a bit of humor into the proceedings.

"I would respect you no matter what," he said, realizing as he spoke that he really meant it. That was the difference in his relationships with Chloe and Liss—and in a flash of insight, he realized that being able to respect the woman he was with increased his own self-esteem. A man of worth required a woman of worth. Simple, but a profound bit of self-discovery in this stage of his life.

"And I you. Let's sleep on it, Ben. I've got a big day tomorrow. The meeting with Patrice in Palm Beach."

He didn't try to hide his disappointment. Her face was cast in darkness now, and she moved away.

"Good night, Ben."

"Good night."

She went inside, and he heard the creak of the hall stairs as she walked to her room, the *snick!* of the latch as she shut the door.

When Ben was sure that Chloe had disappeared into her room for good, he headed for the shower in his own quarters. A very hot one, which took care of the problem.

THE NEXT MORNING, when Chloe drove to Palm Beach to meet with Patrice, she had more than enough to contemplate along the way. Not only the incident with Ben last night, which had left her feeling lost and alone. She'd gone downstairs because it was so hot and she couldn't sleep. She'd been fantasizing as she stood on the porch that Ben might step out of the shadows and take her in his arms. When it actually happened, it was like being caught up in a dream.

But in a dream, fantasies were fulfilled. In real life, sometimes they weren't. Practicalities intervened, and in the harsh light of the next day, Chloe realized that backing off was the wisest thing she could have done.

That wasn't the only thing she brooded about. Naomi had called before Chloe left Sanluca to report that Tara was missing again.

Naomi was beside herself. "Marilyn said Tara left her house Saturday night after she was supposed to have gone to bed. She would have had to climb out a window to get out without being seen, since Marilyn had stayed up late to work on a quilting project and was watching TV downstairs. I'm hoping Tara will turn up here at home soon. Last time I talked with her, she said she wanted to get a job."

"A job? Where?" Chloe had asked, exasperated. Work wasn't exactly plentiful in Farish, Texas.

"Tara suggested that maybe your friend Beth would hire her in her interior design business now that she's expecting a baby."

"Beth can handle everything all by herself, and anyway, Tara doesn't know anything about design."

"Tara hasn't figured out that any job not requiring a college degree would be a dead end in Farish. But she'd better go back to high school in the fall, or she'll never get as far as college," Naomi said.

"I'm willing to bet that Tara will be at Farish High on the first day of school in September," Chloe said soothingly, but what if Tara really intended to drop out? The girl needed convincing that she should finish high school. Tara's grades were okay, not spectacular, but Chloe was sure that if Tara was interested in something, she'd learn everything she could about it. She'd been fascinated by dinosaurs when she was younger, and she'd avidly read every book she could find on the subject. She'd learned to make origami dinosaurs, and she'd saved her allowance to buy balsa wood kits so she could build model dinosaurs. She'd completed many dinosaur science projects, some of which were on permanent display in the library at her former elementary school.

But what would inspire Tara to finish school now? What would spike her interest? As much as she cared about her niece, as much as she understood Tara's rebellion, Chloe was as puzzled as her sister over what to do about it.

If anything could take her mind off this perplexing family matter, Palm Beach was it. The town was beautiful, with its long vistas of perfectly manicured boulevards, palm fronds waving in the gentle breeze from the ocean and steady parade of shiny Rolls-Royces proceeding at an elegant pace. Just for fun, Chloe drove along the ocean before heading toward the main shopping area and parking on a quiet side street.

Patrice's shop was called Spindrift and was located in one of the quaint, charming piazzas opening off Worth Avenue. When Chloe entered, a bell on the door chimed, and Patrice emerged from her office, wearing a big smile. "Come in, come in," she said, hooking her arm through Chloe's. "We're not busy in the summer months, and this is a perfect time for us to chat. I'm so glad you're here, Chloe. Tell me, what have you heard from Gwynne?"

In the shop, Chloe had the impression of beautiful clothes artistically displayed, of tastefully dressed sales personnel lingering discreetly in the corners and of rarefied air perfumed with the scent of the sea. But there wasn't much time to study her surroundings with Patrice bringing her a frosty glass of mint iced tea and making sure she was comfortable on the big cushy couch in her office.

It only took a few minutes to discuss Tayloe's marriage to her Mexican bullfighter husband and Gwynne's determination to get her master's degree in speech pathology. Patrice seemed as eager as Chloe to get to the subject of their visit today.

"I'm so curious to see what you have in that briefcase," Patrice said. "Open it up and show me what you do."

Chloe was only too glad to comply, and she was gratified by Patrice's enthusiastic response to her designs.

"My customers are very discriminating and most of them have exquisite taste. Can you make more?"

"I have a backlog of pieces that I can leave with you today if you like."

Patrice smiled. "I'll display them in the window. Now, why don't we go to lunch," she suggested.

They adjourned to an intimate restaurant around the corner and indulged in coconut shrimp, banana muffins and an enormous dessert featuring a copious amount of chocolate. They reminisced about the week Patrice had visited the inn years ago. Patrice recalled that Chloe had helped her bake her special brown-sugar cookies, and they'd held a tea party on the front porch. Afterward, Tayloe and Patrice had challenged Gwynne, Naomi and Chloe in Trivial Pursuit and won handily.

As Patrice and Chloe were on the way out the restaurant door and saying their goodbyes, Chloe's cell phone rang. Since it could be Naomi calling with news of Tara, Chloe dug the phone out of her handbag and clicked it on.

"Chloe," said Ben, his voice crackling through a bad connection. "You need to head home right away."

"What's wrong?"

"There's a girl sitting on the front porch painting her toenails green. She says she's your niece."

WHEN CHLOE REACHED the Frangipani Inn, Tara was lying back in a huge hammock and fanning herself with a magazine.

Chloe tossed her briefcase on a chair and perched her hands on her hips. "Tara! Whatever possessed you to come all the way to Sanluca?"

Tara sat up with a scowl. "Don't freak, Chloe. Anyway, that's not much of a welcome for your favorite niece. You haven't even said hello."

"That's because I'm quite certain that I'll soon be telling you goodbye. I intend to find out when the next plane leaves for

Texas, and you'll be on it." Chloe sagged onto a rocking chair, regarding Tara balefully. Thank goodness Tara was safe, but Chloe didn't care for the green nail polish or the indolent attitude that her niece was, at this very moment, exhibiting.

"Tara, how did you get here?" At sixteen, her niece had lost all vestiges of babyhood; she was slim and pretty, with long blond hair the color that nature should have given Chloe. She was wearing short shorts and a top that barely covered the essentials.

"I caught a bus. It dropped me off at the gas station. I rode over here to the inn with the Turtle Lady. I recognized her from pictures Mom has, except in person she doesn't look so much like the picture, more like a raisin in sneakers."

"Tara, that's not nice. Zephyr is—"

"I know, I know. She's a fixture around here and can't help it if she's as old as the Atlantic. Anyway, she was pumping gas when I got off the bus, and I asked her about turtles and she said she'd drive me to the inn. She was real helpful."

"Why are you here, Tara?"

Tara blew her bangs out of her face. "I didn't like living at Marilyn's, and I'd saved enough money from babysitting and my allowance to leave. Besides, I've heard about Sanluca for what seems like forever from you and Mom. And you're like me, Chloe—you don't settle for the usual. You do your own thing. It'll be fun spending the summer together, you'll see."

Chloe sighed, overwhelmed. Ben strolled around the corner, spared her a curious lift of his brows and began to water the hibiscus hedge.

"We'll call your mom," Chloe decided.

"She'll go ballistic," Tara said in an ominous tone.

"No, she won't. When I talked to her, the only emotions I detected were gratitude and relief that you were okay. You've put her through a lot, Tara."

While Tara was still looking guilty, Chloe produced her cell phone from her handbag, punched the speed dial and passed it to her niece. "I'm going inside for a few minutes. Make peace with your mother, and then I'll chat with her."

Ben, after turning off the water and neatly coiling the hose, followed Chloe into the house, where she had collapsed on a chair in the kitchen.

"Is everything all right?" he asked mildly as he opened the freezer door and dropped a few ice cubes into a glass.

"No," Chloe said mournfully.

"Your niece is kind of uptight," Ben observed. "Care for some ice? I'll get it for you."

"Sure," Chloe said, extending her hand. Ben placed the glass with the ice in it and went to get more for himself. She upended the glass and crunched her teeth down on one of the cubes.

Ben swiveled sharply. "Hey, do you have to do that? It drives me nuts."

"What—chewing ice?"

He seemed abashed. "It's a pet peeve. Sorry."

She swallowed. "That's okay. Compared with the other things going on in my life right now, refraining from chewing ice is minor."

Ben poured water into both glasses and sat down at the table, across from her.

"Tell me about it," he said.

"Tara insists that she's going to stay here."

"Why not let her? She's a charming girl."

"Though significantly underclothed. Yes, Tara's wonderful. Especially when she's getting what she wants. Did you talk with her much?"

"A little. I was replacing glass in the front windows when she walked up. She asked for you, and I told her you weren't here.

Then I called you. Afterward she told me a joke. I like her, Chloe. Maybe she just needs a bit of direction."

"Or a kick in the—"

"Chloe? Chloe!" Tara hollered from the porch. "Mom wants to speak with you."

"Uh-oh, here goes," Chloe muttered. She took another long swig from her glass and went to talk to her sister, ice tinkling as she walked.

"Chloe, can Tara stay? Just for a while? She says she needs to get her head together." Naomi was pleading.

Glass in one hand, phone in the other, Chloe climbed the stairs so she'd be out of Tara's hearing range. "A lot of people ought to regroup, including maybe me. Why can't Tara get her head together in Texas, where she belongs?"

"I've wondered that myself."

"She thinks I don't have rules," Chloe said darkly. "She thinks living here will be a piece of cake."

"Correction—she thinks it will be the whole cake. She likes the idea of meeting new people, and she really enjoyed talking with Ben."

"She told him a joke. I don't have any idea what kind."

"Tara's basically a good kid who is trying to behave herself. We clash, my daughter and I, and it would be good for us to be apart for a while. Let her stay, Chloe. Please. Puh-leeze?"

Chloe gazed ceilingward for a long moment, hoping she wasn't getting into something that would cause her grief down the road, like so many of her other rescue operations. Yet her loneliness here was paramount in her mind; she considered that importing companionship might be more productive than seeking it inappropriately with Ben.

"All right, Mimi," she said after a long sigh. "Tara can stay. But she has to follow my rules, and I'll be strict. No one knows better than I do how kids get around restrictions. I've used all the angles myself. You've got to admit I was a whiz at evading our parents and making excuses."

"My hope is that Tara will be just like you."

"That's touching. You're going to owe me for this, Naomi. Big-time."

"Agreed. So will you tell Tara the happy news, or shall I?"

"I'll do it. I can use the opportunity to lay down the law. She may skedaddle back to Farish tomorrow after she realizes that she can't put anything over on me."

"She won't come home unless we force her. Chloe, you're exactly what she needs."

"We'll see about that." Chloe paused. "Anything else I should do?"

"Only one thing. Tell me more about Ben. Are you having a fling?"

"*Naomi.* He's right here in the house," Chloe hissed after lowering her voice. "I don't want him to hear me talking about him." Downstairs the door slammed, and she looked out her bedroom window. Though she had no view of the porch from the turret room, she heard Tara talking, followed by Ben's low laugh.

"Okay," Chloe said, "he's on the porch talking with Tara." She paused for effect. "Naomi, I really like the guy."

"Like, as in like? Or *like?*"

"Hmm, if this were a questionnaire, I'd have to check neither of the above. He's pleasant, and I enjoy being with him. The thing is, sometimes I've noticed the saddest, most mournful expression in his eyes, but I don't know what's going on with him."

"You'll find out," said Naomi with great conviction. "You always do."

"I'm more or less keeping my distance." Except for a couple of times, but she wasn't about to admit that to her sister.

"Good for you. Are there any other men on the horizon?"

"Let me remind you that I'm here to work. It's therapeutic."

"Do you require therapy?"

"Listen, Naomi, let's not get into that."

"I'm sorry. You worked hard taking care of Grandma, and I'm grateful to you for doing more than your share." Naomi actually did sound contrite.

"She was a delight the whole time, so I really didn't mind. I'm glad to have my own life back at last, though."

"Except for babysitting my daughter," Naomi said ruefully.

"I'll convince her—somehow—to go back to high school in the fall," Chloe vowed. "I'll make her understand that she'd be stupid to do otherwise."

"I hope so."

"Naomi, I'd better run. Love you."

"Love you, too. 'Bye."

After they hung up, Chloe sat on her bed for a long time, listening to Tara and Ben chatting on the front porch. Tara was dramatically telling him about her boring life in Farish, and Ben was calmly asking questions, drawing her out and being his low-key self. At the moment, Chloe appreciated his taking time to visit with Tara while she pulled herself together and figured out how to handle the situation.

When she finally went downstairs to tell Tara that there would be no flouting of the rules, that she'd have to obey and help out around the inn, Chloe felt reasonably optimistic. And she was clear in her own mind that she was doing the right thing by taking charge of Tara for the next couple of months.

Though—and this was a provocative question—if she *were* really going to indulge in a fling with Ben, how would she manage do it with an impressionable teenager on the premises?

Chapter Seven

Tara, after expressing relief at not being shipped back to Texas, offered Chloe the use of her green nail polish. “It would look great on you,” she insisted.

Chloe, having abandoned her adventures with avant-garde hair color and having given up on nail polish years ago, expressed misgivings. “You want me to paint my nails with something the color of moldy cheese?” she asked.

“It’s not the color of mold,” Tara informed her indignantly. “It’s Leapfrog Green.”

“Okay,” Chloe agreed, figuring that if this was what she had to do in order to build rapport between them, she might as well give in.

“Awesome,” Tara declared, and proceeded to give Chloe a manicure. She suggested a pedicure, but that was where Chloe drew the line.

“Sorry, no time. I’ve got to finish a pair of earrings,” she said before fleeing to her workshop. Privately, she had to admit that her newly lacquered nails weren’t half-bad, but having a homegrown manicurist didn’t quite make up for the loss of privacy.

Ben looked askance when he first saw Chloe wearing green

nail polish. "Isn't this backward? Aren't you supposed to be the one who influences Tara, not vice versa?"

"You didn't know me in my younger days," she retorted. "I did worse things than paint my fingernails atrocious colors."

"I did too know you when you were younger," Ben replied thoughtfully.

"Oops, you're right," she conceded before rushing off on a false errand. Maybe he did recall some things about her, she decided. Perhaps he hadn't been so wrapped up in Emily that summer after all. But then, why had he gone and married the woman? Why hadn't he stuck around and been at the inn a year later, after Chloe had finally developed boobs and mastered the intricacies of applying eyeliner? Oh, well, that was then, and she was having enough trouble handling the present without driving herself crazy with questions that probably had no answers.

The kitchen became a gathering place for the three of them, Chloe, Ben and Tara, every morning. Chloe and Tara took turns preparing breakfast, which when Chloe did it tended toward cereal with a banana sliced on top. Tara, on the other hand, offered more exotic fare: scrambled eggs with cream cheese and chives; frozen blueberry pancakes; grilled-cheese sandwiches, which weren't exactly what Chloe considered breakfast fare but were good nevertheless.

Ben discussed his day's repair schedule with Chloe while she and Tara ate their morning meal. He sometimes benefited by Tara's willingness to cook for him, too. She was always willing to toss in another egg or slide another pancake into the toaster on short notice.

One day when Tara had been there about a week, Ben and Chloe were discussing the usual when Tara interrupted.

"I don't see why I can't drink coffee," Tara said. "You two do."

"Wait until you go away to college and crave the caffeine jolt so you can stay awake late at night studying," Chloe told her playfully.

"I'm not going to college," Tara said. "I hate to study."

"So did I," Chloe pointed out. "Until I changed my major to art."

Tara, refusing to be placated, dumped ice cubes from the freezer into her empty orange juice glass and proceeded to chew on them.

Ben spared the girl a pained look. "Tara—" he began.

Chloe interrupted. "Tara, honey, Ben doesn't like to hear anyone chomping on ice."

Tara spit the ice into the glass. "Sorry," she muttered.

"It's one of my pet peeves," Ben said. "Like when people run their fingers down a chalkboard."

Tara blinked at him. "I hate that, too," she said.

"We all have our foibles," Ben said comfortably. He turned his attention to Chloe. "We should get a garbage can with a tighter lid. I chased away another possum last night."

Now that no one was paying attention to her, Tara seemed determined to descend into a sulk. Meanwhile, Chloe wondered where Ben had been until midnight the night before. She and Tara had sat up playing Monopoly until eleven, and although she'd listened for the sound of Ben's Jeep tires crunching the shell-rock driveway, he'd never shown up. She'd intended to ask him to join them, and she'd delayed bringing out the chips and guacamole until really late in case he wanted a snack.

"All right," Chloe said, barring these thoughts from her mind. "Put a garbage can on the list. Tara and I will go to the hardware store and get it along with the other things you requested. Number ten nails, assorted grades of sandpaper and what else?"

"A gallon of white primer."

"Ben, are you really going to take me metal detecting with you?" Tara asked, transparently eager to change the subject back to something concerning her. "Do you think we'll find anything?"

"Maybe." Ben stirred his coffee and reached for a piece of leftover toast.

"Chloe, can we stop at the treasure museum?" Tara asked.

"Sure," Chloe said. In all her visits to Sanluca, she'd never been inside.

"I'm going to drive us into town today," Tara bragged to Ben. "Chloe said I could."

"Great," replied Ben.

"Not until you change into some shorts that are more decent," Chloe piped up.

"These are fine," Tara replied indignantly. "They're halfway to my knees."

And show more skin south of your navel than we need to see, Chloe thought. "What are they—a pair of your dad's boxer shorts?" she asked, forcing back a grin. She'd often attempted to escape from the house in strange getups in her teenage years.

"Yes, but—"

"If you want to go out with me, you'll have to find something more appropriate. How about those jeans I saw in your closet?"

"It's too hot for jeans," Tara argued.

As he placed his cup in the dishwasher, Ben's knee accidentally brushed Chloe's. A glance at Tara reassured her that the girl hadn't noticed, but nevertheless, Chloe edged in the opposite direction. Ben retreated to the other end of the room and began scribbling in a spiral notebook that he used to keep track of his work.

Tara stood up and stalked from the room. After a couple of minutes, she returned, wearing shorts with a drawstring waist. "How's this?" she asked.

"Wonderful," Chloe said, relieved.

Tara started to clear the breakfast things off the table, her previous mood forgotten. "I met some kids on the beach yesterday. Jill lives down the road in Stuart's Point. I like her. She's been to Europe. The guys are Aaron, Greg and Sam. The other girls might be Marla and Judy, or maybe it's Marta and Julie. I watched them surf."

"I'll be working on the windows again today," Ben interjected. "Anything else you want me to do, Chloe?"

She thought, *Kiss me,* then wondered where that had come from. "Um, no." A tension headache began to build behind her eyes, and she tried to remember when she had last slept with a man. Last year. No, this year, when she became interested in a man that she'd met at a friend's wedding, a recent transplant from Kansas. He turned out to be another rescue project, and she'd dropped him almost immediately. He'd stopped by every night for dinner with her and her grandmother, watching their TV afterward until he felt asleep snoring on the couch. Chloe, after a few inquiries around town, found out that he was separated and his wife had kicked him out of the house.

Chloe hadn't been mightily attracted to him, however, as she was to Ben. He even now made her tremble by merely glancing at her in that secretly covetous way that got around any misgivings she might have had.

"Let's get going, Tara," she said briskly. She tossed her the car keys, and Tara let out a delighted shriek.

"See you later, Ben," Tara said as she jumped up and slammed out the back door.

This left Ben and Chloe staring at each other across the kitchen table.

"See you later," he said softly, his meaning entirely different from Tara's. Chloe didn't reply. She merely followed Tara out the door, knowing that something was bound to happen between her and Ben sooner or later. She hoped it would be sooner.

"SO WE WENT to the treasure museum, and they're looking for student volunteers," Tara said to Ben that night. "I signed up. Kids work in the gift shop, relieve the cashier, run errands, things like that."

"Good for you," Ben said easily. He had knocked on the back door with the intention of reporting that he was finished repairing the porch railing. Tara had insisted he come in and eat chicken salad with them. She'd prepared it herself, arranging it with fruit slices on crystal plates, and was obviously proud of her cooking skills. He liked Tara; she was exuberant and cheerful, and she eased the almost constant sexual tension between Chloe and him.

They were sitting in the library, and Chloe, on a narrow love seat, was sorting jewelry findings into small boxes. Ben was perusing the shelves for a book to read, thinking that it might help him get through the lonely nights when he wasn't at one of his meetings or hanging out at the Sand Bar.

A knock sounded on the door, and Chloe went to answer it. She expected it to be Zephyr, who—she had learned from experience—might show up any time of the day or night. But it turned out to be the tall boy called Aaron, his friend Greg, and Jill, the girl with whom Tara had struck up a friendship on the beach.

"Is Tara here?" asked Greg.

Tara came to see who it was. "Greg! And Aaron, and Jill! Y'all, this is my aunt, Chloe Timberlake." She gestured over her shoulder, where Ben offered a genial wave. "And that's Ben. Remember, I told you about him, the treasure-hunting guy?"

Chloe held the door open and the three teenagers trooped inside. The boys shook hands with Ben, and a moment of awkwardness ensued.

"Chloe, would it be okay if the four of us sat out on the

porch?" Tara seemed thrilled to have visitors, but clearly she didn't want to subject them to the stiff scrutiny of adults.

"Of course," Chloe said. "I'll bring cold drinks. Does everyone like iced tea?"

This met with nods all around, and as the young people followed Tara out onto the porch, Chloe headed for the kitchen.

Ben ambled in and began to refill empty ice trays. "Nice kids," he said.

"I'm glad Tara's making friends," she replied.

"I've met Jill's parents, Lorena and Barry Pettus. It was years ago."

"Tara took an instant liking to Jill." She loaded four glasses of tea onto a tray and carried them out to the front porch.

"Thanks," Tara said with a bright smile, and the other kids thanked her, too. Greg was sitting beside Tara, and Chloe wondered briefly if he'd be considered a hottie. Jill was pretty, with glossy dark hair and brightly animated expressions. It was Aaron who didn't seem to fit into the group. He seemed older than the others and slightly aloof.

Chloe went back inside and continued to the kitchen, where Ben was closing the refrigerator door. "Could I talk you into helping me chaperone?" she asked. The truth was that she didn't feel she could go to bed and leave the four young people to themselves; she wanted to make sure the visitors went home at a decent hour.

"I wouldn't mind staying," Ben said, perking up as if she'd thrown him a lifeline. "I'll help you sort those jewelry things if you like."

They went back into the library, where Chloe had a partial view of the front porch. Tara and her new friends were talking loudly and laughing, their talk punctuated by slang that Chloe didn't recognize.

"This really makes me feel old," she confided to Ben after they'd divided the jewelry findings into boxes and put them away. "I have no idea what they're saying to one another. Really."

"Me, neither," he told her with a chuckle.

"My sister says that there's nothing like having a couple of teenagers around to keep you feeling young, but she's wrong."

"There's something to be said for it," Ben said reflectively, and his tone caused her to aim a sharp look in his direction.

At that point, the visitors prepared to leave. Amid all the goodbyes, Ben's expression took on a somberness that seemed out of place. Chloe didn't have a chance to ponder this because Tara soon came bouncing inside, her face alight with pleasure.

"Isn't it sweet that they all came to see me, Chloe? Greg has the prettiest hazel eyes, don't you think? Jill told me she's in love with Aaron, and she's only seventeen. Greg asked me to go to the movies with him some night. Would that be okay?"

Realizing that Tara didn't really expect answers to all her questions, Chloe tried anyway. "Yes, yes and maybe, after I get to know Greg better."

"Greg wants to volunteer at the treasure museum, too. Jill says she's trying to find a paying job, but there aren't any. I'm going to bed now, Chloe. Can I use your phone to call Mom?"

"Sure, but make sure you give it back to me so I can charge the battery. Good night, Tara. Sweet dreams."

Tara went running upstairs, and Chloe rolled her eyes. "So much energy."

Ben laughed. "More than I have, that's for sure. By the way, how did your visit with Patrice go? I never had a chance to ask."

"Very well. She's planning to sell my things at astronomical prices. Any news on when your job might come through?"

"No clue."

Chloe stretched elaborately. "Well, I guess I'd better go

upstairs and grab the phone from Tara. I'd like to chat with Naomi and reassure her that everything is okay."

Ben's attention flicked toward the stairwell, where Tara's voice rose and fell behind her closed door. "I don't think you'll have any trouble with Tara this summer."

"I hope not," Chloe said fervently.

"Has she mentioned that she's interested in diving? She's welcome to attend some of my scuba classes if you wouldn't mind."

"I'll ask Naomi. I doubt that she'll object."

"Well, then, good night," Ben said.

"See you tomorrow," she replied. He watched her as she mounted the stairs.

It was clear to her, and probably to him as well, that if anything were going to happen between them, they would have to choose their time carefully. *If* anything were going to happen. Just in case, she'd refilled her prescription for birth control pills. She'd let it expire when her skin cleared up. Now she might need the pills for an entirely different reason.

SHE HAD WRITTEN on this date sixteen years ago.

> Dear Trees, I saw Gold on the beach today, just the two of us! He didn't notice me at first. He was walking along and staring down at the sand as if he was a million miles away. I had gone to look for the Turtle Lady but couldn't find her. Wind wanted to invite her to eat dinner with us. Well, anyway, I was trying to find a good piece of driftwood for a crafts project (I want to drill some holes in it and stick air plants in, cause the Turtle Lady said she has some growing right on the oak tree at her house). And there was Gold! He was wearing nothing but a bathing suit and his bare chest. Well, you know what I mean. It's really hairy, not like the

boys at school. I said, "Ben?" (I had to use his real name when I spoke to him since he doesn't know he's Gold.)

He said, "Huh?" Then he looked at me. Really studied me up and down. I was so embarrassed because I was wearing Ocean's old bikini, the one that's too small for both of us. (Mine wasn't dry from swimming that morning and I'd hung it out to dry.) He looked at me the way a man looks at a woman, you know? As if I was something he liked seeing.

I wanted to kiss him then and there. But he just smiled in a sort of unfocused way. He called me Carrots and kept walking.

I know what happens between a man and a woman. I want it to happen to me sometime. But when I look at Gold and he looks at me, I want it to happen right now.

This has to be the most fantastic summer of my life. Aren't you glad I'm telling you all about it?

Love,

Fire (Chloe D. Timberlake, who is passionately in love with Gold)

AFTER TARA'S ARRIVAL at the Frangipani Inn, Ben made himself scarce. The Sand Bar was his refuge, except when Liss was around.

"I can't figure out what's with that girl," Joe said to him one evening during a lull. "She's always been a little spacey, but last week she didn't show up for work for a couple of days, said she needed time off to get a tattoo. In Liss's case, that's gilding the lily."

Joe went to the kitchen to ask for clean glasses, and Ben studied the newly inked hearts and roses on Liss's shoulder as best he could from that distance. This earned him an inquiring glance from Liss, and when she headed toward him he quickly swiveled around to face the bar, hoping she wouldn't stop to talk.

"Ben?"

He made himself turn and smile, though he was gritting his teeth. "Hi, Liss. What's happening?"

"I saw you admiring my tattoo."

"Well—"

"You don't like it?" She appeared worried, her brow furrowing into an unbecoming line.

"Of course not," he lied. He firmly believed that sometimes, in social situations, it was better to fudge than to hurt someone's feelings.

"Have you ever had a tattoo?"

"Never had the urge," he told her.

"If you do, I can tell you the name of the guy who did mine."

"Sure," he said. Across the room, a group in one of the booths was casting annoyed glances in their direction, no doubt wanting their server to pay attention to them. "I believe you've got some needy customers over there," he said with a nod in that direction.

"They'll wait. I want to ask you something, Ben." Her expression was more serious than he'd ever seen it, and he braced himself for what she might say.

"That night when we went to my place," she said. "I didn't do anything to turn you off, did I?"

He figured he might as well be kind. "No, Liss. You're a beautiful woman," he said carefully. "I—have other interests, that's all."

"You mean the person you brought to eat dinner here? The one with all the earrings?"

But not a navel ring, he thought as he pulled his focus away from hers. "Chloe. Yes."

"You're, well, boyfriend and girlfriend?"

This was getting too personal for him, so he bolted down the rest of his tonic and lime and stood up. "You could say that," he allowed. Considering that he and Chloe hadn't even slept together yet, claiming a relationship was a little premature.

"That's too bad," she said. "I'm sorry to hear it."

At least this conversation might put an end to Liss's pursuit of him. "Like I said that night, you can find someone else."

"Maybe I already have," Liss said defensively. "Maybe I'm not all that crazy about you anyway."

"Then I'd be happy for you and whomever," he said, tossing a couple of bills on the bar for Joe.

"I wish I could say the same about you and—what's her name? Zoe?"

"Chloe," he said, starting toward the door.

"You'll get tired of her real fast," Liss said, tossing her head.

He didn't like her tone or her attitude, so he wheeled and walked back to her. "I won't," he said, not even trying to keep the anger out of his voice. "And if you ever say anything against Chloe again while you're here and supposed to be working, I'll talk to the manager. Got it?"

"Got it," Liss said faintly.

He nodded curtly. "Okay."

He sauntered out. Behind him, Liss was bristling with indignation. In a way, he was grateful for the exchange because it allowed feelings to surface that he hadn't realized he felt toward Chloe. Protectiveness, for one, and a degree of caring that he'd thought was beyond him. He'd been a treasure hunter most of his life. And now, in Chloe, he recognized a treasure of real value. The only trouble was that he had nothing to offer her—no job, no real prospects, not even a place to live.

TARA HAD SETTLED into her room, Sea Oats, with little effort. She told Chloe that she liked the room's yellow-and-gold color scheme; she'd brought a picture of her mother, father and twin sisters and propped it on the dresser beside her well-worn teddy bear. Chloe, who had to keep reminding herself that Tara was growing up, found it touching that she had brought her childhood toy along. However, as her niece, in a skimpy bikini, headed for the beach with her new friends, Chloe noted that Tara was definitely more woman than child nowadays.

It didn't take long, after Chloe consulted with Naomi and Ray, to grant dating privileges to Tara and Greg. Chloe liked Greg and found him unerringly polite. Tara began to spend two days a week at the treasure museum, and she and Greg often manned the gift shop together. As for the rest of Tara's friends, Chloe had grown fond of Jill, who often drove over in her mother's car to visit in the evening. Jill wanted a job so she could save money to buy her own car, something sportier than her mother's Lincoln Town Car, and Chloe admired her determination. In her experience, too many kids never learned the satisfaction of working toward a goal and achieving it, and the fact that Jill's parents were well-to-do but refused to buy her a car was a pleasant surprise. As for Aaron, Jill's boyfriend, Chloe still hadn't warmed to him. In every situation, he seemed to be assessing those present and, judging from the smug expression on his face, feeling superior.

She mentioned this observation to Ben one day when he stopped in to ask if she needed to mail anything. She had been pouring herself a beer, and it felt strange not to offer him one.

"How about a glass of water?" she offered.

He hesitated. "You can drink a beer," he told her. "It won't bother me. I'll get my own water." He found a glass in the cupboard and proceeded to pour water out of the jug she kept in the fridge.

Three weeks had elapsed since their romantic interlude on the porch. Chloe wondered if Ben ever wished that things had gone further than they had, if he had any desire to resume where they'd left off. Leaning against the kitchen counter, she took a long pull from the bottle. Ben stood near the door, one thumb hooked through his belt loop, the other hand curved around the glass, which was damp with condensation from the humid air. Automatically, she handed him a napkin to wrap around it.

"How long have you been sober?" she asked. He'd be within his rights to remind her that it was none of her business, but he didn't.

His gaze didn't waver. "It's been over a year, but sobriety is never easy. I've only backslid once, on the anniversary—well, some things are hard to get through."

Before she could frame an appropriate reply, she heard the crunch of tires on the shell-rock driveway. Jill and Aaron pulled up next to her Volvo. When they met at the back of Aaron's car to remove beach paraphernalia from the trunk, Aaron gathered an acquiescent Jill, who was wearing only a brief bikini, close for a long and passionate kiss.

Chloe nodded in their direction. "See that? I hope Tara doesn't follow Jill's example."

"She won't. She confides in me some, you know."

"I'm glad she talks to you. Naomi would be, too."

"Tara likes Greg, but she has a sensible head on her shoulders. They're just friends."

"Greg seems like a good influence. Aaron has a quality, though, that I don't care for. I'm not sure what it is."

"Tara said he's older than the others. He's eighteen and joining the navy in the fall."

She narrowed her eyes as she glanced out the window at Aaron and Jill. "If he's older, why does he want to hang out with younger kids?"

"Jill's dynamite."

"You're right." She remembered the passions of her youth and sighed, feeling old all of a sudden. It hadn't been so many years since she'd wandered around in a too-revealing swimsuit at the Farish Country Club, not realizing how titillating she must have been to the guys.

Ben drained his glass and set it beside the sink. "When I get back, will you have time to go over the bills we need to send to Gwynne?"

"Sure. I'm through working for the day."

"I'll check in with you in a while."

She watched Ben as he walked to his Jeep. What was that someone had said—something about youth being wasted on the young? Not that she and Ben were exactly over the hill, which reminded her that she hadn't taken her birth control pill this morning. She ran upstairs, unwilling to risk forgetting it, even though she couldn't figure out how she and Ben would ever manage enough privacy to make love.

Chloe had begun to refer to the sex act in her own mind as lovemaking. So was she falling in love with Ben Derrick? Were his constant presence in her life, and his kindness to her niece, and his helpful attitude wearing her down? Or were her own memories enough to do the trick? Perhaps they should sleep together so she'd have a chance of getting him out of her system. Sometimes, when the guy wasn't any good in bed, that finished it for her. She could say goodbye without regret.

However, she didn't think Ben would turn out to be a dud. And even if he were, he might prove to be a fast learner.

Chapter Eight

Ben didn't return until late in the afternoon, and by that time, Tara had already asked for and received Chloe's blessing to spend the night with Jill. After a reassuring conversation with Jill's mother, who said she was eager to meet Tara, Chloe helped her niece pack an overnight bag.

"I can't wait to see Jill's house," Tara said. "Greg says it's enormous."

"You'll be home when?" Chloe asked. Jill and Aaron were waiting outside to drive Tara to Jill's house, but they'd made no plans for Tara's return home.

"Jill's going to drop me off at the museum in the morning for my shift. Afterward, she's planning to drive to Vero to interview for a job. She thinks she might be able to work at the newspaper."

"Call me before you leave Jill's house, okay?"

"Do I have to?" Tara wailed.

"Absolutely. Help me out here, Tara. I'm not accustomed to keeping tabs on a busy teenager, and I wouldn't feel right if you didn't check in."

"Okay," Tara said, resigned. After kissing Chloe quickly on the cheek, she clattered downstairs and hailed Jill and Aaron from the back porch.

Chloe overheard them talking. "My aunt says I have to call her in the morning. Isn't that psycho?" Tara said.

"Psycho," agreed Aaron, but Jill only laughed.

"She's acting like a parent," Jill said. "Get used to it, Tara."

And then they were off, wheeling out of the parking area and sending up plumes of white dust in their wake.

From her vantage point in Tara's room, which overlooked the back of the house, Chloe saw Ben come around the corner of the house, carrying a sheaf of papers. He'd want to go over those bills now, and she might as well.

"I BOUGHT A WHOLE CHICKEN at the fresh market in Vero," Ben said after they'd sealed the receipts in an envelope to send to Gwynne. "Also an artichoke salad and a bottle of white wine. For you," he added hastily.

"Did we have a dinner date?" she asked archly.

"We do now. Besides, I ran into Zephyr at the vegetable stand, and she was all atwitter over having houseguests on the way when she wanted to mark a nest on the beach that the park ranger reported this morning. She gave me the orange flags and netting and requested that I do it for her. I figure that we'll honor her request, and while we're at it, we'll have a sunset picnic. Are you game?"

"Of course. With Tara gone for the evening, I'm ready anytime." She smiled at him.

"I'll pack a picnic basket—there's one on a closet shelf in the annex—and be back in half an hour. We might want to go for a swim to cool off." The temperature had been in the debilitating nineties all week.

"You're on," Chloe said.

When Ben climbed up the slope from the annex, she was ready. "I'll carry that," she said, appropriating the small cooler. She peeked inside. Water for him, wine for her, plus two glasses.

"I forgot beach towels. Do you have any handy?" he asked.

Chloe dodged inside and returned with towels and a blanket. With Ben carrying Zephyr's nest-marking equipment, they set off down the boardwalk, greeting several beachgoers who were walking back to their cars.

To find the turtle crawl and mark the nest didn't take long. Afterward, Ben spread the blanket nearby, and they sat cross-legged to eat in a leisurely fashion. Chloe was in a rare mood, happy to be communicating with someone on an adult level for a change. This evening the ocean, calm now, was tinged rosy pink by the sun dipping low in the west. The waves rose and fell, whispering on the shore.

With dinner out of the way and its remains packed in the basket, they lay on the blanket to watch the stars come out. Except for the two of them, the beach was deserted. Ben reached for her hand.

"Moonlight swim?" he asked.

"Or a facsimile of," she added, shooting him a mischievous smile.

Her smile faded as she stared at him, his face illuminated by starlight. As a girl, she had dreamed of a moment when the two of them would be alone together, but this reality was so much better than her old fantasies that she couldn't speak. Without a word, he stood, pulling her up with him.

Chloe, mindful of a day years ago when she'd met him alone on the beach and had wanted more than anything to run her fingers through the soft dark hair on his chest, did so now. He rewarded her by his sharp intake of breath, by his bending over and touching his cheek briefly to her forehead. Neither of them spoke as he led her to the edge of the sea.

He kissed her as the waves purled around their feet, kissed her again more lingeringly when they lapped waist high. All her senses aroused, Chloe felt lit with a bright passion, more brilliant and hotter than the brightest star above.

But the heat was not derived from the heavens; it was his body that warmed her. His mouth captured hers, fierce with desire. She closed her eyes, losing herself with him, giving and surrendering to his touch.

Slowly, so slowly, he loosened the top of her bikini, his touch gentle, his fingers sure. The fabric fell away, still fastened around her waist, but now Ben's hands glided over her wet skin, caressing and exploring. He cupped her breasts, stooped to kiss them, and she arched against him until his hands slid lower to hold her derriere. She tugged at his swimsuit and released the hardness within. Before she knew it, he had lifted her and her legs were wrapped around his waist.

Fabric, still too much of it. He feathered his lips to her shoulders and along her throat as she rocked against him in the rhythm of the sea.

"Make love with me now, Chloe," he said, his voice urgent in her ear. "Let's not wait any longer."

Instead of answering, she swam out of his arms and dove deep below the moon path, coming up in a shimmer of silver leading the way toward shore. Her arms dipped and swung, flinging water spangles into the air, and Ben was close behind her. When her feet struck a line of rocks at the edge of the surf, she stumbled and nearly fell. He caught her, skin against skin for a long moment, until she shivered and drew him into a long kiss.

She led him the short distance to the blanket and knelt, gazing up at his dark shape silhouetted against the moonlit ocean.

Quickly, he slipped out of his swim trunks, and even more quickly, he knelt beside her, bringing his face into focus. He tipped one breast with a finger. "Beautiful," he said, his voice low in his throat. "You're lovely, Chloe."

For an answer, she lay back and pulled him on top of her. He supported himself on his elbows as she rippled her fingers over each vertebra in turn and down his smooth flanks. The scent of the sea was mysterious, tantalizing; she opened her mouth to his and tasted salt. She learned all the textures of him: skin, hair, fingernails, teeth, tongue. Gloried in the contrast, savored the magical effect of man and woman together, doing what they were made to do.

He reached for the picnic basket. "This time I'm prepared," he said, withdrawing a foil packet.

"Don't worry. I can't get pregnant," she said, but he readied himself anyway. She helped, guiding him to her center, holding him tightly as he hesitated.

"Chloe," he murmured, "I've wanted this since I saw you on that first night."

"I've wanted you since—" But she didn't finish the sentence. Nothing could be gained by confessing that she'd been wildly in love with him when she was a teenager and he was an Older Man.

"Don't talk," he said. "Just enjoy." He was teasing her, nipping at her neck, not entering her when he could have, and so easily.

"You, too," she said, rising to meet him so that he slid, silky and slick, into her.

"Ah," he said, a word like a prayer. Her lips found his, and together they flowed into each other as if they had been doing this forever. He wrapped his arms around her, held her fast. Chloe had never known the act to be so beautiful, so caring and giving, so joyous. She trembled beneath him, couldn't help it, and felt him, the essence of him, in every cell of her body.

He was spectacular, focused and real, and at the moment of climax, they joined in something more magical than the moonlight, more majestic than the sea. He sank on top of her, spent.

His lips tasted the hollow of her throat as he said her name and perhaps something else.

"Chloe, I—"

The rest of his sentence was lost in the rush of the waves on the shore, but she thought Ben had said, *Chloe, I think I love you.*

"LET'S GO FOR A SWIM this morning," Tara said two days later when she was getting ready to meet her friends on the beach. "I told the others that you might want to come with us."

Chloe, who was concentrating on fitting a bit of fourteen-karat gold wire around a small wedge of azure sea glass, replied without looking up. "I'll need to go shopping to buy a new swimsuit," she said without thinking.

"Why can't you wear your old one?" Tara asked.

Chloe felt her face flush, though she kept her back to Tara so her niece wouldn't notice. Her bikini had washed away with the tide; or at least, she presumed it had. Neither top nor bottom had reappeared after the impassioned lovemaking on the beach, and she'd had to wrap herself in her blouse and a beach towel for the short walk to the house.

"I can't do it today," Chloe said firmly. "Could you please take that box of canning jars and put it on the back porch for Zephyr? I told her I'd leave them there so she won't disturb me while I'm working. Which I wish you'd consider once in a while," she added pointedly.

"I was only asking you if you'd like to swim with us," Tara said, adopting a mock-aggrieved tone.

"I have to finish these things for the Sanluca gift shop," she said, shifting in her seat. Her nipples were sore and her thighs still ached from making love with Ben, but she could hardly wait to do it again.

"Isn't it great that I'm not around all the time, bothering you and pestering you and things?"

"I like having you here," Chloe said truthfully, though she certainly contemplated the downside of Tara's presence a lot these days.

"That's what Ben said. He told me so yesterday after I hammered him with a whole bunch of questions about searching for buried treasure. I found a couple of quarters on the beach with the metal detector. And I really love the scuba class."

"Hobbies are good," Chloe replied absently. The wire bent around the sea glass, but the cage it made was too elaborate to show off the glass's qualities. Patiently, she unwound the wire and started over.

"I don't mean for treasure hunting to be a hobby, or scuba, either. Florida State University has an oceanography program. Isn't that exciting? Ben says I could become a marine archaeologist and work in his field."

Good for Ben, Chloe thought, then said casually, "Why don't you get some brochures. Find out the requirements for that major."

"Jill has a Florida State course catalog. I'll check next time I'm at her house. Oh, by the way, she didn't get that job at the newspaper."

"Mmm," Chloe said.

"Are you going to open the Frangipani Inn as a bed-and-breakfast again, Chloe? Ben said you might."

"I've been considering. Right now it's too much work to contemplate, not to mention that the bedrooms provide a pleasant habitat for a whole slew of spiders, as well as the chameleon that took up residence under the dressing table in Driftwood after Butch kept chasing it." Driftwood was the bedroom across the hall from her room, tastefully decorated in shades of gray.

"Hire Jill and me to clean for you. We could get the place shaped up by fall, when tourists start fleeing those cold northern winters."

"Why would you want to clean house?" Tara's parents sent her a weekly allowance.

"I'd like to save money so I can come back next summer and volunteer at the treasure museum full-time. That way I'd learn a lot and be ready for Florida State the following fall."

"You're planning on going back to Farish High this year, then?" Chloe asked, trying not to reveal her trepidation.

Tara appeared puzzled. "Well, sure. If I'm going to Florida State, I'll have to graduate."

"Good idea," Chloe said. She certainly wasn't breaking into a happy dance yet, since Tara had been known to change her mind on a whim.

"Ben gave me lemons that he bought at the produce stand," Tara said. "I might as well make lemonade for the group." She scampered off, leaving Chloe shaking her head in wonderment. What a difference a few weeks made, she marveled. How far Tara had come in the short time she'd lived at the inn!

BEN WAS CRAZY about this woman who had so amazingly appeared in his life, and the thing was, he wasn't sure how to keep her there. She talked about staying at the Frangipani Inn through the fall and winter, and she'd mentioned renting rooms the way Tayloe and Gwynne had done. But every time he tried to pin her down, she deliberately shifted the conversation. Or maybe it just seemed that way. The two of them always had so much to talk about. Her business, his treasure hunting, Tara.

Sometimes he considered what it would be like being married to Chloe. To wake up in the morning and gaze into those lovely lavender-blue eyes. To walk up behind her when she was standing at the kitchen sink and reach around her to caress one of those lush breasts. Thinking about it wasn't enough. He wanted to broach the subject to Chloe, though he sensed that she wasn't ready, and neither was he. It rankled that his life and career were still on hold and that he couldn't plan a future. So it was that he decided to confront Andy McGehee.

The city marina in Sanluca baked in the hot noon sunshine, but Ben didn't allow himself to be distracted by the billowing sails of the boats on the water or the boisterous shouts of boys casting nets in the nearby shallows. As he passed several of the Sea Search boats, he was transported back to those heady days of the hunt. The clatter of the compressors that drove the airlift as it washed sand away from the crumbling hull of a wreck, the excitement as divers dug to uncover artifacts hidden for three hundred years. He missed it and longed to be part of it again.

As Ben approached, Andy was supervising the loading of supplies onto one of his dive boats, *Vision Quest*. He smiled in welcome when he saw Ben.

"Good to see you, Ben," Andy said, shaking his hand. "How's it going?"

"Pretty good," Ben replied.

"Hey," Andy hollered when a man walked past with two cardboard boxes, "watch it! That's my own private stock of Kit Kat bars!" Andy loved Kit Kat bars and claimed he could live on them for days at a time.

Ben hid a smile, but Andy noticed. "What are you laughing at?" he demanded.

The two of them had often engaged in good-natured ribbing, and Ben was encouraged that Andy seemed inclined to relate to him in the same old way.

"Nothing," Ben said hastily. "Nothing at all. Say, Andy, do you have a minute? We could walk up to the Sand Bar, have lunch."

"Sure," Andy said, and he called out a few instructions to his crew before they set off up the dock.

At the Sand Bar, Andy slid into one side of a booth, Ben into the other. Liss was working behind the bar, for which Ben was thankful, considering that she kept aiming frosty glances in his direction.

After they placed their orders with a new waitress, one Ben had never seen before, Andy leaned across the table. "You've been on my mind, Ben," he said slowly. "Are things really going okay?"

Ben nodded. "Yeah, on the personal side." He was thinking of Chloe, her body glistening with sea water as he'd made love to her on the beach.

"I heard you're staying at the Frangipani Inn, but wasn't it closed?"

Ben explained about Tayloe and Gwynne, and, hesitantly, about Chloe moving from Texas.

The waitress brought their sandwiches and left.

Ben cleared his throat. "About that job," he said. "I'm sober, I'm stable and I want to dive again."

Andy chewed and swallowed. He had gone a bit grayer since Ben had worked for him, and he was starting to put on weight. All those Kit Kat bars probably didn't help.

"What're the chances, Andy?" Ben asked. "Are you going to hire me?"

Andy regarded him for a long moment. "I'd like to, believe me, but you nearly caused the death of one of my men. I feel responsible for each and every diver who goes down on one of my missions. I haven't gotten over it, Ben. Maybe I never will."

"Even if I give you my word that I won't drink again, ever? Even if I promise that I've changed?"

Andy stared out the window at the royal poinciana tree, where a cardinal landed in a flash of red feathers. "It hasn't been that long, Ben, since you got sober."

"I learned my lesson," Ben said heavily.

"I believe you. Look, you'd been through a horrible experience. What happened to Ashley was horrible, more than any parent should have to bear."

Ben felt a lump in his throat at the mention of his daughter's name. "Losing Ashley is the hardest thing I've ever had to face," he said, giving every single word due emphasis. "I didn't care what happened to me, and so I drank. I do care what happens to others, and when Rick nearly died, it brought me up short. I deserve a second chance, Andy, for old times' sake."

Andy sighed and gazed out the window again. "I'm not going to hire you, Ben. As far as I'm concerned, you need to prove that you can stay sober."

Ben pushed back in the booth, feeling numb. "For how long?" he asked.

"Next season, we'll talk again." Andy polished off his sandwich, wiped his hands on the paper napkin. "That doesn't mean you can't come around and chat once in a while. I miss you, Ben, but I can't endanger my crew. You understand."

"I guess I do," Ben said dully, staring down at his uneaten lunch.

"Well, I'd better get back to the dock. See you around, Ben."

"Sure," Ben said, and he stood to shake hands with Andy before his former boss left.

"Anything wrong?" asked the waitress when she saw his untouched lunch.

"Not with lunch," Ben said. *Only everything else,* he added to himself.

WHEN BEN GOT HOME after riding around aimlessly in his Jeep for a couple of hours, Chloe was vigorously sweeping the back porch. Butch lounged in the shadows, indolently flipping the tip of his tail now and then as he dreamed.

"Hi," Chloe said, stashing the broom near the kitchen door. She shaded her eyes against the slanting afternoon sun.

"Hi," he said dispiritedly. She was beautiful in her cutoff jeans and a little halter top that covered the essentials but left a lot of skin exposed. Her hair was piled on top of her head in a knot from which wayward wisps escaped, and she wore no makeup. He liked the way she was so unpretentious, how she was always so aboveboard about her thought processes and emotions.

"Anything wrong?" she asked.

"The usual," he said as he walked up and lifted one foot to the bottom step. "I talked with Andy McGehee today, asked him about getting my old job back."

"What did he say?"

"He didn't give me any hope for this year."

He flinched when her face fell. "So, I guess I'll clean the cabinets in the annex," Ben added.

"Sure. Good plan. Have you eaten lunch?" Chloe asked.

"I'm not hungry," he shot back, regretting his surly tone immediately. "I mean, maybe later." He sensed immediately that he'd hurt her feelings.

"All right," she said. She picked up the broom and recommenced sweeping.

Feeling even more depressed, Ben continued around the house to the annex. He felt like a failure for not getting his old job back and like a cad for speaking to Chloe so sharply. He flung himself on the couch. He'd worked so hard to fight his way back from where he'd been, but in the end, he couldn't do anything right. He'd lost the friendship of his ex-wife, Emily, and he didn't have his daughter anymore. Ashley had been the light of his life, the joy of his existence. When she'd died, his life was over.

Yet out of the depths of his misery had risen the determination not to give up. Ever. And so he'd kept on keeping on, even though things weren't, at present, going his way.

Well, maybe they were, sort of. He cared about Chloe and was eager to make amends to her for this afternoon's sharp words. First, he'd get cleaned up, maybe offer to treat Chloe and Tara to dinner at Paquita Juanita's.

After he showered, he decided to take a short nap. Sleep would revive him, perhaps dispel the tension he felt over the morning's conversation with Andy.

He switched on the ceiling fan and let the cool breeze wash over him, and he closed his eyes. Sleep, the healer. Sleep, where he didn't chastise himself for past mistakes.

Sleep. It was better than booze any day.

CHLOE HAD CHORES to do that afternoon. She called Gwynne's godmother, verified that Patrice had sold two major pieces of jewelry at ridiculous prices, and promised to send more. She talked with Gwynne, who offered to pay half the cost of hiring cleaners to get Frangipani Inn in shape for boarders in the fall. She finished work on a particularly lovely sea-glass piece, which included a garnet. And through it all, she wondered about Ben.

When she finished her work, she went to the refrigerator and found the rest of the pizza that Tara had brought home from the mall's food court yesterday. Since it had been quiet in the annex, she decided to check on Ben's progress in cleaning the cabinets and provide him a snack at the same time. He had seemed so down after his talk with Andy.

Carrying the plate of pizza, she walked around to the sliding glass door, where she could look through the screen.

"Ben?" she called. "May I come in?"

No answer, and it was awfully quiet. "Ben?"

What if something had happened to him? He could have fallen, hit his head on the bathroom tile. He could have— Oh, no. He wouldn't have taken a drink; she was sure of it.

She slid the screen open and stepped inside. Nothing was amiss. The steady whoosh of the ceiling fan emitted from the bedroom, and the door was half-closed. She called Ben's name again, but he still didn't answer, so she moved slightly to her right, where she'd be able to see through the bedroom door.

Ben was lying on the bed, stretched out on his back and naked. His skin was dark with tan, the hair on his arms bleached golden by the sun. She drew a sharp breath at the sight of his taut, muscled stomach and what lay below.

She moved softly across the room, went into the bedroom. She put the plate with the pizza on the dresser and let her clothes fall to the floor.

The radio beside the bed played soulful saxophone music. She dipped the forefinger of one hand in a glass of water on the night-stand and drew a wet line around his navel.

No reaction. She bent over and touched her tongue to one of his nipples, and his eyes opened slowly.

"Chloe," he said.

"It's so hot. I want to cool you off," she said, half smiling at the perplexed but delighted expression on his face. She picked up the glass of water and spilled some onto his stomach, then used her palm and a lazy movement to run it across his chest, his abdomen.

"I'm not sure this is the right way to do it," he said. He was exhibiting signs of arousal. Well, one major sign, at least, as her fingers teased and pressed, found erogenous zones, explored. He stroked her back, her breasts, took them in his mouth one by one as she bent over him.

"Long, sweet afternoon," he murmured. "You're so special, Chloe. I love doing this with you."

The statement, though welcome, was only a few words removed from the one thing she would have liked to hear. *I love you.* Would that be difficult for him to say when the time came? Or would that time never come? Guys didn't tell her they loved her. They took, she gave. At the moment, however, that seemed irrelevant. She was lost in the tenderness, the pleasure of this experience.

"When will Tara be home?" he asked before he rolled her over on her side.

"Later," she said. She didn't want her niece to know what was going on with Ben. When two adults consensually engaged in making love, it wasn't anyone else's business. Or so Chloe had believed before she had to worry about setting a good example.

Ben's lips traversed the back of her neck, his hands sweet torture on her breasts. He entered her, and she gasped. The sunlight filtering through the curtains seemed suddenly too bright, blindingly white. She rode the waves of sensation, giving herself up to them.

Afterward, he held her tight. She kept her eyes closed, not wanting to see mundane objects such as the radio, the chipped dresser across the room, the plate of pizza slices, which were probably soggy now.

He kissed her ear—a loud smack that brought her back to reality.

"What shall we do now?" he said before getting up and going into the bathroom.

"Sleep?" she said, too drowsy to move, her limbs slowed by the heat and exertion.

He must have decided it was a good idea, because he came back in a few minutes. They drowsed, curled together spoon-style, until a car door slammed outside.

Chapter Nine

Chloe was instantly awake. "Who's that?"

Ben was out of bed immediately, pulling aside the curtain for a sliver's view of the driveway.

"Tara," he said. "She's back."

Chloe scrambled to grab her panties and stepped into them, nearly falling in the process. Ben was laughing, and so was she.

"Hey, do you two want to go out to dinner?" he called as she flew out of the bedroom and down the corridor to the kitchen.

She only skewered him with a frantic look before she opened the door. Good grief, wasn't it bad enough that Tara had almost caught them in the act? Did he have to suggest that the three of them sit down in a restaurant while she and Ben were still worn out from too much sex?

If there was such a thing. With Ben, too much was an impossibility. Chloe didn't think she'd ever get enough of this man, even if they spent a lifetime together.

A few hours later, Ben drove them to the Mexican restaurant. Tara wore a new outfit, and Chloe, freshly showered and with her hair caught up in a barrette, had donned her best white linen slacks and a print sleeveless jersey in colors of the rainbow. Ben, next to Chloe in the restaurant, reached over and caressed her thigh when Tara wasn't looking.

Tara kept them laughing throughout the meal with descriptions of various characters who'd come into the museum, including some who had been part of the Sea Search crew when Ben had worked the wrecks offshore.

"And this guy, his name is Lundy something or other, he, like, strolls in every day to marvel over the things on display that he says he found on the *Spiritu* wreck. Did you ever dive on that one, Ben?"

"Lundy and I worked together, but I expect he's retired now."

"Yeah, but he has stories. Chloe, maybe you could make your famous fajitas some night and we could invite Lundy over to tell the kids these things. It would be something nice I could do for Jill, Greg and Aaron, and they have friends they could bring—Suzette, Marta and Julie. I'd like to meet their whole crowd for when I come back next year."

"I don't mind having people over, but we have to clean house first," Chloe said. "At least the parlor and porch."

"I'll help."

"Gwynne and I are going to split the cost of hiring someone."

"Hire me and Jill. Please?" Tara leaned forward expectantly.

"Well, I—"

"Why not?" Ben asked. "You said you appreciated the fact that Jill was saving her money to buy a car, and I bet she's a hard worker."

"When Aaron's not around," Tara agreed. "If he's there, they're usually stuck in a lip-lock."

"Tara!" Chloe said, laughing.

"I'm going to the ladies' room," Tara said. "Think it over, Chloe. Jill and I could work three afternoons a week, if you'd like."

As Tara disappeared into the group of people waiting to be seated, Ben leaned over and whispered in Chloe's ear. "I could work every afternoon, too," he said. "Pleasing you."

"You've been doing an admirable job," she admitted.

"So have you."

"Let's cool it until later," she murmured as a party of two advanced to the table next to theirs.

"Will there be a later?" he asked with interest.

"After Tara's asleep, I'll sneak downstairs. Meet me on the porch."

"This time, I'll—"

"You'll keep quiet about it," she said as Tara began to wend her way between the tables.

"But I'll go on savoring my anticipation," Ben retorted with a twinkle in his eyes.

"Hey, Ben," Tara said as she sat down. "You promised a ride on the beach in your Jeep. How about tonight?"

Inwardly, Chloe groaned. The sooner Tara went to sleep, the better. A ride on the beach would only delay getting together with Ben.

With an understanding wink at Chloe, he said, "Tonight would be good. Maybe we'll even catch one of those mama turtles laying her eggs."

This was something that Tara had heard about but hadn't yet seen. "Wow," she said, wide-eyed. "I hope so."

Chloe kept her eyes downcast. She was pleased that Tara and Ben got along so famously. It was almost as if Tara filled some sort of need in Ben. But what? She still had much to learn about him, even now.

THE MOON WAS FULL, the beach brightly illuminated, when Ben jumped out of the Jeep and removed the chain barring the entrance to the state park.

"I'm glad that you've got special permission to ride on the trails through the dunes," Tara said.

"The ranger said not to disturb the wildlife. She lets Zephyr in, too," Ben said. He steered along a rutted path littered with dried palmetto fronds, which increased traction and crunched noisily beneath the Jeep's wheels. Trees slid by, shadowy and dark. Encroaching vines snagged Chloe's hair, and she loosened it from her barrette.

Ben had rolled up the canvas on the sides of the Jeep, so that the air rushed past their faces as he picked up speed when they drove into the open. Tara shrieked with delight as dune grass whipped past, slapping against the Jeep's sides. "Let's get out," Ben said, slamming to a stop. And then the three of them held hands and ran down the winding path to the water. When they reached the beach, Tara danced in front of them, the full sleeves of her blouse blowing in the wind. Chloe and Ben followed at a more sedate pace. He took her hand for a moment, squeezing it before letting it go.

"Look!" Tara shouted. "It must be a turtle!" Her feet kicked up sand as she rushed to see.

"Of course it's a turtle," Zephyr said as she materialized beside them, huffing and puffing with exertion.

"Zephyr!" exclaimed Chloe. "How long have you been following us?"

"Only for a ways," she said. "Now, how about getting that child to be quiet so she doesn't scare the darling thing."

The "darling thing" weighed something like three hundred pounds, had heaved herself out of the surf and was laboring up the incline toward the dunes. The loggerhead carried with her the scent of the sea; her shell was layered with barnacles and flossy strands of bright green moss. She continued up the beach until she reached an area above the seaweed heaped at the high-tide line, and there she started to scoop away the sand with her back flippers.

Tara watched, enthralled, as the turtle began, with much effort, dropping eggs the size and color of ping-pong balls into the nest she had made.

"Why is she crying? Does it hurt?" Tara asked in alarm.

"When she dug her nest, sand flew all around. Tears wash the sand out of turtles' eyes," Zephyr replied.

After an hour or so, when the turtle had finished depositing her eggs, she covered the nest with sand and headed back to the ocean, leaving the characteristic U-shaped track on the beach. Once the turtle disappeared into the froth of surf, Zephyr marked the nest. "I've got some clutches that are almost ready for the babies to hatch," she said to Tara. "Want me to tell you when their time comes? I can always use help herding them toward the ocean so they don't wind up in the dunes and get eaten by predators."

"I feel so sorry for little turtles," Tara said thoughtfully. "Their parents aren't there to guide them."

"That's true," Zephyr said. "Those of us who have parents should be thankful."

Tara was uncharacteristically quiet as they left Zephyr to prowl the beach alone. Ben slid his arms around Tara and Chloe, one on each side. "How about ice cream before bedtime?" he asked on the way back to the Jeep.

"Especially if it's mint chocolate chip," Tara said, breaking her silence.

"Which you bought when you went to the store for us the other day," Chloe reminded her.

"Aren't you glad I can drive, Chloe? Am I a big help?"

"Yes, sweetie, you are," Chloe said, meaning it.

Tara hugged her impulsively. "I want to be," she said. "But I miss my parents and my sisters. I'm just realizing that."

"That's a valuable lesson, isn't it?" Chloe said as they clambered into the Jeep.

"Hmm, I suppose it is. I'm definitely going back to Farish in the fall. I can't wait to tell my classmates about my wonderful summer."

Chloe and Ben, looking over his shoulder at her in the backseat, exchanged triumphant glances at this declaration. When they reached the inn, Tara climbed down from the Jeep first. "I'll go dish out the ice cream. Don't be long, you two."

"Tara's done a lot of maturing, hasn't she?" Ben said as Chloe helped him roll down the Jeep's side curtains.

"I'd say so, thank goodness. Let's walk for a little while, okay?" She finished fastening the curtains and met him on the other side of the vehicle.

"It's plain that Tara's having a good time, but what about *your* summer?" Ben teased, his hand lifting to curve around the back of Chloe's neck as they stepped onto the boardwalk.

"It didn't get special until recently, but I'd say that as summers go, this one is fantastic so far." She walked a short way, leaned on the railing and gazed up at Ben.

"Hey, Chloe and Ben, I've got the ice cream ready," Tara called from the inn.

Ben sneaked a quick kiss. "We'll be there in a minute," Chloe called back.

"It will be all melted by the time you get here," Tara warned. They heard the back door slam.

Ben turned Chloe around and pulled her to him.

"I'm mad about you, Chloe Timberlake," he murmured as her ear came within nibbling distance. "Totally."

"Maybe it's just the sex," she said, though she was sure she'd never felt happier in her life.

"And maybe not," he told her.

Chloe wasn't ready to confront either her emotions or his. She cast her arms around his neck, reveling in the crush of his rough beard against her cheek. His lips were tender, his arms tight around her. She didn't want to leave him now, but Tara was calling again.

No, Chloe thought, it wasn't only sex. It was companionship and being able to depend on each other. It was exchanging confidences and becoming best friends.

Although the sex was pretty good, too.

AT THE INN after his short walk with Chloe, Ben stood in the foyer, taking in the big parlor, where Tara sat at the piano idly fingering the keys. Chloe was curled up on the sofa, eating ice cream. Is this what it was like to be part of a family? Ben wondered. To be comfortable in the presence of other people who were comfortable with you?

In his family of origin, his mother had spent a lot of time in her room, weeping. His father arrived home roaring drunk most nights and took out his rage on his cowering children. As soon as he was of age, Ben had left that cramped concrete-block house in Yahola and struck out on his own. When Ben had been gone for six months, his father had been knifed by another man in a bar. Afterward, his mother had moved in with her aunt in Oklahoma and eventually died. His two sisters lived in California, and his brother was in the air force and stationed in Korea. They were no longer close.

For a while he and Ashley had formed a circle of two. They'd made their own jokes, created a short-cut language and enjoyed each other's company. Now that Ashley was gone, Ben was on his own. He'd made a mess of his life in the past, but here he was with Chloe and Tara, and what he felt was a solid affection for both of them. And gratitude for allowing him to be part of their family group.

"Play 'Polynesian Nocturne,'" Chloe suggested to Tara.

"The piano is out of tune," Tara pointed out.

"If you'll practice, I'll have it tuned soon," Chloe said.

"My dad likes this one, too," Tara said. The notes began to ripple from her fingers in cascading crescendos, and Chloe smiled across the room at Ben. He sat down beside her and finished his ice cream. Chloe had already eaten hers and was keeping time to the music by tapping her foot.

Tara wound up with a flourish before turning to Chloe. "Now can I use your computer to get online, Chloe? I promised Amy that I'd send her some pictures that Greg took of all of us on the beach." Amy was Tara's best friend in Farish.

"Go ahead," Chloe said, yawning. "I'm sleepy. I'm going to crash soon."

Tara disappeared into Chloe's workroom, where they heard her booting up the laptop.

Ben reached for Chloe's hand. She pulled it away.

"Stop, I'm all sticky from the ice cream."

He retained his hold on her and playfully licked the ice cream from her fingers, one by one. She tried to contain her laughter but failed, and he chuckled along with her.

"What's going on in there, you two?" Tara called.

"Nothing," Chloe said, and she stood and picked up the three bowls that had held the ice cream. "We'll be in the kitchen, Tara," she answered.

Ben followed Chloe and helped her stack the bowls and spoons in the dishwasher.

"The ride was fun tonight," Chloe said. He slid out a chair for her at the table.

"Want to sit and talk awhile?"

She sat and so did he. Even in the harsh light from the overhead fluorescents, Chloe was beautiful. Her skin was lightly tanned, and though she'd worn her hair caught up in a barrette earlier, it now hung loose around her face. She kept combing it back with the fingers of one hand, a graceful movement more charming than she seemed to realize.

"I like this," he said in a rush of happiness, his gesture encompassing the kitchen, the house beyond, the click of the keyboard as Tara used the computer.

"The inn? Oh, so do—"

"No," he said. "I meant being here with you and Tara."

"Oh," she said, seeming perplexed.

He poured out the story of his difficult childhood and all that it had entailed. "When I was a kid, I believed that every father came home and yelled at his kids and that every mother hid in her room, paralyzed with fear," he said. "Not something like this—people together, enjoying one another."

Chloe listened solemnly, studying his face as he talked. "I've taken my upbringing for granted," she said. "It was normal—well, as much as anyone's. A mother and father who loved each other, my sister, my grandparents. A small town where everyone knew everyone else."

"You're lucky," he told her.

"I wanted out of Farish," she said. She lowered her voice. "The way Tara does now."

"It's good to spread our wings, to find out if what we grew up to believe was normal really is."

"Yes, and sometimes we fall flat on our faces," Chloe said wryly. "Like when I almost flunked out of freshman year at the University of Texas because I was bored with the courses. My parents expected me to be a teacher, and I was an artist at heart." She shrugged. "My parents and I both learned a valuable lesson. I switched my major, and that's when I came into my own."

"Good for you. You had the courage to try something different from what they expected."

"It helped that Mom and Dad were supportive once I made my decision."

"Where are your parents now, Chloe?"

"They both died young. My father had a heart attack during my last year in college, and my mother soon after."

Tara stuck her head in the door. "I'm going to bed, Chloe."

"I'd better head back to the annex," Ben said as he pushed his chair away from the table. He felt somehow relieved that he'd revealed part of his history tonight, though there was more to tell. That could wait. Talking about the bad time was anything but easy for him. He never discussed it with anyone, ever.

"I'll be right up," Chloe said.

Tara went upstairs, and Ben squeezed Chloe's hand. "I'll leave the door unlocked," he whispered.

He hurried to his place and took off his clothes. The house's old plumbing suffered its usual wheezes and whomps as Chloe and Tara prepared for bed upstairs. He wondered how long it would takc Tara to fall asleep. He wondered when Chloe would be able to sneak into his bed. He contemplated, for a moment, what it would be like to go public with their relationship.

As soon as he lay down on his bed, he dozed. It was over an hour later when he heard the creak of floorboards in the kitchen, then the annex door opening. Soon afterward, Chloe, smelling of soap and talc, slipped into bed beside him.

"I didn't even need a flashlight," she whispered. "I found the way by heart."

"By heart," he mused as he buried his face in her hair. "What a nice way to put it."

She stilled, became quiet. Perhaps he had gone too far if she wasn't really emotionally involved.

"Make love to me," she said urgently as his hands found the places he so longed to touch. He kissed her face, her shoulders, her breasts. As he entered her, she wrapped her arms around him as if she couldn't get close enough. He felt enveloped by her, lost in her. With their bodies pressed so tightly together, it was like being two people in one skin.

Chloe took the act of making love and shaped it into something beautiful, just as she did with her jewelry. The act of sex was instinct, and sometimes no more than that. Nothing special, nothing new. Yet with this woman he'd experienced an expansion of all his senses and the hope that this could be more than a shallow affair.

They fell asleep after midnight, and as the first rays of dawn crept up over the dunes, Chloe left him. Her fragrance lingered on his pillow, and he went back to sleep hugging it to his chest.

Later, when he woke, he heard Chloe and Tara laughing on the front porch. He fixed himself a bowl of cereal, planning his day's work. First he'd take the metal detector down the beach and do some treasure hunting close to where the mother turtle had laid her eggs last night. Then he'd start painting the porch railings. Perhaps he'd invite Tara and Chloe to join him at his place for hamburgers for dinner.

He was walking the beach with the metal detector when he realized that he hadn't thought about Ashley all day. Guilt assailed him; how could he go for hours at a time without thinking of his daughter? He pictured her, those blue eyes with such long lashes, her round face, the mouth that almost always smiled. She'd had blond hair. That hair flowing almost to her waist in loose curls was the feature that had set her apart from every other thirteen-year-old he knew.

By the time he got home an hour or so later, he wasn't thinking about Ashley anymore. He showered, dressed, then pulled the shoe box out from under his bed, intending to count the coins and various other items he'd gleaned on past metal-detecting expeditions. An Indian head nickel, a corroded belt buckle that might be sterling silver, and six gold coins. He removed the nickel and buckle from the box for cleaning, then picked up the coin he'd discovered on his first day here.

The cob had uneven edges, but it was beautiful with its stamped design on each side. Women often mounted cobs in bezel frames to wear on chains around their necks, or attached them to charm bracelets. He could combine this coin and the chain he'd found to make a gift for Chloe.

He turned the coin this way and that in the streamer of light admitted by the bedroom window. Yes, that was what he would do with it. He'd give it to Chloe, who was a treasure in and of herself. Always giving to others, never expecting anything in return. It was about time that someone recognized her worth, and this would be the perfect way to let her know that he held her in high esteem.

TARA AND JILL REPORTED for work at the end of the week by marching into Chloe's workshop, addressing her with smart salutes and asking for their orders.

Chloe couldn't help but laugh. Tara wore a kerchief over her hair, and Jill was dressed in a tattered pair of shorts and an old T-shirt—a marked difference from her boutique beach ensembles and expensive sandals.

"The way to clean a room," Chloe directed as she accompanied the girls into the parlor, "is to start high up. In other words, wipe the cobwebs from the ceilings first, move on to cleaning the chandeliers—and the one in the dining room is an antique Waterford, so handle it carefully. Then woodwork, walls, upholstery, floor, rugs."

"Which room should we start in?" asked Jill.

"Parlor, then library, then the dining room and porch. We'll talk about the upstairs after you've finished those."

"Yes, ma'am," they shouted in unison. Chloe, grateful in the extreme for their help, retreated to her workshop and did her best to ignore the vacuum cleaner roar, the grating of furniture on the floor as the girls moved it and the silences that often erupted into girlish laughter.

The thing that gave her the most concern was that Aaron, Jill's boyfriend, stopped by and stayed for over an hour. When Jill playfully asked him if he'd like to help clean the prismed sconces in the parlor, he refused and sat on the hall settee with his arms folded over his chest, scowling at the girls. Chloe, in her workshop, was party to the whole conversation, and Aaron was visible to her when she looked up from her work. He saw her watching him and favored her with a sardonic grin.

Tara and Jill finished their work on the chandelier, and Chloe wasn't happy when they offered him lunch. The three of them gathered around the back-porch table, scarfing down quantities of tomato sandwiches. From what Chloe could figure out as she heated up leftover macaroni and cheese for herself, most of the conversation was between Tara and Jill, with an occasional uninterested grunt from Aaron.

Later, Tara came inside to tell Chloe that they were adjourning to the beach to go surfing. "Aaron borrowed a board from somebody. He wants to try it out."

"You're surfing, too?"

Tara shook her head. "Jill and I are going to hunt for shells that I can send my sisters. Greg's coming over later." She hurried away, and Chloe soon heard her engaging in banter with her friends while they filled an insulated jug to take to the beach with them.

Chloe got up and went into the kitchen to tell Tara what time to be back for dinner. "I was thinking," she said to the kids. "How about if we have that party Tara's been talking about? I'll make fajitas."

"Her *famous* fajitas," Tara said with obvious glee.

"It sounds wonderful," Jill said.

Aaron merely lifted his brows as if to say, *Who cares?*

"My mom will make brownies if I ask her. She likes to bake," Jill said.

"Ooh, that would be great." Tara beamed.

"How about next Saturday night?"

"Sure," chorused Tara and Jill.

At that moment, Ben arrived at the back door. "What's next Saturday night?"

"A party. You're invited," Tara told him.

The door slammed after them as they left, and Ben rubbed the back of his neck. "What was that all about?"

"Tara's going to ask a bunch of kids over, and I'm hoping you'll help me keep an eye on things."

"No problem. Say, do you have a minute?"

She leaned over and kissed his cheek. "More than."

He curved his hands around her waist. "You smell wonderful."

"Same as I did yesterday."

"You smelled wonderful then, too."

She let him hug her, marveling as she always did how well they fit together. They quickly broke apart, mostly because Chloe didn't trust Tara not to run back into the house to get something she'd forgotten.

"How long will we have to sneak around like this?" Ben asked mildly. His brown eyes regarded her with equanimity.

"As long as we wish to keep our relationship a secret." She busied herself wiping spatters from the counter.

"Is that such a good idea?"

"Depends," Chloe said, avoiding his gaze.

"We're a couple," he told her. "Maybe we should act like one."

"By advertising that we sleep together?" Chloe's eyebrows rose straight up into her hairline.

He walked around the table and leaned on the counter beside her, arms and ankles crossed. "No, not exactly. Tara could know that we like each other, couldn't she?"

"She already does."

"I mean, that we're romantically involved. There's nothing wrong with a healthy, caring relationship."

"Tara's had a good example in her parents. Naomi and Ray are in love after all this time, and they're happy. I don't need to muddy the waters for her. It might be confusing to see us—uh, gazing into each other's eyes. Or something."

"It might be more confusing if she figures out that we're crazy about each other but never touch. Or kiss," he added.

"Ben, I—"

"Uh-oh," he said. "Here it comes."

She smiled. "It's not as if we—as if—oh, I'm not sure how to say this."

"Just spit it out," he suggested helpfully.

"We've only been 'romantically involved' for a short time. If Tara finds out we, um, sleep together, she may jump to conclusions."

"So?"

"I don't want her getting the idea that this is more than it is," she said, rinsing the sponge under the faucet.

"Have you ever considered that this might be more than a fling?"

"I'm not sure what you mean."

"I care about you a great deal, Chloe. I'm proud for the world to know that I'm with such a wonderful, charming, although admittedly wacky, woman." He noted the way her face lit up. "Now it's your turn," he said. "Have at it." He uncrossed his legs and arms, inviting her to close the distance between them.

She moved forward one large step and placed her hands on his chest, looking up at him. "You honor me," she said softly. "I haven't figured out what I feel yet, other than excited and eager and pleasured intensely."

"That's enough," he said agreeably. "That's more than I hoped for."

She stood on tiptoe to kiss the tip of his nose. "I don't trust this, Ben," she said. "It seems too easy, too happy, too...wonderful?"

"It'll do," Ben said before cupping her head between his palms and tilting her face up for his kiss. It was openmouthed and hungry, eager and demanding. When they finally surfaced for air, he grinned. "I'll let you call the shots. I don't like hiding my feelings for you, that's all."

"We'll take it easy," she said, her knees weak from his kisses. "I'll handle Tara, okay? She's on the brink of steering her life in a new direction, partly thanks to you. I don't want to upset her so that she disappears again to parts unknown, changes her mind about going back to school or falls back into bad habits."

Ben nodded soberly. "I understand. Well, now that this is settled, what do you say we make good use of the kids being down on the beach and retire to somewhere private? I could use a bit of afternoon delight."

"So could I," she said, as eager as he was.

"We'd better hurry," he urged, reaching for her buttons. She laughed, sidestepping him neatly, but he was already unzipping his pants. She broke away, ran upstairs and threw herself across her bed, the white wicker bed of her girlhood, as he kicked the door closed behind him. Through her window, they could keep an eye on the teenagers down by the surf, would notice right away if one of them started toward the house. The forbidden aspect of making love with those four people close by made

Chloe desire Ben even more, and her heart was beating fast as she reached up to pull him down beside her.

He fumbled with her shirt, pushed it up to kiss the round, firm buds of her nipples. She traced his back, the whole length of his spine, while he slid her shorts aside and entered her. Their mouths found each other, mingled lips, teeth, tongue. Stayed together as long as it lasted and then beyond.

This time they didn't linger. They didn't need to make love for long hours; this time, their purpose was to consummate a new understanding of their relationship. What they had together was more than mere like. And less than love. But more than either of them had expected, all the same.

Chapter Ten

On the night of Tara's party, Chloe stayed busy grilling the meat for the fajitas, chopping vegetables and warming tortillas. Ben iced down cold drinks in the tub of the washing machine, delivered a preventive lecture to Aaron and Greg about underage drinking and made a last-minute run to the store for more paper plates, since Chloe didn't want to use Gwynne's good dishes.

Tara enjoyed being the center of attention as she described with gusto how she'd ridden all the way from Texas on a bus by herself, and later when she taught dance steps to Jill and a couple of goggle-eyed boys. After everyone ate, Lundy, the man Tara had met at the treasure museum, stopped by and told a few of his treasure-hunting yarns, which were embellished with sound effects and grand gestures. His stories were well received by the kids, but he begged off early, saying he had to pick up his grandchild.

Ben saw Lundy to the door. Afterward, he walked up behind Chloe while she was at the stove and kissed the back of her neck, dodging as she threatened to clobber him with the frying pan.

"We need more ice," she said. "Do you have any in your apartment?"

"A whole bag of it, set aside in my freezer for such an emergency," he told her.

"Ben," Tara called from the parlor. "Did you move Greg's guitar somewhere? He said he left it by the front door."

"It's in the library, where it's out of the way. I'll get it," he said.

Chloe started for the annex, glad that she wasn't keeping tabs on this lively group of kids all by herself.

In Ben's apartment, all the lights were on, and as she entered the room, Chloe spotted a couple sitting on the plastic chairs on the patio. The glass doors were open, their faces outlined in profile against the line of the dunes.

"I don't want to do that," Jill said forcefully.

"Do it for me," Aaron pleaded.

"I can't."

"Jill, if you love me, you'll—"

Chloe did a one-eighty, thinking to get out of there as fast as she could before she heard more. She stumbled over a doorstop, and two heads whipped around so that she could see their faces clearly in the light from the room. "Just getting ice out of the freezer," she caroled, embarrassed.

"Can I help, Chloe?" Jill asked, and Chloe detected relief in her tone.

"No, thanks," Chloe told her, carrying the big bag of ice to the screen. "I'm going to turn off the lights in the apartment, so why don't you two go up to the parlor. Greg is ready to play his guitar."

Aaron didn't seem pleased at this suggestion, but considering the previous conversation, Chloe wouldn't have expected him to be. Jill bounced up out of the chair, her smile tight and forced. "Sure, that sounds like fun. Those fajitas were really good, just like Tara said, Chloe. I wish my mom had that recipe."

"I'll write it down for her," Chloe promised. She switched on the outside light over the door. "See you upstairs."

Chloe watched as the two of them headed around the house, then closed and locked the glass door. Lost in thought, toting the bag of ice, she hurried through Ben's apartment, turning off lights as she went. Aaron, of course, wasn't the first boy to pressure his girlfriend for more than she wanted to give, but Chloe preferred not to hear his impassioned pleas on her own turf.

When Chloe arrived back in the kitchen, Aaron and Jill were walking through the front door, Aaron frowning and Jill doing her best to appear nonchalant. The two of them slipped back into the crowd sitting on the parlor floor as some of the kids began to sing along with the music. Ben appeared from somewhere, took Chloe's hand and led her to the library, where they stood in the shadows listening to the young voices raised in song.

The party lasted until midnight, and then everyone piled into cars to go home. Tara, once she had said goodbye to her friends, came in from the front porch as the taillights of the last car disappeared up the driveway.

She stretched elaborately. "It was a wonderful party, Chloe," she said. "Thanks. You, too, Ben."

"We'll clean up," Chloe said.

"I'll help." Tara went into the parlor and returned with a bag full of soiled cups and plates.

"Hey," Ben said to Tara, "I've been meaning to ask you and Jill if you could clean my apartment soon."

"Jill and I will work it into our busy schedule," Tara told Ben. "Oops—that is, in between other things. Greg and Aaron invited us to tour the Kennedy Space Center one day this week. It's only about an hour away. Can I go, Chloe? It sounds sooo cool."

"Sure, but who's driving?" Chloe asked.

"Greg's got his mother's car while she's on a trip to see her parents."

"Let me know when you figure out what day you're going."

"I will," Tara said. "Is it okay if I call Mom? She asked me to call no matter how late, and I can't wait to tell her how well Greg plays the guitar."

"Go ahead," Chloe said, glad that Tara felt like talking with Naomi.

Chloe and Ben worked side by side in the kitchen, wiping up spills and washing dishes. By the time they had finished, Tara was no longer talking on the phone, and she'd turned off the lamp in her room.

Ben and Chloe exchanged a glance, and he kept his arm around her all the way through the annex hallway to his apartment. Butch came with them, waited patiently while they got into bed, then curled up beside Chloe's feet.

"I don't have a litter box in here," Ben said, almost as an afterthought before he fell asleep.

"You don't need one," Chloe replied, nestling her head into the hollow of his shoulder, where it fit so well.

"Huh?"

She smiled into the darkness and promised before she closed her eyes, "I'll explain later."

Chapter Eleven

Ben smelled the fire before he saw the flames. Smoke stung his nostrils, blocked his vision. He began to run as his eyes watered and his nose became congested. The flames licked at his feet, burned his skin.

"Daddy! Daddy!"

It was always the same. Ashley calling out for him, terrified, lost, scared. Sometimes he could hardly hear her voice over the roar and crackle of the fire. Often, he shouted, "I'm coming, honey!" though he had no recollection of what he'd actually said. Again, he fought through the crowd, which was milling around, some people running, some people scrambling over the fallen bodies of others. He could never find Ashley. Couldn't reach her. All he had to go by was the sound of her voice, and sometimes it came from one direction, sometimes from another. He would twist and turn, struggling to get to Ashley. He'd run and shout her name and tell her Daddy would help her, find her, save her. And he never did. Never could.

This time was different. Always before when he woke up, he was alone. This time when the dream was over, someone was holding him close. He gasped, still struggling, and heard Chloe's alarmed voice.

"Ben? You're having a bad dream. Wake up, Ben."

In his anguish, he was trembling, shaking, and he went limp in her arms. He allowed himself to cherish her kisses, letting the tears dry cool upon his face.

His heart rate slowly returned to normal, and he wrapped his arms around her. Chloe was soft and warm and welcoming, her curves fitting his angles, her breath gentle beside his ear. Ben closed his eyes against the unspeakable horror of his memories. Ashley was dead. He couldn't have saved her; everyone said so. But that didn't make his failure any easier to bear.

"Okay now?" Chloe pushed herself up on an elbow and brushed the hair back from his forehead.

"Yes. I'm sorry I woke you, Chloe. Let's go back to sleep."

She was a shape above him in the dim room, and he couldn't discern her expression. "Do you need to talk about it? You were so upset."

"No, let's cuddle. It was just a bad dream."

She seemed to accept this and curled up beside him. "Did it have to do with your childhood?"

For a moment, he didn't connect what she'd said to their conversation in the kitchen that night. Then he recalled that he'd told her about his home life, and he supposed it was natural that she'd connect the two things.

"No," he said. "It was another kind of dream." *The worst kind,* he could have added but didn't—a nightmare from which there was no relief and one that would haunt him for the rest of his life.

"Mmm," Chloe said, sounding as if she were already half asleep.

If she had pushed him, he might have told her, but he never would come right out and say that it was his fault he no longer had a daughter. He blamed himself every single day of his life and would until the day he died. But rather than confess his shortcomings to Chloe, he preferred that she never find out that Ashley had existed.

CHLOE DIDN'T FALL ASLEEP AGAIN for a long while. Not for the first time, she sensed that Ben had deeper, sadder memories than he wished to reveal.

To be honest, she was glad he hadn't told her about them. Once Ben let her in on what was bothering him, she'd feel duty-bound to make things right. That, at this point in her life, wasn't supposed to be an option. She was trying her hardest to focus on herself, never mind that she'd taken on responsibility for Tara. That job was turning out to be easier than Chloe had expected. Ben was another story. And she was planning to stay uninvolved in his problems, whatever they were and no matter how sympathetic she might be.

This didn't mean that she didn't care. Oh, far from it. Ben was more important to her than she would have deemed possible when she'd first arrived at Frangipani Inn. The key was to keep things in perspective.

When she woke up, she reached over and felt the bed beside her, but Ben wasn't there. She smelled the bracing scent of fresh-brewed coffee wafting in from the kitchen and rolled onto her side just in time for Ben to swoop into the room and hand her a mug.

"For you," he said.

She pushed herself to a sitting position, suddenly frantic. "Tara," she said, panicky at the thought of her niece knocking on Chloe's bedroom door and finding her gone.

"Don't worry," Ben said. "Zephyr stopped by earlier and threw seashells at her window. They left in a rush to help a bunch of turtle babies find their way to the sea."

Chloe sagged against the pillow. "Tara didn't look for me in my room?"

"I was on the back porch when Zephyr arrived, and Tara ran out to join her without even washing her face."

"You're observant," Chloe said, taking a long sip of coffee. She brightened. "Also, you make better coffee than I do," she said.

"Not true. Anyway, before Tara left, I was trying to invent a cover story for your whereabouts. I'd decided to say that you fell asleep on my couch last night after we cleaned up after the party."

"My clever niece would see through that in a minute," Chloe said.

"I didn't have to use that story, thank goodness. Want some breakfast?"

Chloe shook her head. "I'd better hurry upstairs, shower and get dressed before Tara comes back."

She slid out of bed, and Butch ran in to twine through her ankles.

"By the way," Ben said meaningfully, "I was treated to Butch's performance in the bathroom this morning. Now I understand why he doesn't need a litter box."

"Amazing, isn't it?" Chloe grinned.

"I mean, there he was, squatting on the toilet seat and—"

"You can spare me the details," she said with a grimace.

"Was he born that way? Is that normal?" Ben regarded Butch with a bemused frown.

Chloe laughed. "I taught him."

"Brilliant, but how?"

"Oh, it was a kit I bought in a pet store. It includes a toilet seat adapter and herbs that you sprinkle in the litter, which goes inside the adapter, and then when you take the adapter away, the cat's toilet trained."

Ben stared at her. “Chloe, you should stop making jewelry and take up toilet training cats for other people.”

“Yuck. Once was enough.” She picked up Butch and kissed Ben on the cheek. “See you later.”

“Yeah. You, too, smart boy.” He scratched the cat under the chin.

Chloe rushed off to begin her day, but she was smiling. She could have sworn Butch was, too.

PATRICE CALLED during the next week and asked Chloe to provide more jewelry. “I have a couple of customers who have been telling their friends about your unique designs,” she said.

“I’ll bring some to you as soon as I can,” Chloe said.

Tara hurried into her office as Chloe was hanging up. She was wearing a skirt—a rarity in her wardrobe—and a conservative white blouse. “Chloe? Can you run me to the museum, or shall I drive myself?”

Chloe glanced up from her work. “I’d love to go into town. I have errands to do.”

“Is it okay if Greg picks me up from the museum at the end of my shift? His mom asked if I could eat dinner with them, and afterward, we’ll all watch the space shuttle launch from their backyard. I’m so excited about it. I never expected to see one.” Tara had been bowled over by her tour of the Kennedy Space Center and had been keeping her fingers crossed that the shuttle launch, long scheduled for this date, wouldn’t be postponed.

“Sure,” Chloe said, who was also looking forward to the launch. She’d never seen a shuttle blast off in all the times she’d summered at the Frangipani Inn, though she’d caught a couple of minor satellite liftoffs years ago.

“Can we leave in ten minutes?”

“I’ll be ready. Hey, Tara, bring the brownie pan that belongs to Jill’s mom. I’ll drop it off at her house this morning before it gets lost in the shuffle." Chloe shut off her lamp and set aside the necklace she'd been crafting. She didn't mind stopping what she was doing when it involved time alone with her niece. She'd learned that solid communication often happened when she least expected it—riding in the car, walking to the mailbox to get the mail, even while helping Tara pump up the tires of Gwynne's old bike.

Shortly afterward, as she and Tara were driving across the bridge toward the blue blur of the mainland, Chloe used the opportunity to tackle a subject that she wished she didn't feel compelled to mention.

"I've been meaning to speak to you about something that concerns me," she said to Tara, easing into the topic.

"Oh?" Tara turned puzzled eyes upon her.

"Jill and Aaron seemed, well, a bit intense at the fajita party."

"I'm not sure what you mean."

"I heard them talking. Does she ever confide in you?"

Tara considered. "Only that she's crazy about Aaron and will miss him terribly when he leaves for basic training in the fall."

This Chloe could handle. "She'll do fine. She's pretty, fun, and there's a whole world of boys out there."

"Sometimes you only want a special boy," Tara said.

"At Jill's age, there will probably be a dozen or more such boys before she settles down. Perhaps you could talk to her about playing the field."

A long silence. "I tried that, but Jill told me to mind my own business. She and Aaron are in love, and I'm such a kid because I don't understand how it is when you really love someone." Despite her blithe delivery of the words, Tara appeared troubled.

"Tara, I hope Jill won't make any decisions she'll regret when she's older and more mature."

"Me, too."

"Do you—well, would it be a good idea if I spoke to Jill's mom?"

Tara turned horrified eyes on her. "Oh, my gosh! No! I'd be so embarrassed, and if Jill found out you'd said anything, she'd hate me! She'd think I ratted on her."

"I doubt—"

"Honest, Chloe, she would. You've got to promise me you won't say anything to Mrs. Pettus when you take the brownie pan to their house. I'd *die* if you did."

Chloe sighed. "Okay. I'll keep quiet."

"Not a word?"

"Not a word," Chloe assured her.

Tara, mollified, faced front again. "Jill will be all right, no matter what her problems with Aaron. I've certainly made decisions that I now realize were dumb. I've learned from them and moved on. Like about this summer, when I decided to get away from home for a while. That was a bad decision that turned into a good one, wasn't it? It's fun being with you and Ben, and I met Greg, and maybe he's going to visit me in Farish sometime."

"I'm happy that you don't regret coming here," Chloe said warmly.

"Why would I?" Tara said, staring at her wide-eyed as Chloe braked to a stop in front of the museum.

Chloe smiled at her. "I can't imagine," she said, and the two of them laughed.

On her way home from town, instead of heading toward the Frangipani Inn on Beach Road, Chloe drove the other way toward Stuart's Point. The road led past Ibis Trail, a sanctuary where birdwatchers frequently congregated. Salt marshes bordered both sides of the road, edged with saw grass and populated with various forms of wildlife. Here, far away from the usual tourist attractions, it was possible to appreciate the way Florida had looked before the developers arrived. Pristine and unspoiled, quiet and unhurried. And because of the preserve, this small area would stay that way forever.

Stuart's Point was an unguarded, gated community, with big homes that lined meandering, palm-lined lanes. Chloe found the Pettus house readily, since Tara had described it in detail. Jill's mother, Lorena, an older, more staid version of Jill, greeted Chloe at the door.

"I brought this back," Chloe said, holding out the pan. She had printed out a copy of her fajita recipe and tucked it inside.

Jill's mother smiled. "Please come in."

Chloe started to shake her head, but Lorena appropriated her arm. "Jill has spoken of you so many times. Let's sit in the living room."

Chloe allowed herself to be propelled into a large open space whose main feature was an enormous waterfall cascading over native coquina rock set into the wall. She took in high ceilings, polished bamboo floors that seemed to go on forever, an aviary positioned between living and dining rooms.

"Your house is wonderful," Chloe said. Outside, a jewellike swimming pool was set in the midst of a tropical bower. The ocean view beyond was as stunning as the house's interior.

"Thanks, but this place is my husband's doing. He's an architect."

Lorena expressed delight at the fajita recipe, saying that no one believed her, but she loved to cook. "Aren't teenagers the toughest critics around? When Jill says she likes something, it must be fantastic."

Chloe didn't stay long, making the excuse that she had work to do at home, and Lorena slowly walked her to the door. "Thank you, Chloe, for giving Jill a job for the summer. She's got a fierce streak of independence, wanting to buy her own car when she can use mine almost anytime."

Chloe complimented Lorena sincerely on daughter's willingness to work and her eagerness to please. "I'm grateful for Tara's and Jill's help at the inn. They earn every cent of their money."

"Another thing about this job," Lorena said more thoughtfully. "It's good for Jill to have something constructive to do. I don't like her spending too much time with Aaron."

This would have been the perfect opening to mention her own concern about Jill and her boyfriend, but she had promised Tara. "I understand," was the most Chloe felt comfortable saying. Lorena, however, was inclined to be talkative.

"You have to be so careful with teenagers," she commented with a rueful smile.

"Very true," Chloe murmured. She rested her hand on the doorknob, eager for a quick escape.

"Tell me, Chloe, what's your opinion of Aaron?"

Chloe squirmed at this loaded question. "I've just met him," she said.

Lorena sighed. "The one good thing is that he'll be leaving soon."

"That's what Tara said," Chloe replied. She couldn't wait to be out of there. "And now I really must run along."

"Maybe we could get together one of these days with the girls," Lorena suggested. "Perhaps take them out to a nice lunch at a good restaurant. I've enjoyed knowing Tara so much."

"It sounds like fun," Chloe said. She liked Lorena tremendously, despite her discomfort at being put on the spot about Aaron.

BEN WAS WASHING paintbrushes in the spigot beside the back porch when she arrived at the Frangipani Inn. "What are you doing today?" he asked.

"I just left Jill's parents' house. Lorena and I had a chat." Chloe was more agitated than usual, and Ben picked up on it.

"Oh?" He stopped rinsing brushes, regarding her with raised brows.

"I doubt that Lorena likes Aaron any more than I do. That's not such a big surprise." She paused. "Say, do you want to have dinner together? And watch the launch afterward?"

"Launches are always beautiful at night, and this one is scheduled for nine o'clock. Sure, I'd like that."

"Stop in around seven. I'll make spaghetti sauce."

"I thought you didn't like to cook."

"All I have to do is brown some ground beef and throw in sauce from a jar. I can handle that." Chloe smiled at him, continued into the house and settled down to work. The afternoon went quickly, and when Ben showed up in the kitchen after she'd started the pasta, she told him that Tara was going to eat with Greg's family.

"That means it's just you and me, darlin'," he said as he wrapped his arms around her.

"Careful," she warned with a laugh, "or you'll get spaghetti sauce all over my shirt."

"Which would be a good reason to take it off, wouldn't it?" he said mischievously, unbuttoning her top button.

She rebuttoned it. "Not," she retorted with good humor.

After they'd gorged themselves on spaghetti, salad and French bread, Ben helped her clean up.

"We'll see if we can find a secluded spot in the dunes, lie back on the blanket and get naked," he said.

She eyed him doubtfully. "I hope you're joking."

"Yes, about the blanket," and she snapped her dish towel at him.

"I was only trying to find out if you were listening," he said reprovingly.

"We should pack a cooler with some sodas and potato chips," Chloe suggested.

Ben went to find the cooler, and then he and Chloe joined others who were thronging down the boardwalk to the beach. Someone had set up several tiki torches in the sand, and one of the park rangers was giving a talk about the space program.

"Let's get away from everybody," Ben said, leading her back into the dunes and winding along on a path past a grove of oaks. Here there were no people, and Ben spread the blanket out. Chloe sprawled on it first, and he glanced down at her with a half smile. "I haven't forgotten my original idea of getting naked," he said.

"Well, I have. With people around? And kids and dogs and who knows what? Sit down, Ben Derrick, and stop blathering." She laughed up at him, and as if to prove her point, a dog romped by with its tongue hanging out.

"Shorty! Come back here," shouted its apparent owner, who with a gaggle of children in tow was laboring southward at the edge of the surf.

"See? They didn't even know we were here," murmured Ben. He sat beside her and took her hand.

"All right, what happens now?"

"You take your clothes off." He waggled his eyebrows at her.

She couldn't help laughing at his persistence. "I mean about the launch."

"Some people will have radios or maybe small battery-operated televisions, and as the countdown to launch progresses, they'll start chanting. We'll probably hear them down the beach." Ben opened a bag of potato chips and offered her some before helping himself to a handful.

Chloe munched for a while, then twisted the top off a bottle of cola. "Have some," she offered, and they companionably shared the same bottle until all the cola was gone.

"Do you ever miss it? Alcohol, I mean?" Chloe asked Ben.

"No, though I used to enjoy drinking a beer now and then. Why do you ask?"

She shrugged. "It's something I wondered about. I've had addictions of my own," she said as Ben's brows lifted clear into his hairline.

"Not to substances," she hastened to add. "To people. Or rather, to certain people who need my help. I get a rush from looking after them, enjoy their praise, and in some cases actually require it. Even when they take advantage of me, I don't want to give them up. To my own detriment a lot of times," she added.

He studied her face curiously. "Like now?" he asked softly. "With Tara?"

She shook her head and crumpled up the potato chip bag before tossing it into the cooler. "Tara's making progress, and she's short-term. No, not with Tara."

"With me, then?" Ben asked gently. "Are you trying to tell me something, Chloe?"

She was aghast that he had mistaken her meaning. "No, Ben, I've never—I mean—"

"Sweet Chloe," he said, brushing a bit of sand off her face. "If you ever feel that I'm too much responsibility, that I'm in your way, tell me. I wouldn't harm you for the world."

"Oh, Ben," she said. "You've given and given to me and Tara, and I'm forever grateful."

He kissed her tenderly, and her arms went around his neck. "I can't stay away from you, Chloe," he said as he slid his hand inside her shorts. "If it is possible to be addicted to a person, then that's what this is, but so far I haven't found anything wrong with this. With us."

She focused on his face above her. "Nor have I," she said.

He kissed her, kept kissing her until she thought she would

die of wanting him. Her mind filled with images: herself at sixteen, meeting him on the beach; Ben thanking her back then when she'd poured his coffee with her hands trembling because she'd been so attracted to him; the serious way he had talked to Aaron and Greg about underage drinking. So many memories, so many moods. She took his hand, placed it on one of her breasts. Needing him to touch her in intimate places, needing the reassurance that she meant something to him.

They heard people down the beach chanting the countdown, and a dog barked, but they were so well hidden away in the dunes that no one noticed the two of them.

"Dearest Chloe," Ben murmured, kissing each breast. By this time her shorts were somewhere on the blanket, and she hoped they weren't going the way of her lost swimsuit. She pulled the edges of the blanket over Ben and her, effectively blending them into the cover of oaks.

Nine, eight, seven, six, five, four, three, two, one—

The sky erupted golden when the rocket blasted off, its trail blazing red and silver and yellow as it arced over the ocean. The blast started a rumble deep inside the earth, shaking the ground where they lay.

"Ooh," sighed the crowds as the rocket spun away, and "Aah" as Chloe began to wish that she and Ben could be lost in space together and never return to Earth. But, she decided, inner space had proved to be even more intriguing, considering how it could bend to accommodate all sorts of people.

Under the blanket, as the rocket sped into the night, Ben held her close for a long time. Tucked into their own secret hideaway, they were utterly private and discreet. She traced the lines of his face with her finger as if she were sculpting him; he curved himself around her, his angles to her curves.

"So, uh, what did you think about the launch?" he ventured.

"I felt the earth move," she said truthfully.

He laughed and kissed the tip of her nose. "I hope the experience will be as moving next time," he said.

"It probably will, but meanwhile, could you please help me find my clothes?"

"Against my better judgment," Ben said, reaching down inside the blanket and coming up with her shorts.

"Judgment had nothing to do with it," Chloe said, but she was smiling all the same.

Chapter Twelve

The next day, Chloe was hulling strawberries that Zephyr had brought early that morning when an unfamiliar car nosed into the parking space normally reserved for her Volvo. Curious, she peeked out the window and saw a tall woman step out. The visitor stood staring at the inn for a long moment, then seemed to pull herself together before determinedly setting off along the path leading to the front door.

Chloe quickly dried her hands on a towel and hurried through the foyer. Probably another former guest who hadn't heard that the place no longer operated as a bed-and-breakfast.

The woman knocked sharply. Chloe opened the door, meeting the stranger's cool gaze.

"Yes?" she inquired politely, taking in her visitor's manicured nails, glossy brown hair fastened in a neat roll at her nape and the long skirt worn with sandals.

"Is Ben here? They told me at the post office that this is where he's staying."

"Well," Chloe said, "he actually lives in the annex. He has his own entrance down by the dunes." She inclined her head to indicate direction.

"Oh," said the woman, clearly distressed. "I'm sorry to

cause you any trouble, Ms—? I'm sorry, but I don't know your name."

"It's Chloe...Chloe Timberlake. I'm looking after the inn for my aunt and cousin. If you'd like to come in, I'll call Ben."

"Yes," murmured the woman as she stepped inside. Her sweeping glance encompassed the gleaming parlor, the newly cleaned library, the elegant chandelier overhead.

"Who shall I tell him is here?" Chloe asked.

The woman hesitated, then met Chloe's eyes squarely. "Emily Derrick. I'm Ben's ex-wife."

Chloe was stunned. Ben had mentioned that his ex lived in Colorado. "I—I'll tell him," she stammered, hurrying out. Behind her, Emily settled on the wide Victorian sofa, folded her hands in her lap and commenced staring at the ocean in the distance as if it were the most fascinating sight in the world.

Chloe didn't stop to knock at the door to the annex. She flung it open. "Ben! Ben, are you in here?"

"As it happens, I am," he said amiably as she burst into his living room. "I'm polishing up my day's treasure-hunting finds. Sit down and join me." He indicated a stool beside the kitchen counter.

Chloe ignored the fine but tarnished locket that Ben was rubbing with a soft cloth. "Someone's here. She says she's your former wife."

The locket clattered to the floor, but Ben didn't notice. "Emily?" he exclaimed, striding around the counter. "She's *here?*"

"In the parlor," Chloe said as he rushed along the hallway and into the kitchen of the inn. She could barely keep up with him.

At their approach, Emily Derrick rose. Ben halted in the archway between parlor and foyer. Chloe stood frozen behind them, knowing that neither was any longer aware of her presence. They had eyes only for each other.

"Ben," Emily said, stepping forward. She held out her hands.

Chloe's first instinct was to leave, but at the moment, she found herself totally incapable of movement.

Ben clasped Emily's hands in his. "Emily. I didn't expect you."

Emily smiled slightly. "I was surprised to learn you were back in Sanluca. After—after you said you were leaving for good."

"I should have left immediately after the fire. Then nothing would have happened to Rick."

"He's well and working for an oceanographic institute in Maine. His boys are getting big. Trevor is six, and Lang is ten."

"And you, Em?"

She bit her lip. "My life in Colorado is unexpectedly fulfilling, and I've made a lot of new friends."

"I'm glad."

"How are you, Ben?"

"I still don't have my old job back, but if I can stay sober, I believe Andy will hire me again."

"I hope so." Emily hesitated. "I'm here to tell you something. I'm going to be married in the fall, to a wonderful man I met in Colorado. He owns a ski-rental business, and he has two children, a boy and a girl. They're delightful kids, and we get along great. I'm finally going to have that family I wanted." Her eyes sparkled.

"That's good, Em," Ben said, though his words fell flat.

"One other thing, the most important." Emily's eyes searched his face. "I came here to forgive you, Ben. I'm beginning a new life, relegating the past to the past. I don't want to start my new marriage under shadows of bitterness."

"Em—"

"Please stop blaming yourself for what happened. If I can forgive you for our daughter's death, surely you can forgive yourself. Please, Ben?"

Chloe's mind reeled as Emily spoke. Ben was a father? Had a daughter who had died? Ben was speaking now, but Chloe couldn't hear his words over the rush in her ears, and all she wanted was to get out of there. She backed into her workshop, groped for the door handle and pulled the door closed behind her. She leaned against it and closed her eyes.

In all the conversations they'd had, all the times that Chloe had congratulated herself on their open and honest relationship, Ben had never mentioned a daughter. Dear God, from what Emily said, Ben must have been responsible for her death. But how? And why?

Ben had always been a man of mystery, even going back to that summer when she'd first met him. Then, he'd lived at the inn for a couple of months, charming the other guests, earning the admiration of two teenage girls who hung on his every word and disappearing without a word to anyone. Now, when she thought she knew this man, it turned out that she didn't at all.

The murmur of voices rose and fell in the parlor. Chloe sat down and tried to work, found it difficult to concentrate. She buried her head in her hands. After a while, a tap on the door startled her.

When she opened it, Ben stood there. "Chloe, I have a favor to ask," he said.

"Yes?"

"Emily rented a vacant RV from Ducky Hester, but I hate the idea of her staying there. She'll be glad to pay you if you'll let her room at the inn for a few nights."

Chloe herself would have hated to stay at Ducky's, and Emily wouldn't be here long. Still, she fumbled around for an out.

"The girls are going to start cleaning upstairs next week. There'll be a lot of noise and mess."

"Tara and Jill could rearrange their schedule while Emily is here so that they're working in the annex instead of upstairs."

"As long as Emily understands that the inn isn't ready for guests, I suppose I wouldn't mind," Chloe said reluctantly.

Ben's face lit up. "Thanks, Chloe. I know she'll appreciate it. Say, would you like to have dinner at the Sand Bar with Em and me? She has a thing for their hamburgers, always has."

Chloe shook her head. "I'll be cooking for Tara tonight. Afterward, we're going to go over the information she found about the oceanography program at Florida State." She'd expected Ben to be here while she and Tara examined the brochures.

"Tara could join the three of us at the Sand Bar."

"She's excited about studying oceanography, Ben. It wouldn't be wise to put this off."

"Well then, which room do you want Emily to take? Driftwood?"

This was the one directly across the room from hers, and probably the cleanest, except for the chameleon living under the dresser. "Sure. Ben—" She broke off her sentence.

"Yes?" He regarded her with mild interest.

Chloe wanted to say, *Don't you think you have some explaining to do?* She wanted to blurt out her doubts and concerns; she wanted to talk with him. But she could see that he was itching to get back to Emily.

"Nothing," she said.

"I'm sorry you won't be going with us," he told her.

"Wc need to talk," she said evenly. "About—"

"About my daughter? About Ashley?"

Chloe had never heard that name before. "Yes," she said evenly. "About Ashley."

For a moment that all-too-familiar desolate expression flitted across Ben's features. "We will," he said. "After Emily leaves."

He brushed her cheek with the knuckles of one hand. She wanted to lean into that touch, be held in his arms. But she kept her expression neutral. This wasn't the time for that.

Later, she watched as Ben and Emily drove away. She felt betrayed. Not because Ben had taken Emily to dinner, but because he had been less than forthright about his past. She'd accepted his status as a recovering alcoholic, and it didn't bother her that he had been married. But she was accustomed to being manipulated by men, and she'd been determined to avoid such situations in her new life. If Ben had omitted mentioning such an important part of his history, what else wasn't he telling her? What skeletons were likely to tumble out of his closet later on?

AFTER DINNER THAT NIGHT, when she and Tara were sifting through the many materials about the oceanography program, Chloe found it difficult to pay attention even though Tara was enthused about her new direction. Chloe couldn't help but notice that Ben and Emily had been gone a really long time, and maybe they were dancing to blues music on the Sand Bar's tiny scuffed dance floor, and then they would drive back to the inn and…

No. Emily had said she was getting married. Surely she wasn't here to make a play for her ex-husband.

"Chloe? Did you hear what I said?"

Chloe pulled herself back to matters at hand. "Something about maybe you wouldn't have to live in a dorm your first year at Florida State."

"Would Gwynne mind if I lived with her?"

"She'll have finished work on her master's degree by the time you start college, but you could ask. She may intend to stay in Tallahassee and work."

"Mom said that she and Dad would be supportive of my plans to go to Florida State even though they'd have to spring for out-of-state tuition. I bet I could get a paying job at the treasure museum next summer to help out. They said maybe they could use me in the lab where they clean the treasure they've brought up from the wrecks."

"You're planning to come back to Sanluca? For sure?"

"I could live with you here at the inn again."

"Tara, dear, I may not be here that long."

Tara's brow wrinkled in dismay. "But you have to stay, Chloe! You have to! Aren't you planning to run the inn as a B and B again?"

"We'll see," Chloe said faintly, but if her relationship with Ben went sour, she wouldn't want to be anywhere in the vicinity. She'd go somewhere else—maybe even back to Farish. That was something she had never even vaguely contemplated before, and the fact that she'd even consider it certainly was an indicator of her present distress.

Tara surprised her by enveloping her in a big hug. The burst of affection heartened her, but it didn't quite make up for Ben's going off with Emily. Even if his absence was only temporary, it still rankled.

"LET ME GET THIS STRAIGHT, Chloe. Ben has moved his former wife into the inn?"

"Uh-huh," Chloe said, picking at a loose thread on the bedspread as she talked with Naomi. She lay on her stomach across the bed where she had a good view of the beach through the window. Ben and Emily were there, walking and earnestly engaged in conversation. Ever since Emily had arrived yesterday, they'd been together. Except for last night. Emily had disappeared into her room early and hadn't emerged until morning.

"You should have your head examined," Naomi told her.

"Thanks, Naomi. I needed to hear that."

"Isn't this just another manifestation of your rescue personality? Emily has to have a place to stay, so you help her out?"

"Ben asked. I could hardly refuse, considering that there's really no decent motel around here."

"And now the two of them are on the beach together, holding hands and—"

"They're not holding hands," Chloe said unhappily. "They're actually about three feet apart. Emily's pointing out at something in the ocean. A freighter, most likely. Ben's shaking his head. She's—"

"I don't require a blow-by-blow description of the action," Naomi said. "Let's talk about where you go from here."

"Maybe back home to Farish. There is something wrong with a man who doesn't mention that he had a daughter who died. How many other things hasn't he told me?"

"Who knows? Who cares?"

"I do," Chloe said unhappily. "This is my life we're talking about."

"You and Tara could drive back to Farish together at the end of the summer. You're invited to stay with us until you find a place of your own."

A picture of Farish flashed through Chloe's mind. The big courthouse, the church steeple, rough guys in cowboy boots ogling her at the supermarket. Farish would be her last choice.

"No, Mimi. I'll find someplace where I can make a fresh start," she said unhappily.

Naomi, sounding exasperated, asked to speak with her daughter. After Tara took the call in her own room, Chloe stared broodingly at the couple on the beach. There was nothing like a little well-placed jealousy to clarify matters in one's mind, and Emily's reappearance in Ben's life certainly had done that. Watching Ben and his ex-wife on the beach from her bedroom window, Chloe decided, was not the best way to spend her day, so she phoned Zephyr and asked her if she could come over.

"You're welcome any time," Zephyr said firmly. "What's happening?"

"A lot," Chloe said. "Too much."

"You might as well get on over here and tell me what's on your mind."

Chloe gave one last long, exasperated look at Ben and Emily and hurried to get her car keys. "I'm leaving right now," she said.

Chapter Thirteen

Zephyr lived on the mainland only a few miles from town past acres and acres of orange groves. Even though she'd invited Chloe to visit many times, Chloe had never gone. Now she was glad of a place where she could escape Ben, Emily and her own dire imaginings about what might be transpiring between them.

Once across the bridge and past the groves, the landscape was taken over by stands of palmettos and sweet bay, with a few plant nurseries thrown in for good measure. At a scruffy mailbox painted with a loggerhead turtle, Chloe turned off the highway and continued down a bumpy driveway to the house.

Zephyr lived in a typical tin-roofed cracker shack, painted shiny white and featuring a wide porch running around three sides. When Chloe drove up, her friend was sitting in the shade on a lawn chair placed under a spreading oak hung with a few long wisps of Spanish moss.

"Why didn't you tell me that Ben had a daughter?" Chloe asked no sooner than she'd sat down beside Zephyr, who was shelling peas.

"It was none of my business," Zephyr said.

"He could have mentioned *something*. All the time we've known each other, all this time we've been falling in—" She stopped, horrified at what she'd been about to admit. She hadn't even admitted it to herself.

"Falling in love?"

A lump in her throat, Chloe nodded.

"It would be easy to fall for Ben," Zephyr said as she tossed another hull into a brown paper bag. "He's a nice guy."

"Oh, sure," Chloe replied with irony. "Ben's a recovering alcoholic who almost killed a man and is responsible for the death of his daughter. Why do I keep finding these people?"

"You don't find them. They find you," Zephyr said succinctly. "At least, I suspect that's what happens."

"Do I have a sign across my forehead that says, 'Make me do something stupid'?" Chloe said, exasperated with herself.

"No, but you have an empathetic attitude. You act as if you care about other people."

"Well, I do. But I'm tired of fixing things for everyone else and screwing up my own life in the process."

"You haven't exactly done that. Yet."

"Oh, Zephyr. I'm like one of your baby turtles. I've headed in a whole bunch of wrong directions, and I need to be set on the right course."

"Hatchlings find their own way. Turtles have magnetite in their brains. It's an iron compound that draws them to the North Pole like a compass and helps them navigate. That's how female turtles manage to return to the same nesting beach over and over again."

"I don't have any powers like that," Chloe objected.

"You came back to Sanluca, didn't you? Something drew you here."

"Zephyr—"

"Listen to me, Chloe. You'd better depend on your own self, because I can't offer magic spells to get you out of trouble. I certainly wish I'd had magnetic navigation or voodoo, one or the other, when I fell in love with a cowboy from Okeechobee City."

Okeechobee City was located inland in a major cattle-growing area of Florida, and Chloe had gone to a rodeo there once with Tayloe and Gwynne. "You've mentioned a cowboy before," Chloe recalled.

"Uh-huh. Want to hear about it?"

"Sure," Chloe said.

Zephyr reached for more peas. "I fell for my cowboy over a dinner of catfish and hush puppies at the Sand Bar, and he invited me to move closer to him so we could explore our mutual interests. Mutual interests! That's highfalutin talk for a cowboy. Like a fool, I did it. Closed up this house, packed all my stuff, and took up residence in an apartment over a Laundromat near the ranch where he worked. Dumb thing to do," she said.

"Maybe not, since you were in love with him," Chloe pointed out.

"I suspect he was having an ego trip and liked the idea of some woman—any woman—following him to the ends of the earth, which Okeechobee might be, though it's a pleasant enough little town." Forgetting for a moment about her task, Zephyr stared reflectively off into the distance.

"You were telling me about the cowboy," Chloe reminded her gently.

"His ex-wife showed up one day."

"Like Emily?"

"Not quite. Ex Mrs. Cowboy weighed two hundred and fifty pounds, and she said he owed her money. She tracked him down at my place and, like a fool, I let her in the door. She hit him upside the head and sat on him until he turned purple. Then I gave her the money and she went away."

"Didn't he pay you back?"

"Nope. He didn't see a need to do that. Knew I was in love and would do whatever it took to keep him."

"What happened after that?"

"I figured that for the amount of money I paid to get rid of his ex-wife, I could have bought me a decent guy. Kicked the cowboy out and moved back to Sanluca. My second husband followed me from Okeechobee and proposed the day after he arrived in town. We were married thirty years, God rest his soul."

"That's an interesting story, Zephyr. What does it have to do with me?"

Zephyr regarded her with a challenging grin. "Who says it has anything to do with you?"

"I thought—"

"I was merely indulging in a bit of reminiscing. And now that it's getting dark, how about if I fry up some pork chops and redeye gravy."

Since Tara and Jill were going to dinner and a movie at the mall in Melbourne, Chloe was free for dinner. Staying would mean that she wouldn't be subjected to halfhearted invitations from Ben and Emily, and that was good, too.

"Thanks, Zephyr," she said. "I'd love to."

"Good. Can't have you mooning over Ben. Emily will be gone before long, and then you and Ben can thrash things out. Just be glad Emily doesn't weight two hundred and fifty pounds and want money."

"I guess that is something," Chloe said, unable to keep from laughing.

Zephyr's excellent pork chops and gravy served up with rice and fresh peas was the first decent meal Chloe had eaten in two days, and when she went back to her room at the inn, she could hear Emily humming across the hall as she moved around Driftwood. As for Ben, his Jeep wasn't parked outside.

After Tara came home and went to bed, Chloe stayed awake listening for the crunch of the Jeep's tires on the driveway. Ben showed up around midnight, and she heard the sliding glass door open and close beneath her window. The creak of the floorboards across the hall told her that Emily was still in Driftwood.

Chloe didn't fall asleep right away, so she sat up in bed and reached for the old diary.

Dear Trees, I want to die. Gold hasn't spoken to me in three whole days! In fact, I don't know where he's been. Maybe on the dive boat or someplace. Mrs. Mixon, a lady who lives at the inn all year round, says Gold is gone for good. I don't know how she knows this. He still has things in his room, I sneaked in one day and looked around. His room still smells like him. He left his old plaid shirt on the chair. His clothes are in the closet.

Wind says his rent is paid up to the end of the month, and that's when I'm going back to Farish. I want to see him so badly you can't imagine. And I can't tell Ocean or Wind—they'd think it's ridiculous. Ocean keeps trying to get me to meet this friend of hers, Hank Something Or Other. I am not interested. I'm in love with Gold.

But where is he?????

Worried and wondering,

Fire (Chloe D. Timberlake)

She'd drawn a remarkably good likeness of Ben as he'd been in those days, capturing the warm light in his eyes and the boyish charm that had made him a favorite with the other residents at the Frangipani Inn.

Now, unlike then, at least Chloe knew where Ben was. But since it wasn't with her, the knowledge gave her no comfort at all.

ON THE DAY EMILY LEFT, Ben was glad to see her go. It meant he could patch things up with Chloe.

Chloe prepared a breakfast of eggs, bacon and English muffins, and while Emily ate alone in the dining room, he went upstairs to get her suitcase. On his way outside with it, he heard Chloe refuse payment. Afterward, his ex came out of the inn alone.

"That's it, then," Emily said, lingering where he stood to put the suitcase in her car. "I hope everything goes well for you from now on."

"Thanks, Em."

After a moment of awkwardness, she kissed him lightly on the cheek. "Be happy, Ben." He may have detected the sheen of tears in her eyes, but she climbed in the car too quickly to be sure.

As he slammed the trunk lid, Chloe barged out of the house. She immediately noticed that the garbage can had been overturned again, probably by the hungry possum that kept mounting night raids, and she went to pick it up and stuff the bags of garbage back in. He watched her out of the corner of his eye as she weighed the lid of the can down with a chunk of coquina rock and tested it to see if it would hold.

"Goodbye," Emily called out the car window. She waved at Chloe, who returned the wave in an unenthusiastic fashion. Ben stood, hands on hips, feeling relieved as he watched Emily back out of the parking space.

With Emily here, he hadn't felt free to be himself. To be truthful, he'd been eager to reconnect with his ex-wife, but only because she was the mother of his child and he would forever feel guilty that Ashley had died. His guilt had thrown up a wall between them where none had been before; when he and Emily should have been able to support each other, he'd had nothing to give. Now that she was on the threshold of a new beginning, he'd been able accept her forgiveness. During the past few days, she had convinced him that this was key to their moving on with their lives.

How was he going to explain all this to Chloe, who was presently stalking back to the porch, her eyes boring holes through him? He was going to give it his best try.

"You could have charged Emily for the room," he said conversationally as he approached.

Chloe pivoted on her heel, regarded him for a long moment and shrugged—a careless movement that didn't fool him. She was perturbed, and rightly so. "Emily is family," Chloe said abruptly before turning toward the kitchen door.

He was right behind her when they reached the kitchen. "*Was* family," he said, touching Chloe's shoulder in a gesture of supplication.

Eyes flashing, hands clenched at her sides, she said, "You told me you'd been married before, Ben, but you never mentioned a daughter."

"She died," he replied helplessly. "It was painful to discuss it."

"You could have told *me*."

"I didn't talk about Ashley to anyone. When she died, it was—it was—" He didn't know how to describe the utter hopelessness, the futility of his life. The anguish, the heartbreak, the guilt. He closed his eyes, opened them again, and saw Chloe. The anger had gone out of her expression, leaving only disappointment. In a moment of empathy, he knew how she must feel.

"It was horrible. I felt empty. I couldn't function. I couldn't manage even the most simple aspects of my life," he finished.

Chloe's expression softened, and then, after a wavering moment, her face crumpled. She buried it in her hands. "Oh, Ben. I'm sorry," she said, her voice muffled.

"It's okay," he said. "We should talk about it."

"You and Emily," she said, dropping her hands and staring at him with a bleakness he'd never seen in her before. "What is that all about?"

The words poured out, and he said things about grief and guilt and ultimate forgiveness. He was repeating what Emily had so earnestly told him, but because it was what he had come to believe, too, there was no falseness. Chloe stood staring at him, and she must have been somewhat surprised because she didn't interrupt, she didn't speak.

"It's about moving on," he said. "Emily and I were never really in love."

"You married her, Ben. That summer I was crazy in love with you, and you went and married Emily. I was devastated."

He stared at her, shocked. "You were just a kid," he said finally. "I was much older, twenty-one to your sixteen. We hardly knew each other."

"What I felt was a teenage crush, but to me it was the real thing. You broke my heart, Ben."

"Are you going to blame me for that? When it would have been wrong for me to show any interest in you, considering the age difference?" He spoke heatedly, but he didn't derive pleasure from the way she deflated in the face of his logic.

"No," she said. "No. I never thought of it that way."

He forced himself to remain calm, to ignore his urge to take Chloe in his arms and comfort her.

"Emily and I married very young when she discovered she was pregnant that summer. I was her child's father. I respected Em, I liked her, and I didn't want her to be alone even though a pregnancy was the last thing I'd expected to happen. We used precautions, and they didn't work, and—she got pregnant. Anyway, from the beginning, it was a disastrous marriage, because even though we were friends, we were unable to live together. When Ashley was six months old, we divorced. I'm happy that Em's found someone who really cares about her. She's not too old to have more kids of her own."

Chloe sank onto a chair. "So while she was here, you weren't falling in love with each other all over again?"

He stared incredulously. "Is that what you thought?"

"I've even considered that you might be seeing someone else besides me."

"Absolutely not." His denial was vehement. "Whatever gave you that impression?"

"You go out at night and stay out late."

"I go to AA meetings, Chloe. It helps me stay sober. I thought you knew that."

"You never said," she pointed out.

"I hang at the Sand Bar sometimes. It's a good place to pick up information about treasure hunting, which I find necessary in order to keep up now that I'm not working in the field. There's no one but you, Chloe. Why didn't you ask me about it if you were concerned?"

"I didn't want to pry."

"I haven't been interested in any other woman since I moved into the inn, and that's the truth."

"What about Emily?"

"Chloe, Em and I are like oil and water. We'll never mix. This may have been the last time I'll ever see Emily. She says it's too painful to come back to Sanluca. We parted friends—again. That's what we both wanted."

"I liked her," Chloe said. "It surprised me that she was so nice."

Ben rubbed the back of his neck. "I wouldn't have married her in the first place if she hadn't been, as you say, nice. It was a mistake, but one I made in good faith and for a good reason. I wanted Ashley to have my name and I wanted to contribute to her support. I was a presence in my daughter's short life. That's important to me."

Chloe nodded, then looked away. "When did Ashley die, Ben?"

"A little over two years ago."

Chloe swiveled abruptly and went to the sideboard in the dining room, where Emily had eaten a solitary breakfast that morning. "Emily left these," she said, thrusting a sheaf of yellowing newspaper clippings in front of Ben's nose.

For a moment, he didn't comprehend. Then he understood.

"That's Em's way of putting the past behind her," he said heavily. "She said she was going to get rid of them."

"Well, her way of doing that was to dump them here at the inn."

"She probably thinks it will bring closure to me if I'm the one to destroy them. She mentioned that." He shook his head at Emily's tactic. She'd always been one to insist on other people doing things her way. "I'll take care of it," he told Chloe. "Then we can talk."

"Why don't you let me read these," she said quietly. "Wouldn't that make it easier on you?"

"Nothing makes it easier, but go ahead, if you like," he said, keeping his voice low.

"If it upsets you…"

"No," he said. He reached out to touch her cheek, wanting things to be right between them again.

"I've got things to do in the annex," he said. "I'll be back later and we can have lunch."

She smiled, but it was a pained smile.

Not knowing what else he might say to make things better he left her, going to his apartment to sit for a long time in the armchair facing the patio. He, like Emily, needed to put the bad time to rest. Say goodbye to it and move on.

With a sigh, he got up and cleared a stack of old magazines off the kitchen counter. Several were women's magazines that Emily had brought, and he set them aside in case Chloe and Tara might like to read them. Emily had also left a bottle of excellent Scotch, which she liked to drink on occasion. She'd probably forgotten it, so he stashed it away in a cabinet where he wouldn't see it every time he came into the kitchen. Joe, the bartender at the Sand Bar, had proved a loyal friend. Ben would give the bottle to Joe next time he saw him.

He could ask Chloe if she'd drink it, but she didn't care for anything more potent than beer or wine. Of course, he and Chloe would have other things to talk about when he next saw her. And it was time, definitely time, to discuss them.

CHLOE DIDN'T READ the clippings as soon as Ben left her. She was already operating on emotional overload and reluctant to take on any more. After she cleaned the sink and swept the kitchen floor, taking her time about both, she sat down at thc table and steeled herself to read about his daughter's death.

The fire had been big news when it happened, and all the major newspapers in the country had covered it.

> *THE MIAMI POST-EXPRESS*
> TAMPA—Terrified fans leaped from windows and trampled fellow concertgoers as a fire at a rock concert Friday night gutted a theater in the town's historic Ybor City district.
>
> The blaze killed at least ten people, most of them teenagers, and injured dozens more.
>
> The concert, featuring the Latino band, Chico Chico, was a performance to benefit music programs in the public schools. No band members were injured.

"I smelled smoke, and someone yelled 'Fire.' Flames shot off the stage and went everywhere," said Maria Torres-Ola, 25, who attended the concert with her boyfriend.

"The girl in front of me started screaming for her father," said Brant Senecal, 17. "Her long blue dress was on fire. I ran up the aisle, choking in the smoke."

"I saw people scrambling up the walls, trying to get out the windows," said a shaken parent, John Schultz, 48. "I was lucky. My kids and me crawled on our hands and knees toward an exit door."

Attendees at the concert numbered around 600. Many parents were in the audience, since Chico Chico tends to appeal to young teenagers.

Francis O'Rourke, head of security for Flo-Star Productions, the sponsor of the event, said that the hall was filled to capacity. "It's an old theater, but we thought we had adequate fire alarms and escape routes. The flames spread fast, and people didn't have time to reach the exits. I can't tell you how shocked and sad I am."

The fire apparently started around 9:00 p.m. in pyrotechnic equipment used onstage.

A fire department official told reporters that when rescue workers reached the scene, they found ten people dead and many wounded. About twenty survivors were brought down extension ladders that reached the higher windows.

Bringing the fire under control took an hour, according to O'Rourke, but eight hours after the blaze began, the building was still smoldering and the street was cordoned off. About a hundred firefighters battled the blaze.

"We will be looking into any safety violations. You can be sure of that," said the fire department official, who declined to be named.

"This is one of the worst fires in our city," said Mayor Beaujames Chadwick. "I've never seen anything like it."

Police said they will begin an investigation into possible involuntary manslaughter.

The picture accompanying the article showed the ruins of a building. Smoke still rose from the charred rubble. Chloe shivered with terror for the poor souls who had been caught in that all-consuming conflagration.

She folded the bit of newsprint and set it aside. She was too horrified to read any of the others until a small one caught her eye. It was a scrap clipped from the local weekly, the *Sanluca Courier:*

OBITUARIES

Ashley Martyne Derrick

Ashley Martyne Derrick, thirteen-year-old daughter of Emily Martyne Derrick and Benjamin J. Derrick, both of Sanluca, died Saturday in Tampa as the result of a fire.

Ashley was born on December 10, 1990, in Vero Beach. She was an honor student at Jerome Ruby Middle School and a champion speller who represented Indian River County at the state spelling bee in Orlando last year.

A clarinetist in the school band, Ashley also sang soprano in the Trinity Community Church choir. She played the lead in the seventh-grade play *Princess P. Green and the Dragon.*

She is survived by her parents, and her maternal grandfather, Leonard D. Martyn, of Palm Beach Gardens, as well as her maternal great-aunt Talitha M. Surrency (Samuel) of Denver. Other survivors are uncles William Derrick (Judy), serving in the U.S. Army in Iraq; Jane D.

Zillessen (Joseph) of Merced, California, and Mindy Carman (Michael) of Atascadero, California; as well as several cousins.

The obituary, though it gave many details, seemed so cold and unfeeling. It didn't attempt to express or record the wrenching emotions that the death of such a promising young girl must have brought to the lives of her loved ones. Chloe's heart ached for them, and for Ben especially. She couldn't begin to imagine the agony of losing a child.

Chloe blinked her eyes to clear the tears away. As she did so, a shadow fell across the table. She lifted her head. "Ben, I'm so sorry."

"I couldn't tell you," he said. "I don't talk about it. Up until now, I mean."

"Until Emily came to see you?"

He shook his head. "No. Until I cared about you. The full story isn't in the newspaper articles. Those are cut-and-dried factual accounts. They say nothing about Ashley, who she was. That she loved animals, that she cared about kids with disabilities, that she wanted to be a doctor so she could help people. They don't say what really happened that night."

Chloe stood up and reached out to him. Her hand found his. "Tell me, Ben."

Wordlessly, he led her to his apartment, where he lay down on the bed and she settled beside him with her head on his shoulder. Outside, over the sound of the waves, they heard children shouting. A car door slammed. Someone on the boardwalk laughed.

Those were the outside noises. Inside, it was quiet. Not even the sound of a dripping faucet marred the silence.

"It was Ashley's birthday," Ben began after a long time.

"Chico Chico, Ashley's favorite band, was giving a concert in Tampa, and I was going there to see a man about selling some boat equipment to Andy. Ashley was spending the week with me because Emily was away taking care of her mother, who was in the hospital.

"I remember when Ashley came to me with a flyer about Chico Chico. She'd picked it up in the music room at school and was eager to go to the concert. A percentage of the proceeds was supposed to benefit music programs in the schools, and since she was in both band and choir, this was a big deal to her.

"'Daddy, can we go? Katy and Roma could go with us,' she said. Katy and Roma were her two best friends. Ashley suggested that I drop them off at the mall so they could shop while I talked to the guy about the equipment. The day of the concert was Ashley's thirteenth birthday, and it was supposed to be a special treat." He was quiet for a long time before resuming the story.

"As it turned out, Katy's parents had plans for that day, and Roma woke up with bronchitis and called at the last minute to say she couldn't go. Ashley said, 'It'll be fun, just you and me,' and…it was."

For the first time, his voice broke.

Chloe closed her eyes, unable to avoid seeing the chaos, the panic that must have accompanied the fire.

"Before the concert, we went to see the guy about the equipment together, and Ashley waited in the car reading a book while I wrapped up the deal. It took much less time than I'd anticipated, so I suggested we go to the mall. She was thrilled, and as we were strolling past a shop, she fell in love with a dress in the window. It was long and blue and made of a filmy material like gauze or something. I told her to try the dress on, and she looked so pretty in it.

"'I'll buy it for you for your birthday,' I said, and Ashley squealed with delight. She refused to take the dress off, said she'd wear it to the concert. She was crazy about the boys in Chico Chico, had a poster of them in her room, wanted to look her best. I was a reasonably indulgent father, so I didn't object. I was glad to see her so happy.

"We sat right down in front. I was lucky, I thought, to get such good tickets. Ashley was ecstatic when those guys strutted onstage. She had stars in her eyes when they played her favorite song, and the lead singer sang directly to her. I couldn't stop marveling at the way that my daughter was becoming a beautiful woman right before my eyes.

"At intermission, I asked her if she wanted something to drink, and she said yes, so I went to the lobby to the refreshment counter. There was a long line, and I stood back, letting the kids go first. I figured it didn't matter if I missed some of the concert when it resumed. It was more important for those kids to get back to their seats. I was the last person to purchase drinks, and I was turning toward the door to the theater when I heard the first screams.

"Smoke began to pour out of the seating area, thick black coils of it. I ran toward the entrance, only to be met by a wall of panicked people. I fought my way through, was knocked down, struggled to my feet and was carried backward. All that time I was screaming for Ashley, and I heard her calling to me over the roar of the flames.

"'Daddy, Daddy, help!' I'd know her voice anywhere."

Chloe swallowed and felt tears falling from Ben's cheek to hers. She didn't wipe them away.

"Then, the theater turned into a tunnel of fire, and I heard only screams. I was trampled, couldn't get up. Everything went black." He paused. "I woke up in the hospital. I'd suffered smoke inhalation. Had two broken fingers and bruises all over my body.

My first words were, 'Where's Ashley?' The pitying expressions on the nurses' faces told me that she was gone. I wanted to die."

He wrapped both arms around Chloe, held her so close that the beating of his heart was loud in her ear. "Sometimes, I still do. I'm sure Ashley's the one mentioned in one of those articles, the girl with the blue dress. It was long and flowing, no doubt very flammable. Just a spark from that fire, and she would have turned into a human torch. If I'd never bought her that dress, maybe she'd have escaped. But it was Ashley's birthday."

Chloe swallowed past the lump in her throat, fighting the image of a lovely young girl in a flaming blue dress. "Emily is right. You need to stop blaming yourself," she said, her heart heavy.

"Afterward, my life was in tatters. Ripped apart. I couldn't concentrate, couldn't live with myself. During what I call the bad time, I started drinking. I was responsible for what happened to Rick, and all because I wished I'd died in that fire. After a rough time, I realized that dying wouldn't bring Ashley back. It wouldn't solve anything. I quit drinking, got into AA, and I've been sober ever since. Well, except for the anniversary of Ashley's death. I went on a binge and hated myself for it. It'll never happen again, I swear."

"I admire you, Ben," Chloe said quietly. She had no doubt that Ben was a good person. But good people slipped up sometimes. It was a mark of his character that he'd straightened himself out and was striving to put his life back together.

"I'm different since I've been sober. If only I could convince Andy McGehee of that."

"You will, Ben. I have faith in you."

"That means a lot. You have no idea how much."

She held her breath, watching his face as his emotions played themselves out. Pain, remorse, and something even more powerful, though she wouldn't—couldn't—put a name to it.

"I have something to live for now. I have you, Chloe," and his lips grazed her forehead. "You're special in my life. You're someone to care about besides myself, and I needed that. I need *you.* Do you understand what I'm saying?"

"Yes," she whispered. "I think so." Underlying her relief was a niggling voice of doubt; that was what all the others had said. People tended to need her, which ultimately got her into situations that became unworkable.

"I'm trying to say that I'd like to see where this goes with you, Chloe. I gave up any idea of having a family after Ashley died. I didn't want the pain of starting over. Now I've begun to dream about having a second family. You're the kind of person I would want to raise my children if I were lucky enough to have any, and I hope you feel the same way about me."

"I'm honored," she said, though she had reservations. Being a mother was Naomi's destiny, and her friend Beth's, but not hers. Of course, the men she'd known before this were losers, and maybe that had affected her thinking. She'd never met a man she'd deemed suitable to father any child of hers.

She had fallen in love with Ben Derrick. What that would mean to them in the future, she couldn't say.

Later, after they drowsed in each other's arms, Chloe got up and made lunch. Tara arrived home from the museum and asked if she could visit Jill, so Chloe told her she could drive the Volvo. Ben started building a fence around the garbage cans, sinking it in a deep trench so that possums and other varmints wouldn't be able to burrow underneath. Every so often, he came into the house for a drink of water and touched her lovingly and lingeringly before going away again.

One such time, he went through the door in the kitchen to the annex, and she didn't hear him return for a long time. When he did, he slammed into the kitchen, the sound of his work boots striking heavily on the kitchen floor.

When he reached her workshop, she glanced up. "Anything wrong?" she asked mildly when she saw the disturbed expression on his face. But of course nothing could be wrong after this morning; they were again in sync, connected.

Ben flung himself down in the chair beside the door, the one that Tara usually occupied when she stopped to talk.

"I should say so," he said. "The gold coins I kept in the shoe box beneath my bed—the ones I've been finding on the beach—are gone!"

Chapter Fourteen

"Tara wouldn't take them," Chloe said. "I'm sure of it."

"She had the opportunity. She and Jill—"

"Yes, I remember. They cleaned your place," she said. She didn't add, *while you and Emily were strolling down the beach together.* That would have been unfair, and besides, she was over that. Or was supposed to be.

"Who else could have done it?"

"Any of the kids who were here for the party," Chloe said. "Have you checked since then—before today, I mean—to check if all the coins were there?"

He shook his head. "Not lately. There were six of them."

"Tara expects to eat dinner at Jill's. She won't be home until later."

"I'm going to ask her if she did it, Chloe." He said it with worry in his eyes, and now that he'd calmed down, she was sure that Ben didn't want Tara to be the thief any more than she did.

"Please don't undo all the good work we've both done with Tara since she arrived. Confronting her will only make her angry, rebellious." Her words were more of a plea than a request, but Ben's jaw had set into a grim line.

"Tara has a history of shoplifting. She was the only person who knew the shoe box with the coins was hidden under the bed. I showed them to her myself after one of our metal-detecting jaunts."

"Other people could have known about them," Chloe said stubbornly.

"How?"

"By snooping around. You often leave the glass doors open and the screen door unlocked."

"That's so if you'd like to come in and make love, you can," he said, his lips twisting with humor. "It worked, too."

She refused to be sidetracked. "Anyone else could come in, also. People from the state park, or vagrants who sleep on the beach. Dog walkers, beachcombers, kite flyers, etcetera."

"I found Zephyr in my apartment one day," Ben admitted. "She asked if I had any sunscreen, since she'd forgotten hers. She was going to help herself."

"Zephyr wouldn't be interested in gold coins. She's the least materialistic person I've ever met, and one of the most honest." She paused. "Back to your suspicions, Ben. If Tara had wanted to steal something, she could have taken my jewelry anytime. She could have stolen the artifacts in your collection or even the emerald ring."

"One-of-a-kind jewelry pieces that you make would be a lot harder to dispose of than coins, which people find here on the beach fairly often," Ben pointed out. "Anyway, you keep your work in the safe when you're not at your bench. As for my artifacts, they'd require some sort of explanation if anyone tried to sell them, since they're rare. The emerald ring is documented in Sea Search's records. To sell it wouldn't be easy without raising questions."

"I have faith in my niece," Chloe countered.

Ben stood up with a sigh. "We're not getting anywhere, Chloe. I'm not buying the theory that unknown interlopers stole those coins, but I promise I won't speak to Tara if you don't approve. Just the same, I'm going to be especially alert for clues."

"I will, too," she said. "Give me some time to get a read on Tara, see if anything seems amiss."

Ben shook his head ruefully. "I have work to do. We'll forget about this for now, okay?"

Chloe was happy he left. She needed time to figure out if her niece could really be the culprit.

No. Not Tara. But then, who?

DINNER THAT NIGHT was a reserved affair, with Ben staying in his apartment to eat alone. Tara was talkative, telling how Suzette Stephens, one of the other teenagers who worked at the museum, was having a party at her house. "Jill and Aaron are going, and Greg will be there after he gets back from a family wedding. Can I borrow your car? I won't be out late—I have my shift at the museum early the next morning. That's the day I'm going to help set up a new display before the museum opens, and I'm real excited that they asked me."

"I'm not sure about letting you use the car," Chloe said doubtfully. She had never allowed Tara to drive the Volvo by herself at night before.

"I'm a safe driver. Haven't I proved it? And the party's only a few miles down the road." Tara stood and started clearing the dishes from the table. "I'll take your cell phone. You can call me whenever you like. I can phone you if there's a problem."

"How about if I consider your request?" Chloe said.

"Okay, but I'm cleaning up the kitchen tonight as a bribe. Hey, Chloe, you seem tired. Have you been working too hard?" She regarded Chloe for a long moment.

Chloe shook her head. "I've got a lot on my mind, that's all."

"Hmm," Tara replied in a teasing voice. "Does it have to do with a certain handsome fellow?" She was clearly and unabashedly scoping out the romance angle.

"I refuse to answer on the grounds that it might incriminate me," Chloe said, more lightly than she felt.

"Clever answer," Tara called as Chloe retreated to her workshop.

The light was still on in her niece's room when Chloe retired for the night. For Chloe to fall asleep, knowing that Tara was suspected of thievery, wasn't easy. The girl's behavior had been above reproach all summer, except for a few instances of pique that, in Chloe's opinion, didn't count for much.

As the week progressed, Ben kept asking Chloe if she had changed her mind about confronting Tara.

"I have a hard time believing that Tara would betray my trust," he told her. "But even if she didn't take the coins, she must know something about their disappearance."

"Please, Ben," Chloe said, her patience beginning to wear thin. "I told you I'd try to find out if she's involved, and I will."

During the next few days, Chloe stayed close to Tara, occasionally attempting to engage her in conversation that might lead to discussion of the missing coins, but such efforts led her to believe that her niece was either skillful at evasion or was completely innocent.

One day, Tara declared her intention to get rid of white marks from her swimsuit and went out to lie on the beach with a book. "I'm way ahead of Amy," she told Chloe. "She's not even halfway through *Pride and Prejudice* yet, and it's on our summer reading list."

"Good for you," Chloe told her, but her praise was halfhearted.

In a conversation that day with Naomi, her sister had picked up on her distractedness and inquired if anything was wrong.

Dodging the question, Chloe directed the conversation to Tara's reading and her interest in oceanography, which switched Naomi to a different track altogether. Chloe could hardly tell her sister that Tara was suspected of stealing; Naomi would demand that Tara return to Farish immediately. Which, as Chloe had told Ben, could undo all the progress Tara had made the past while.

Attempts to draw Tara out continued to go nowhere. Unfortunately, Ben was growing more impatient.

"How long are we going to wait?" he asked one night when he and Chloe were sitting outside on his patio, watching the moon rise over the ocean. "It's been almost a week. Those coins are valuable, Chloe."

"If Tara had any part in their disappearance, she's not letting on. Honestly, Ben, I don't believe she knows anything." Hiding her growing resentment at Ben's suspicion of her niece wasn't easy.

"She's been acting entirely normal—I'll grant you that," Ben said grudgingly. "How about if we talk to her about it the first of next week? We could make it very casual and nonconfrontational."

"We'll see," Chloe said reluctantly.

Ben raised her hand to his lips and kissed her fingers one by one. "I don't want this to come between us," he said.

"It hasn't," she said stoically, but privately she was not so sure. She got up to leave. "I'd better go. I promised Patrice I'd deliver some jewelry soon."

He followed her into the kitchen, where she rinsed out her glass in the sink. Her gaze fell upon a bottle of Scotch in an open cabinct, and it registered as out of place. Ben didn't drink. He said he couldn't. Still, she didn't mention it. It wasn't her responsibility to warn Ben about booze any more than it was his prerogative to keep harping on Tara's supposed guilt.

The day before the big party at Suzette's house, Jill and Tara were taking a break on the front porch, their feet propped on a wicker ottoman as they planned what they were going to wear the next night. Chloe, who was at her workbench inside, heard a car drive up, and soon afterward, Suzette climbed the steps of the porch and plopped into one of the chairs. Chloe went on painstakingly fitting bits of pearly white glass onto a chunky gold bracelet, which would also feature a large amethyst. She didn't feel guilty for eavesdropping; the girls knew she could hear them talking from her workroom.

"Hi, Tara. Hi, Jill," Suzette said. "I stopped by to find out if you were planning to come to the party." Suzette was a tall girl with a bright smile and a cheerful expression that made people like her right away.

"We wouldn't miss it," Tara said. "Sit down and tell us what everyone's going to wear. I can't decide between my new tank top and skirt or my blouse with all the pockets and the awesome denim shorts."

"I vote for the denim," Jill said. "How about you, Suzette?"

"I'm wearing cutoff pants that I'm borrowing from my sister and a red shirt that I've had for a while. Are you going to be able to use your aunt's car to come to the party, Tara?"

"Maybe. She's thinking about it." She raised her voice. "Aren't you, Chloe?"

"Right," Chloe called through the open window.

"I got a fabulous new CD the other day," Suzette said. "I can't wait for you to hear it."

The others asked what the name of the band was. Tara said the group's music was big in Texas right now, and Chloe gradually lost interest in listening. She managed to ignore their typical teenage talk until they mentioned Aaron.

"I'm sorry about what happened to Aaron about the surfboard," Suzette said. "Sam told me about it this morning."

"Maybe you better tell me what you heard," Jill said.

"That Aaron took a surfboard from Hank's shop and the police picked him up."

"Hank gave it to him." There was outrageous indignation from Jill.

Hank Garrison owned a surf shop between Sanluca and Vero Beach, and surfers in the area patronized it heavily.

"Is that what Aaron said? That it was a gift?" Suzette asked. She sounded puzzled.

"I haven't heard about this," interjected Tara. "What happened?"

Jill answered, and Chloe picked up a growing defensiveness in her attitude. "Hank told Aaron he could have the surfboard, and after he tried it out, he didn't like it. He decided to pawn it, but by then Hank was mad at him about something and reported it stolen."

"Oh, wow," Tara said in shocked amazement. "What a bummer."

"Especially after what happened before," Suzette said knowingly. "I can't believe Aaron gets in these situations."

What situations? Chloe wondered. She sat very still, waiting to hear Jill's reaction.

"Aaron was in the wrong place at the wrong time when that happened."

"When *what* happened?" This from Tara.

"Oh, you don't really want to know," Suzette said airily.

"Just something he took the rap for at school," Jill told her. "The principal had it in for him."

"That's too bad," Tara replied. A long silence ensued, and then Tara spoke. "Suzette, would you like a lemonade?"

"No, I'd better go. Mom and I are going out to buy food for the party. I'm glad you'll both be there." She started down the porch steps.

"'Bye. Want us to bring anything?"

"Thanks, but my mom's doing it all. Tell Greg not to forget his guitar."

"Will do."

Suzette hurried away, and Tara spoke after a long while. "Um, Jill. This thing about Aaron and the surfboard. He's not really in trouble, is he?"

Jill heaved a giant sigh. "I hope not. We had a big fight about it. I'm like, why don't you talk to Hank and smooth things over? Hank's a nice guy, all the kids like him, and maybe there's just a misunderstanding between him and Aaron. He got furious, Aaron did. He said I don't trust him or have faith in him, and I told him that's not true. We almost broke up." Jill's voice was quavering.

"Right before the big party?"

"Uh-huh. It'll be awkward, being there with him. Everyone is talking, and I definitely don't want my parents to hear about it."

"You said your mom doesn't like him, anyway."

"Yeah."

Tara spoke next. "Well, Jill, something tells me this isn't a problem we can solve, so we better get back to work. We've still got that big wardrobe to clean in Sandpiper."

The two of them came back inside and passed Chloe's workshop without comment. Chloe, however, couldn't get down to business as easily as the girls could. She mulled over the conversation she had heard and decided to discuss with Tara what she'd overheard.

She waited until after Tara had spent the afternoon on the beach, gone to her room and showered. When Tara appeared downstairs, Chloe was waiting for her in the kitchen with a plate of fresh-baked cookies.

"I knew I smelled something scrumptious," Tara said, swooping in to grab one.

"I'm through working for the day. Want to sit out on the porch?"

"Sure," Tara said. "Front or back?"

"Your choice."

"Back. Is it okay if Butch goes out?"

"Of course."

Chloe poured a glass of milk for each of them, plus a dollop in a saucer for the cat, and joined Tara on the porch. Tara was on the swing, gently pushing it back and forth with one bare foot, the plate of cookies balanced on the cushion beside her.

Ben was working on the shrubbery nearby; he had planted ti plants around the garbage can enclosure earlier and was now trimming the hibiscus hedge. A few curious gulls flew over, their cries muffled by the clamor of the trimmer. After finishing his milk, Butch switched his tail, crouched and pounced on a lizard, which easily escaped.

"All ready for the party tonight?" Chloe asked conversationally.

"Now that you've said I can drive the car, yes," Tara replied. Chloe had given her permission only that morning. Ben had raised his eyebrows at the time; he'd been rooting around in the closets in the annex hallway, looking for gardening tools. He probably didn't approve of her letting Tara take the car tonight, but, as she reminded herself, it wasn't his decision.

"The rules are, you don't give anyone else a ride and you drive straight home afterward."

Tara rolled her eyes. "Okay." She said it good-naturedly as she helped herself to another cookie.

Chloe decided that there was no tactful way to broach the subject of Aaron and thc surfboard. The best thing to do was to ask bluntly, so that was what she did.

"Tara," she said, "I couldn't help but overhear what you girls were talking about earlier. This thing about Aaron—what do you make of it?"

"I believe Jill when she says he was unfairly accused."

"He was in trouble before at school. Did you ever find out what that was about?"

"Somebody slashed the tires on the principal's car. It might have been Aaron."

"That's a fairly serious offense, Tara."

"He may not have done it," she said defensively.

"Maybe not," agreed Chloe.

Tara kept rocking the swing and it was clear that she wasn't going to venture anything more on the subject.

Chloe took the plunge. "Tara, dear, I'm concerned about something."

"Like what?"

"Like the shoe box of coins missing from under Ben's bed." Chloe kept her gaze level.

Tara stopped her swinging. Out on the ocean, the whine of a Jet Ski blended with the roar of the hedge trimmer, which was growing closer as Ben moved toward the back of the house.

"You think I took them?"

This was a tough one. "No, I don't," Chloe said honestly. "But they're gone. Do you know anything about it?"

Two bright spots of color had appeared on Tara's cheeks. "No, of course not. Why would I?"

"Tara, I'm just asking." Around the corner of the house, the racket of the hedge trimmer ceased.

Tara jumped off the swing and glared at her. Chloe grabbed the plate of cookies before it went flying.

"I thought you were different, Chloe. Everyone else—my parents, teachers, practically every adult in Farish, Texas—suspects me of everything that happens. I made a couple of mistakes, okay? But since that shoplifting incident in Austin, I haven't done anything illegal. And you still don't trust me."

By this time, Chloe was on her feet. "I wouldn't be letting you take the Volvo tonight if I didn't," she answered, her anger growing.

"I wouldn't be surprised if you changed your mind," Tara said with bitterness. "Since you've figured out that I'm a thief and all."

"I never said that, Tara. Kids cover up for other kids. I'm speaking from firsthand experience."

"You're a solid citizen now. You reformed. I have, too."

Ben sauntered around the side of the house, his brow knitted with concern. Tara heard his footsteps and whirled to face him. "How about you, Ben? Do you think I took the shoe box with the coins?" Tara said.

"I hope not," Ben replied quietly but his jaw was square and tense.

Tara's eyes sparked with anger. "I don't believe this." Her gaze darted from Chloe to Ben and back again. She started toward the kitchen door. "I've listened to enough. You can both go to hell for all I care." The door slammed in her wake, and Chloe and Ben were left staring at each other.

Chloe sank onto her chair, feeling totally drained. For the first time, she had an appreciation for the distress that Naomi must feel when she and Tara argued.

Ben tossed the hedge trimmer down and came onto the porch, where he sat down beside Chloe. "That didn't go too well," he said wryly.

Chloe only looked at him and held out the plate of cookies in case he wanted one, but he shook his head.

Ben was silent for a long while. "Let's talk about what we should do now," he said.

Before Chloe could frame an answer, the door opened and Tara barged outside dressed in the outfit she planned to wear to Suzette's party. "I'm out of here. I'm going to Suzette's house early." She headed for the Volvo, which was parked in its usual spot beside Ben's Jeep.

"Tara—"

Tara kept walking. "Are you going to tell me I can't take the car now?"

"I've already given my permission," Chloe said with as much patience as she could muster. "Drive carefully, and I hope you have my cell phone." Beside her, Ben favored her with an incredulous glance.

Tara held up Chloe's cell phone before getting into the car and slamming the door. She peeled off in reverse.

When the Volvo was out of sight, Ben stood up abruptly. "I can't believe you let her take the car," he exploded.

Chloe, her emotions still in a turmoil over how her talk with Tara had failed so utterly, turned blank eyes upon him. "What?"

"You let her take the car."

"I'd promised her earlier."

"Tara insulted both of us and got away with it."

"Ben. What was I supposed to do?"

"Tell Tara she's grounded. Make it clear that she hurt your feelings. Putting up with that sort of behavior only encourages more of the same." He spoke emphatically.

"I'm not accustomed to disciplining teenagers." All sorts of issues seemed to be surfacing here: Ben's growing annoyance over the past week, Tara's lack of respect, her own inability to deal with things.

"With Ashley, I always—" Ben blurted the words, was unable to continue.

"With Ashley, you were the perfect father," Chloe said before she thought.

Ben's face went pale as Chloe realized how cutting and cruel her words must have seemed to him. "In the end, I wasn't, was I?" he said softly.

Sick at heart, she ran after him as he headed down the steps. "Ben, I didn't mean that," she cried. If she could have swallowed her words, she would have. He kept walking, eyes focused straight ahead.

"Oh, you knew what you were saying," he retorted bitterly.

"I didn't, I swear! Ben, I'm so sorry." Someday, she would learn to put her mind in gear before her mouth.

For an answer, Ben wheeled and started walking down the slope toward his apartment. Stunned, Chloe watched him go.

The heat, building all day, had suddenly become oppressive. Clouds in the west, formerly wisps of white, had merged into a dark mass. Long curtains of rain in the distance swept in her direction, and if she wasn't mistaken, the air had freshened, foretelling the usual afternoon thunderstorm.

Before she could react to the change in the weather, Ben reappeared.

"Couldn't we discuss this?" she asked.

He only glowered at her.

"Where are you going?"

"Out," he said. He was halfway to his Jeep and still wearing his work clothes, which was unusual. Always, in the past, he'd showered and changed before he went out in the evenings.

"Ben!" she called in alarm. She feared for his safety as he rammed the Jeep into gear and roared down the driveway.

Chloe stared after him. Maybe it was better that he had left the inn. Maybe he'd cool off and be ready to accept her apology when she offered it.

She had no doubt that she owed him one. What she'd said was unforgivable. She'd hit him where he was most vulnerable—his sense of responsibility for the death of his daughter.

So now she had two things to worry about: Tara's rushing off to the party in anger, and Ben headed somewhere, anywhere, to get away from her.

Tears stung her eyes as she contemplated her empty evening. Blinking them away, she wandered from the kitchen into Ben's apartment, wishing he were there. With Tara gone, they could have made love. Maybe sat out on the patio after dark, talking and laughing and enjoying each other's company.

She would never know why she acted on the impulse to open the kitchen cabinet where she'd seen the bottle of Scotch only days ago. It was gone, and what if Ben had taken it with him? He'd been carrying something, which hadn't seemed important at the time. What if Ben decided to go on a drinking binge, and all because of her?

CHLOE FOUND IT IMPOSSIBLE to concentrate on anything. She tried working, lost patience with the intricacies of fitting sea glass onto a silver disc, threw one piece down in disgust. Re-adjusted her gooseneck lamp to shed more light on her work surface, found it didn't help. She halfheartedly started reading her old diary, hoping it would make her feel better.

> Dear Trees, Gold is gone. Gone forever from my life. How this could happen, I don't know. He is the most special person I have ever met. The only one I dream about.
>
> What's even worse is that no one ever knew I loved him, not even him. I never let on to Wind or Ocean. They would be shocked! And to tell them now wouldn't make any sense. I don't want their pity or their sympathy or advice. I just want Gold!
>
> Mrs. Mixon was right. Gold left for good, but no one knows where he went. He came back to the inn one night

when Ocean, Wind and I had gone to a band concert in Vero. He took all his stuff out of his room, leaving it bare and sad-looking, except for that plaid shirt on his chair. He must have forgotten it.

I stole it. Yep, went right in and yanked it off the chair, and now I am wearing it. Ocean has gone to spend the night with her friend Sierra and I said I didn't care to go. I wanted to cry and write in my diary and think about Gold. I didn't want Ocean to know that I was wearing his shirt. I'll never wash it. I'll keep it forever.

I love him so much. I love him so much. I love him so much.

I'm going back to Farish in a few weeks. I guess I won't be writing in here anymore, cuz I won't have anything good to tell.

Love,
Fire (Chloe D. Timberlake)

Well, so much for feeling better. If anything, Chloe's diary entry made her even more aware of the patterns of loss in her life. As for the plaid shirt, she had slept in it for ages. Eventually, she'd forgotten all about it until she came home from college one spring break to find her father using it as a rag to polish his car. By that time, the shirt hadn't mattered.

In her estimation now, she'd been a silly teenager with less common sense than Tara. Which reminded her that she'd better call her niece on the cell phone. But Tara didn't answer. After repeated tries to reach her, Chloe clicked on the radio in her workshop so she could hear the weather reports, went out on the front porch, sank onto one of the rocking chairs and listened to the crash of waves on the sand.

Maybe she'd been better off in Farish, Texas, where day-today life had been predictable. How could she create her designs, find innovative ways to meld sea glass and precious metals, get them ready for the Palm Beach winter season, with all this turmoil going on around her? Had she really expected to get involved with people who have major problems going on in their lives? The answer was a resounding no, yet here she was, stuck in a situation of which she wanted no part whatsoever.

Chloe may have sat there for an hour or more before she started worrying about Ben. If she was responsible for his starting to drink again, she'd never forgive herself. Inside her head, a little voice that sounded a lot like Naomi told her, *You're not responsible if the guy falls off the wagon.* On the other hand, if not for her thoughtless remark, Ben might be beside her here on the porch.

In the kitchen, the phone rang, startling her out of her self-recrimination. She ran to answer it, hoping it was Tara or Ben.

"Chloe?" Tara's voice was drowned out by static, and almost drowned out by party sounds in the background.

"Tara," Chloe said in relief. "I'm glad you called."

"I wanted to tell you—" Tara broke off, but when she spoke again, she was easier to understand.

"Tell me what?" Chloe prompted. "Are you having a problem? Is everything okay?"

"I'm leaving the party. Jill didn't show up, and Aaron…"

Chloe didn't hear the tail end of the sentence. "What about him?" she demanded.

"I can't get into it now, but I'm leaving in a few minutes for Jill's house. Her parents are out tonight, and we'll be able to talk."

"I wish you wouldn't do that, Tara," Chloe said. "There's a storm on the way."

"Jill's house is only a mile or so down the road." Tara interrupted their conversation to speak in an aside to someone at the party.

"Is Greg there? Could he go with you?"

"The wedding lasted longer than expected, and an accident on the turnpike held them up. I'll be fine, Chloe."

She had a sudden inspiration. "Hey, how about if you stop by and I'll go with you."

"I want to talk with Jill alone. I'll be home after I leave her house. 'Bye, Chloe."

Kids! Chloe thought as she clicked off the phone. Why was it so urgent to talk to Jill tonight? Why hadn't Jill attended the party that both of them had been eagerly anticipating for a week or more?

For the next hour, Chloe paced the floor. She kept consulting her watch and wondering how long it would take Tara to drive to Jill's house, engage in a conversation and return home. Perhaps no longer than an hour.

She'd almost forgotten that the radio was on in her workshop until she heard the strident weather bulletin.

"The United States Weather Service issued an alert at nine-thirty p.m. Eastern Daylight Time," said the tinny voice of the automated announcement. "A severe squall is approaching the communities of Sanluca, Wabasso and Vero Beach from the southwest and traveling north-northeast. It is accompanied by high wind gusts and wind-driven rain. The storm is proceeding at approximately twelve miles per hour, and all those in its path are urged to protect themselves by taking cover. Interested parties should—"

Chloe hurried to the front porch. The waves had increased in height and strength since she'd come inside. The wind was whipping around the turret and blowing sand up from the beach. Tara shouldn't be driving in this weather.

She called Tara on the cell phone, but there was no answer. She attempted to reach Jill in the hope that Jill might be able to tell her if Tara was safe at her house or had left. All she heard was an answering-machine message.

Meanwhile, the air had chilled, a sign that the first squall line was almost there. Butch scuttled in from outside when she opened the front door to take stock of the clouds again, and he hid under the parlor couch. Chloe went around and closed all the windows in the inn when rain began to fall.

She knew what she had to do, but she didn't want to do it. She looked up the number of the Sand Bar in the phone directory and waited patiently until someone picked up. A male voice identified himself as Joe the bartender.

"I'm trying to find Ben Derrick," Chloe said over the howl of the rising wind, hoping against hope that he was there.

"He's here. Want to talk to him?"

Chloe breathed a huge sigh of relief. "Please," she said. "It's important."

"Hey, Ben. Phone for you."

A shuffle, a laugh, and Ben came on the line. "Hello?"

"Ben, it's Chloe." She wasted no time in apprising Ben of the situation.

"I'll find her," he said right away. In the background, the blues band played a wailing lament—eerie punctuation for the concern Chloe was feeling at the moment.

"Are you—all right?" she asked, not without trepidation.

"I'm fine," he said, sounding normal.

"I mean, you haven't been drinking, have you?"

A long pause. "Absolutely not. Chloe, what in the world is going through your head?"

"I'll explain later. Can you swing by and pick me up?"

"That would take extra time, and I'd rather ride over to Jill's right away. I don't like the sound of this."

"Nor do I," Chloe said faintly.

"I'll report back ASAP. Keep calling her on the cell."

"Okay, Ben. Thanks."

A long pause. "Chloe, don't worry. I'm sure Tara is okay."

"I hope so," she replied.

They hung up. Again, Chloe dialed the cell phone, and again, no answer. Fear clenched her heart. How would she ever be able to face Naomi, Ray and the twins if anything had happened to Tara?

Chapter Fifteen

When Chloe called, Joe had been relating with relish how Liss was presently involved in a heavy relationship with her tattoo artist. Ben found the story only marginally interesting. After he hung up, he cut Joe's revelations short and ran outside to his Jeep. Palmetto fronds thrashed and flayed in the lot next door, and an empty plastic bag blew across the parking area and wrapped itself around his ankles. Ben peeled it off and kept running.

The rain blew sideways in torrents, and as he drove across the bridge, Ben strained to see ahead. On Beach Road, markings were obscured by standing water. He turned away from the inn, heading north toward Stuart's Point.

Leaning forward, he peered into the dense fog and rain. He was more worried about Tara than he had let on. While he was playing pool earlier in the evening, he'd heard guys talking about Hank Garrison's run-in with Aaron.

"Shoot, that boy is trouble aiming for a place to land," one of the regulars had remarked.

"You better believe it," agreed another guy who hung out there most nights. "Aaron tried to pawn a surfboard, like a fool. Anybody would recognize one of Hank's boards, and he'd already reported it stolen."

Ben had continued lining up his shot and concentrated on knocking the ball into a pocket, but he'd kept his ears open for any other mention of Jill's boyfriend. He hadn't heard anything, but what he'd already learned had given him pause. Whoever had stolen the coins from the box under his bed would have to dispose of them, and the easiest way to do it would be to pawn them. Quick money, few questions asked. People were always finding treasure around Sanluca, and trying to sell artifacts to collectors or the museum would probably produce more questions than a thief would find comfortable. Pawnbrokers weren't overly particular and tended to respect their customers' privacy.

Unless they suspected something was illegal. In that case, they'd report it to the police.

Since Jill hadn't shown up at Suzette's house tonight, maybe she had broken up with Aaron. He'd overheard part of the girls' conversation on the porch the day before, and knew Jill was upset about Aaron's propensity for getting into trouble. And if Tara had gotten wind of anything indicating that Aaron had something to do with the coins' disappearance, she would certainly go to Jill first. That could explain her early departure from the party.

He'd turned on the Jeep's radio when he left the Sand Bar, and suddenly, a blaring emergency message interrupted the soft music. "A tornado warning has been issued—" began the voice of Weather Central.

"Oh, great, that's all we need," Ben muttered as the announcement continued. In his haste to reach Jill's house, he accelerated even though visibility was still severely hampered by the heavy rain. Then, as he rounded the curve near Ibis Trail, the Jeep spun out and fishtailed. He only managed to straighten out in the last moment before bouncing onto the road shoulder. He twisted the wheel hard to the left, regained control. Shaken, he braked to a halt and sat for a moment to compose and orient himself.

For a moment, he was confused by direction. He was about to guide the Jeep back onto the pavement when a collapsed guardrail on the bridge ahead caught his attention.

Down in the marsh, he spotted something shiny. A bit of foil? A beer can? No, it was too big for either of those, but still, it was something that wasn't supposed to be there. He edged the Jeep onto the road and swung it around so that the headlights shone in that direction.

He wished the squall would let up enough to let him get a better look. The Jeep's windshield wipers were scarcely sufficient to keep up with the deluge. Suddenly, a moment of comparative calm commenced, and he saw a face. A frightened face mouthing words that he couldn't hear through the closed window of a car halfway covered with water.

He leaped out of the Jeep and ran across the road, unheedful of the water sloshing in his shoes and blowing in his eyes. Tara. It was Tara down there, in Chloe's car, with blood flowing down her face. He recognized the Volvo's faded blue paint, the squared-off roof and the hood, which jutted out of the water at an odd angle.

For once in his life, Ben was sorry that he'd never acquired a cell phone. He had no way to call for help. No way to reach someone who could help him get Tara out of the car. And he had no doubt that she was in serious trouble. From what he could tell at first assessment, the car had plowed through the guardrail, maybe in a skid and probably because Tara couldn't see well enough to stay on the road. It had landed in shallow water that he knew dropped off sharply several yards from shore. The ghostly remnant of a dock destroyed by last year's hurricane held up the front of the car, but he detected that the back of the vehicle was sinking.

"Tara! Can you hear me?"

She nodded, her face strained and her eyes wild. She was struggling to roll down the window.

"Don't make any quick movements! We don't want the car to slide into deeper water!"

She froze, looking terrified, and nodded again.

"Do you have the cell phone?" Perhaps it was in a convenient pocket in her shirt or in her purse, and if so maybe she could call 911.

Tara shook her head and said something, and though he didn't hear the words over the howl of the wind and rain, he gathered that the phone wasn't available.

Ben knew he had to get Tara out of the sinking car. At the same time, he was assailed by doubt. All the emotions, all the fears, all the pain of that night in the theater two years ago threatened to overwhelm him. He stood poised on the edge of the marsh, waist high in saw grass and ready to jump in, yet couldn't make himself move forward.

What if he failed this time too? What if he couldn't save Tara? What if she died, just as Ashley had, because he couldn't get to her even after trying his best?

CHLOE COULDN'T SIT and do nothing while Tara was out in the storm somewhere. She called Jill's house, and left a frantic message.

"Lorena, Jill, please pick up if you're there. Tara's supposed to be home, and she isn't. It's storming outside and I'm very worried so please, when you get this message, call me immediately."

She also tried Suzette's house, and a boy whose voice she didn't recognize answered. He identified himself as Paul Antonacci and asked politely if he could help her.

"I'm trying to find my niece Tara Clark."

"Just a minute." Paul muffled the phone, but she heard him ask if anyone knew where Tara was.

"Tara's gone to Jill's, maybe to bring her to the party," someone said.

"That was a while ago," Paul replied. He returned his attention to Chloe. "Do you want to talk to Suzette or her parents?"

"Sure," Chloe said, feeling defeated.

A man came on the line and said he was George, Suzette's father. After she related her concerns, George said that he'd be worried, too, if Suzette were missing. "Look," he said. "One of the kids who lives on Stuart's Point just arrived here. He went home to get something earlier, and we can ask him if he saw the Volvo parked at Jill's house. He would have had to pass right by."

"Anything you can do will be appreciated," Chloe said.

George went away, came back. "His name is Flip Atchison, and he's sure that the Volvo wasn't there. He said he'd recognize it. He's seen Tara driving the car more than once."

"Then I have no idea where Tara is," Chloe said, beginning to panic.

"I understand how upset you must be. My wife and I will drive over and get you. We'll ride out to Stuart's Point together and talk to Jill. She must be at home. Some of the kids say she told them she would be there tonight."

"All—all right," Chloe conceded. "If you wouldn't mind." By this time, since she hadn't heard from him, she was terrified that something had happened to Ben, too.

"Livvie and I will be at the inn in a few minutes. Her sister and husband can stay here at the party and keep an eye on things."

"Thanks," Chloe said, feeling totally grateful.

She was wearing her rain jacket and waiting anxiously at the back door for George and Livvie when they drove up. The wind had abated slightly, but rain still poured from the sky. George ran up to the porch with an umbrella, but it turned inside out in the wind before he reached her.

"I don't mind getting wet," Chloe hollered over the noise of the storm. Her face and hair were drenched by the time she slid into the back seat of the Stephenses' minivan. Livvie, her expression somber, handed a towel back to Chloe so she could dry off.

"After you hung up, Flip mentioned noticing a broken guardrail on the Ibis Trail bridge on his way back to our place. We'll check it out."

"A broken guardrail," Chloe murmured, almost to herself.

"Don't worry," Livvie said comfortingly. "My guess is that Tara and Jill are sitting comfortably in the Pettuses' TV room, eating popcorn and watching a movie."

"They didn't answer the phone," Chloe said. "If anyone were at the Pettus house, wouldn't they have answered?"

Neither George nor Livvie replied at first, and the swish of the windshield wipers punctuated their silence. Then Livvie said, "Some kids only answer their own cell phones. They consider the land lines in their homes their parents'."

Chloe supposed this was a reasonable explanation, but even so, as the broken guardrail came into view on the left side of the highway, her heart almost stopped. Ben's Jeep, headlights tilted crazily, was parked on the slope of shell rock that created the road shoulder above the marsh.

George braked sharply and brought the minivan to a halt. As Chloe leaped from it and began to run through the pelting rain toward the Jeep, Livvie was dialing 911. "We have an accident—" was all Chloe heard her say before she spotted the hood of the Volvo canted at a dangerous angle above the marsh.

THE WATER WAS RISING. As he stood there, riveted by his own inadequacies, it covered Tara's shoulders, lapped halfway up her neck. She was crying now, the tears washing the blood from her head wound into the water.

Last time, when he'd tried to save Ashley, he hadn't been able to penetrate the flames that had so quickly consumed the theater. But now, the threat was water. He was at home in the water, a strong swimmer, a fighter. Even as he reasoned with himself, panic seized his chest, kept him from doing what he should do. Frozen motionless, all he could do was watch as the water kept rising.

Suddenly, Ashley in her blue dress appeared superimposed on Tara's form behind the glass. Ashley's face was serene, her eyes solidly on him, entreating, encouraging. He blinked in disbelief, and the image of his daughter faded and became Tara again. Tara sobbing, clawing at the window.

In that moment, a great calm overtook him. He ran to grab a hammer from the tool kit in the back of the Jeep. "Hold on, Tara!" he shouted, kicking off his waterlogged shoes.

Little wind-driven waves sucked at the car, and the water inside continued to rise. Ben plunged into the marsh, sickened as the car lurched backward. The serrated edges of the saw grass cut his cheek, stung. Something dark and slimy wriggled past, brushing against his leg. A fish? A frog? He couldn't tell. Tara was gasping for breath, struggling to hold her mouth and nose above the surface.

He swam, began to tread water. He didn't want to create a current that would send the car backward and sink it. He had no idea how stable it was, how much it would take to tip the Volvo to the bottom of the marsh. He had to do something, and he'd better do it quickly. Grasping the handle of the back door, he hung on to it for balance while he swung the hammer with all his might and struck a mighty blow against the window right behind the front seat where Tara sat.

Water poured out, covered his face as the door swung open. He surfaced in time to see Tara as the rush of water carried her out and away from the car.

The Volvo teetered, and he let go of the handle, swimming as hard as he could away from the vehicle. Tara gasped beside him, went down, fought him when he grabbed her. He yanked her up as she went limp, knowing they had to get away from the car before it fell off the pilings and sucked them down with it.

He dragged Tara through the saw grass. He didn't feel anything as its edges slashed his face, his hands. Blood still rose from the cut on her head, washing away in the rain. He heaved her onto the shore, bent over her, realized that blue emergency lights were flashing on the road.

Ben had no idea how much time had passed since he'd first come upon the scene, but it didn't seem important. He was terrified that Tara might have stopped breathing, and he couldn't detect any movement of her chest and lungs.

"Breathe," he commanded, hoping against hope. "*Breathe,* damn it!"

Nothing. Not a hint of movement or breath, and his eyes filled with tears of frustration. He started CPR, praying that it would work. It seemed like aeons before Tara shuddered, choked, opened her eyes. And inhaled a deep, shuddering breath.

Chloe tumbled toward them, sobbing and slipping in the mud. Rescue workers took over. An ambulance crew teetered down the bank, their white shoes sinking into the mud. Ben stood aside, his chest aching, the cuts on his face stinging, his heart beating fast.

"Ben," Chloe said, moving close, rain indistinguishable from the tears on her face. "Are you all right?"

He nodded, unable to speak. Because he was. He had saved Tara, redeemed himself for his past failings, kept another family from experiencing a terrible, unspeakable loss.

"Yes," he said, curving an arm around Chloe. "Yes, Chloe, I am."

DESPITE THE GASH on Tara's head, which wasn't as serious as it appeared, the doctor who applied sutures in the emergency room said that she was going to be fine. When it was clear that she was not in any immediate danger, she was allowed to go home with Chloe and Ben.

Before they left, the emergency room doctor pulled them aside. He carried a plastic bag containing six gold coins.

"These were in her pockets," the doctor told them. "The nurse who found them went off duty, but she asked me to give them to you."

Ben accepted the coins and thanked him.

"I'm sure we'll get the full story when Tara is able to talk to us," Chloe said.

"In light of what happened tonight, the coins are unimportant," Ben said. "It doesn't matter anymore."

"Of course it does," said Chloe. She wanted Tara's name cleared once and for all.

Chloe called Naomi and Ray when they reached the inn, calmed her sister down and promised Ray she'd call again after they all got some rest. Tara was understandably exhausted and fell into a deep sleep as soon as they tucked her in. Once, she opened her eyes, to see Chloe and Ben hovering over her bed, and told them, with a smile, to go away.

Finally, when she was so tired that she could no longer stay on her feet, Chloe sought the solace of her room and lay down on the bed, where she dozed off and on. After a while, with Tara still sleeping peacefully, Ben joined her and lay down beside her.

"Ben?" Chloe said, confused for a moment.

"Right here," he said. He reached for her hand and held it until she went to sleep.

Long after the sun rose, when they heard Tara stirring in her room, they both got up. Chloe smoothed her hair, wild after her drenching in the rain, and Ben went down to his apartment to shower and shave, though he'd suffered cuts on his face from the saw grass. Chloe prepared a breakfast tray of pancakes and fruit, and carried it to Tara, who sat up in bed while she ate. When Ben arrived, he ate pancakes, too. They all had a lot to talk about, but after a while, it became clear that everyone was avoiding the obvious question.

"I—I had the coins in my pockets," Tara said finally.

"The nurse in the emergency room found them and they were returned to me," Ben hastened to tell her.

Tara drew a deep breath. "Jill took them," Tara said flatly. "I'm really sorry, Ben. It's my fault because I showed the box with the coins in it to Jill when we were cleaning the apartment. I'd told her how you found things on the beach all the time, and I—I thought I could trust her."

Ben's lips set in a grim line. "If Jill's the one who stole the coins, then it's her fault, not yours."

"She did it because Aaron insisted. He said he could get good money for cob coins. Jill kept telling him that stealing was wrong, that she didn't want to be part of it, but he insisted that if she really loved him, she'd do it. He said there were lots more where those came from, and Ben would find more to replace them."

"Did Aaron need the money?" Chloe asked.

"Jill says so. He agreed to pay restitution to the high school principal for the tires he slashed, and his parents washed their hands of the whole situation, said they weren't going to pay Aaron's debts because he was eighteen years old and they weren't responsible for his wrongdoing. So the pressure was on him to raise the amount before he goes in the service, or the principal might prosecute. Aaron figured that hocking the coins was the best way to get quick money."

"Why didn't he pawn them right away?" Ben asked.

"He was going to, but then he got in trouble over the surfboard he took from Mr. Garrison. Jill was holding the coins at her house and was scared that someone—her mother or dad—would discover them. Aaron said he'd find another pawn shop, maybe up the coast, or he'd auction them online. Either way, he promised to take them off Jill's hands, but he got spooked by the surfboard incident and never did. Jill was so angry and felt so duped that she spilled the story as soon as I confronted her."

"What happened after that?"

Tara swallowed a bite of her pancakes. "Last night when I got to Jill's house, she was crying and all alone. I figured she was sad because she and Aaron broke up, and we sat down in the breakfast nook to talk about it. I wanted to ask her about the coins, but she was practically hysterical, and then she blurts out that she stole them. She's like, 'You can take the coins with you please, I don't want them and never did.' She runs upstairs, I guess to her room, and she comes down with the shoe box with the coins in it. I said, 'Why don't you give them back to Ben yourself?' and she says no, she's too embarrassed, won't I take them and put them back."

"What did you say?" Chloe wanted to know.

"Not much, because while we were having this conversation, the phone was ringing and ringing," Tara said. "Jill said it must be Aaron, but she didn't want to talk to him, so she'd turned off her cell phone and was letting the answering machine pick up the land line."

"The persistent caller was me, calling to find out if you were there," Chloe said.

"I didn't think of that. Suddenly, Jill dumped the coins out on the table and stuffed them in my shirt pockets. I said, 'This doesn't seem right,' and she said, 'It's more right than when I took them.' I told her, 'How can I take them back? Ben knows someone took them,' which is when Jill started to cry. I got wigged out then, all the emotional things about how she abused our friendship and because she did, two of my favorite people in the world suspect I'm a thief, so I jumped up and ran out of the house. It was raining really hard, but I didn't care. I just wanted to get out of there."

"I'm sorry you had to go through that, Tara," Ben said, looking uncomfortable.

"It doesn't matter now," Tara said. "As long as you believe I didn't have anything to do with stealing them. Jill said she did it to prove to Aaron that she loved him, that he was pressuring her about other things and she thought he'd stop if she took the coins."

Chloe exchanged glances with Ben. "We both believe you," she said as she reached for Tara's hand.

"I skidded on the curve near Ibis Trail. I remember the Volvo's wheels leaving the road and the screech of metal on metal. The cell phone was beside me, but it must have been knocked into the back seat. I was probably unconscious awhile, because I banged my head pretty hard on the windshield. The back of the car filled with water, and—and—" She swallowed and bit her lip.

"You don't have to talk about all that until you're ready," Ben told her.

"I'm sorry about the Volvo, Chloe."

"The important thing is that you're safe," Chloe replied firmly. "You scared us both nearly to death."

"I wish none of it had happened," Tara said. "Except for getting the coins back, that is. I want to get up and take a shower. Can I? And maybe call my friends afterward?"

"Sure," Chloe said. "Ben and I will clear out of here for a while."

"We have a few things to talk about," Ben said, smiling at both of them.

"Whatever," Tara said, and they left to go downstairs.

When they reached the foyer, Chloe was reminded of that first night here when Ben had saved her from the mouse and exterminated the palmetto bug. Now they knew each other in a different way than they had then, a better way. They had endured difficulties in their relationship, repaired and mended it. She felt closer to Ben than she ever had before.

Ben opened his hand to show her the coins. They gleamed in the stream of sunshine coming through the parlor windows. "Thank goodness everyone's all right," he said.

Before Chloe could reply, they heard someone drive into the inn's parking area. It was Lorena Pettus with a penitent-looking Jill in tow.

Chloe opened the back door as soon as they stepped onto the porch. "Come in," she said gravely. She introduced Ben to Lorena, and suggested that they all go into the parlor.

"We stopped in to make sure that Tara is really okay," Lorena said after drawing a long breath. Chloe could only imagine how difficult this was for her and for Jill.

"And to apologize," Jill added. "I shouldn't have taken those coins. It was wrong, and—and it caused everyone a lot of problems, including me. I've broken up with Aaron for good. He managed to convince me—" Here Jill couldn't continue. She pulled a tissue out of her pocket and wiped her eyes.

Chloe, though she felt her trust had been abused, couldn't help feeling pity for Jill. She herself had endured unhealthy relationships, unduly influenced by a smart-talking guy. Any woman could be a victim at any age. It had happened to Zephyr, as well. Even though Jill had barely begun her dating experience, she was certainly not immune.

"What Jill means to say," Lorena went on carefully, with a sideways glance at her daughter, "is that she'll understand if you prefer never to see her again. She likes Tara very much, and she wishes they could go on being friends, but if you don't approve, she can accept that."

"I want to try to be friends," said Tara, freshly showered and dressed in record time. She had been walking down the stairs when Lorena had begun her speech, and she came into the parlor now.

Jill sniffed and put away her tissue. She offered a tentative smile. "You mean it? You can forgive me?"

"I understand, sort of, why you did what you did, Jill. It's up to Chloe and Ben to forgive you."

"I—um, well, I'll try," Chloe said. She glanced at Ben. He sat on the couch with his arms folded across his chest, listening as everyone else spoke.

"I feel so—so guilty for what I did," Jill whispered. "It's like a pain right here," and she pressed her fingers against her chest. "It's a physical hurt, knowing that I caused all of you so much trouble."

"I can understand that one," Ben said. "I've been there myself."

"Would it be okay if Jill and I go out on the porch and talk?" Tara asked.

"Yes," Lorena said. "But only for a few minutes."

The two girls left the room and went outside, where they murmured in low tones.

"I'm sure Jill is telling Tara the latest developments about Aaron," Lorena said to Chloe and Ben. "The police stopped by our house this morning. They'll question Jill about that surfboard that was stolen, and we're going to take her to the Sanluca police station this afternoon to tell what she knows. Aaron may be part of a burglary ring that has been stealing from houses up and down the coast for months."

"Does that make Jill an accessory to his crimes?" Ben asked.

"She insists that she knew nothing about it. She's been

through a lot with Aaron, and I wish I'd known all of the things she's been telling me this morning. I'd have put a stop to that romance long before now," Lorena said. She looked tired, defeated, and Chloe's heart went out to her.

"One thing you don't have to worry about," Ben said. "I haven't reported the theft of the coins to the police, and as far as I'm concerned, it never happened. As long as Jill enters counseling, I'm willing to forget the whole thing."

Lorena managed a wavering smile. "Her father and I are committed to getting her the help she needs," she said.

After the girls came back inside, Lorena and Jill left. Ben stood with his arms around Chloe and Tara, watching the pair go.

"Jill and I are going to cool it for the rest of the summer. When I come back next year, maybe we can pick up where we left off," Tara said.

As the Pettus car disappeared from sight, a carload of teenagers screeched to a stop in the parking lot. "It's Suzette!" Tara said with glee. "And Greg and—oh, it's Marta and Julie." She ran outside to greet her friends, all of whom trooped through the house to the front porch, where someone produced a cooler full of soft drinks. "They're left over from last night's party," Suzette said. "We brought them to drink while we cheered you up after your accident."

Exclamations ensued as Tara elaborated on how she'd gone off the road into the marsh and how Ben had rescued her.

"It's good that they're gathering around Tara after her accident," Ben said. "I wonder if any of them knows how close it was."

"They'll hear about it." Chloe paused. "Naomi and Ray want to thank you in person. They may visit soon."

"Good. I'd like to meet them." He grew quiet.

"You were wonderful last night," Chloe told him. "I haven't thanked you properly for saving my niece's life."

"We can take care of that tonight, if you're free." He grinned at her.

"Seriously, Ben. Tara would have—would have died if you hadn't found her. And gone in after her." She didn't have the words to express her gratitude to this man for saving Tara. She would never have the words.

"I had help," Ben said with conviction. He explained how Ashley had appeared in her blue dress, how seeing his daughter in the Volvo had driven him into action. "Maybe the vision of Ashley was only my own imagination or the way my mind dealt with my indecision. We'll never know, but I was scared before I saw her, Chloe. Afraid I'd fail again."

"You're a real hero, Ben. No one in town will ever forget what you did," Chloe said with great conviction.

Ben's eyes went soft, and he moved around the back of Chloe's chair. He put his arms around her before bending to kiss her nape. "Let's get out of the inn," he murmured close to her ear. "Make some time for ourselves."

"Good idea," Chloe replied, taking heart that things were comfortable between them again. She felt a surge of relief, followed by an overpowering and incredible happiness.

"We could slip off for a walk along the beach," he suggested. "Alone."

Hand in hand, they escaped out the back door, around the annex and through the dunes. The smell of sunbaked sand and the salty tang of the air underscored Chloe's happy mood. Near the high-tide line, newly exuberant, Ben crouched and offered an impromptu piggyback ride. Chloe laughed and climbed on. He carried her a hundred feet or so down the beach, finally dumping her near one of Zephyr's marked turtle nests.

Ben took her hand and pulled her over to a large driftwood log. "Let's sit while we discuss a few things." He slid over to one side of the log to make room for her, and then he slid the recovered coins from his pocket.

"I'd like to make a necklace for you out of one of these," he said. "A memento of the summer."

Her heart sank. "Are you going somewhere?" she asked him as loss, heartbreak and misery crowded out the joy. In that instant, she foundered in grief. Felt bereft.

"No," he said slowly. "Only out on one of Andy's boats now and then."

Realization of his meaning struck her, and she stared at him. "You mean—you mean you got your job back?"

"I sure did. While I was bringing Tara up from the sinking car, Andy drove up on his way home to his house on Manatee Island. He watched the whole rescue. We talked while you were with Tara in the cubicle in the hospital emergency room. He said that he no longer had any doubts about my ability to function under pressure, that he wants me to work with him again. Of course it helped that one of his divers quit last week because of family issues, but he's chosen not to hire someone new. I'm going to send Andy a whole case of Kit Kat bars as a thank-you present."

"Oh, Ben," Chloe said, unable to keep from laughing. "It's what you've been waiting for."

"There's something else I've been wanting, Chloe."

Her laughter trailed off as she sensed a new purpose and seriousness in his attitude.

"I've been ready to make a commitment to you," he said slowly, "but without a real job or a future, I was sure you wouldn't want me."

"Want you? Ben, I've wanted you ever since I was Tara's age!"

"That was then. This is now. We're older and wiser, and we've been tested by life. I got to thinking about that, and it occurred to me that those shards of sea glass that you pick up on the beach have been scoured by the sand and made more beautiful than the original object. They're like us, Chloe. When we met before, we were new, unscoured by life. We've struggled and endured and perhaps become better people in the process."

She gazed at him, knowing that what he said was true. Her problems with the men in her life, her role in perpetuating their problems, had made her stronger. Had helped her to recognize a promising relationship when she finally found it, and that was a major step forward in her life. So many of the men in her past, guys on whom she had pinned her hopes and who had left her disappointed, all those she hadn't been able to save from themselves—they were nothing now.

He didn't stop talking. She wished he never would.

"I love you, Chloe Timberlake. You're a sweet sorceress who spends her days conjuring beauty out of glass and metal. Is it any wonder that you've created love where none existed? I want you to marry me. I want to make you pregnant so you can have my babies. *Our* babies, part of me and part of you. Can you? Will you?" He appeared nervous, which struck her as amusing. Everything, she was realizing right now, had been clear in her own mind for a long time.

She wrapped her arms around his neck and stared deeply into his eyes. She saw devotion and caring and, most of all, love. "Of course, at least to the first part. I'll marry you, but as for babies—well, let's just say that I'll have to get used to the idea. After my experience in being a temporary mother to Tara for the summer, I'm not sure I'm cut out to have a family."

"You've been wonderful with Tara. You'll be a terrific mommy." He spoke with the utmost sincerity.

"And you will be—you *were*—a great dad, Ben." She was serious now, searching his eyes for a hint of the old pain, the hidden suffering. She saw none.

"As long as you're with me, Chloe, I can handle any challenge." He sounded convinced of that; she only hoped it was true.

"Even twins?" she asked impishly. "They run in my family." Naomi and Ray had Jennifer and Jodie, and her mother had also been a twin.

"Two for one would be a bonus," he replied with a twinkle. "I'm game if you are."

"Can't wait till you toilet train our kids. You've had experience with Butch."

"Ha! You can't train kids using a pan of kitty litter sitting on top of the toilet. What do you do when it's a baby, anyway?"

"I'll be glad to give you pointers when the time comes. I know all about it. So, do you want a ring made out of sea glass? Or would something more traditional suit you better?"

"Must I decide right now?"

"You've only had sixteen years to think about it," he teased. He reached into a shirt pocket. "Would you wear this? Or is it too old-fashioned?"

She stared down at the emerald-and-gold ring that he'd found on the wreck in Key West. It gleamed in the sunshine, shining with promise.

"Oh, Ben," she said, her heart filled to the brim. "Of course I would."

He lifted her hand and slid the ring onto her finger. It fit perfectly. "It's yours. You're mine. What could be better?" His lips curved into a smile.

"You're turning me into a traditional, ordinary sort of woman," she said warningly and with some surprise.

He laughed. "That, my love, you will never be, but in the past few minutes you have agreed to some traditional, ordinary things. Like getting married. Like having children." He pulled her close, kissed her cheek.

"We can live at the inn," Chloe said. "We'll run it as a bed and breakfast, for a while, anyway. Tara can visit next summer. You wouldn't mind, would you?"

He shook his head. "Tara is welcome anytime as long as she doesn't chew ice."

Chloe started to laugh. "If that's your only objection, we're okay."

"You won't miss Farish, Chloe?"

"No, Ben. I've found my true home here in Sanluca with you." Secure in her newfound bliss, she could say this and mean it.

The sun was setting in the west, casting the rippling surface of the ocean in molten light. From the porch of the inn came the pealing laughter of Tara and her friends. Chloe and Ben and Tara—all three of them had been castaways from their previous lives. All three lost, in a way, but now found.

Sometimes the treasures that mean the most are hidden deepest in our hearts, Chloe reflected. The shifting sands of our lives don't always part voluntarily to reveal what lies beneath. Sometimes you have to dig deep, and have to have faith that something of value will eventually surface. And it could be a long wait.

"Look," Ben said softly. "The baby turtles are hatching."

She followed his line of sight to the nest and saw several small hatchlings struggling free. Others began to surge up out of the sand, standing motionless for a few moments as they oriented themselves to the world. Most headed toward the ocean, which was close to low tide, and since the nest had been created above the high-tide line, this was a long walk.

Chloe and Ben hurried to help them find their way. One or two of the baby turtles seemed confused and headed toward the dunes. Chloe picked them up and pointed them in the right direction.

"We're setting them off on the right course," Ben observed. "Like you did with Tara."

"Like *we* did with Tara," she corrected him.

When the first tiny turtle caught the roll of a wave, Chloe felt like cheering. It disappeared into the surf, safe from land predators. Soon, its brothers and sisters followed. She recalled from Zephyr's explanations that for a day or two, the hatchlings would paddle in the direction of the oncoming waves, until they reached the open sea.

"There they go," Ben said when they had all disappeared into the surf. "All safe."

"As are we," Chloe murmured.

"Yes," he answered. "Finally."

He held her close, their hearts beating in cadence with the rhythm of the sea, their love a cherished treasure that would sustain them for the rest of their lives.

That night, Chloe wrote in the diary of her sixteenth summer one last time.

> Dear Trees, He loves me. I love him. So now I can close out this diary and let you know that everything turned out all right.
>
> Ben disappeared from my life that summer, and when I learned he'd married someone else, I thought my heart was broken. It wasn't. It was only bruised. I found a boyfriend before the year was out, and lots more after that. As for Ben, he didn't stay married to Emily, and their only child died tragically. It was very sad, but our life experiences during all those years prepared us for what happened next. Made us appreciate finding each other, and made our love even more precious to both of us.
>
> It seems kind of silly, my telling you at the ripe old age

of thirty-two what finally happened with Ben and me. But, you know, some things take a while. Like getting back to the place where you really belong. Like finding out that someone really is pure Gold.

Ben and I plan to be married in the fall, at Lost Galleons Beach. I'll wear the cob coin on a chain around my neck, and he'll put the emerald ring on my finger. And, God willing, we'll never be apart again.

Love,
Chloe D. Timberlake (formerly known as Fire, and soon to be Mrs. Benjamin J. Derrick)

Epilogue

From the *Sanluca Courier*:

BIRTH ANNOUNCEMENTS
OCTOBER 7, 2007—At Melbourne Municipal Hospital, to Mr. and Mrs. Benjamin Joel Derrick (Chloe Dionne Timberlake) of the Frangipani Inn, Sanluca, twin daughters, Mariah Beth and Bryony Rose.

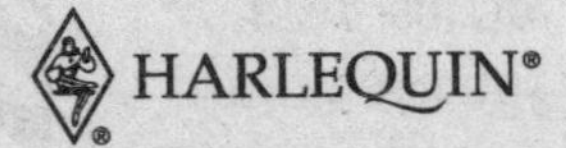

American ROMANCE®

COMING NEXT MONTH

#1113 MASON'S MARRIAGE by Tina Leonard

Cowboys by the Dozen

When the sheriff from Malfunction Junction discovers he's a father, he's delighted, even if the news comes four years late. Naturally, Mason assumes he'll finally have the only two women he's ever wanted. But Mimi Cannady expects to be wooed, and for a lifelong bachelor that's a tall order—like being asked to do the two-step with two left feet.

#1114 ONE DADDY TOO MANY by Debra Salonen

Sisters of the Silver Dollar

Kate's ex-husband wants joint custody of their daughter, but Kate can't forgive his betrayal. She hires lawyer Rob Brighten to fight the case and finds herself falling in love. But little Maya only wants her "real" daddy. Now, what's a good mother to do?

#1115 TEXAS BORN by Ann DeFee

Olivia Alvarado, vet and local coroner in Port Serenity, Texas, can't stay away from sexy sheriff C. J. Baker, even though she wants to. (Or does she?) She and C.J. are professionally connected by murder—and by mutts (once C.J. gets a dog). And if he has his way, they'll be *personally* connected, too. By marriage...

#1116 CAPTURING THE COP by Michele Dunaway

In the Family

Thirty years of good behavior was enough for anyone, even perpetual virgin Olivia Johnson, minister's daughter. And that was an understatement! Fortunately, it took just a glance at handsome detective Garrett Krause for her to get a few good ideas about some bad behavior—and how to make up for lost time.

www.eHarlequin.com

HARCNM0406